GHOST SHADOW

Maria Schneider

Bear Mountain Books

A Bear Mountain Books Production
www.BearMountainBooks.com

Maria E. Schneider

Printing History:
POD printing November 2015
POD printing June 30, 2024

Cover Art: Elements of the cover from depositphotos.com

ISBN-13: 978-0692578353 (Bear Mountain Books)
ISBN-10: 0692578358

Acknowledgments

For my nephew Kyle: You left this world too early and you are missed. Thanks to all my readers who have stuck with me, especially my beta readers. April, thanks for the gargoyle. John Levitt, you added some much needed sanity with your suggestion to streamline the plot. Scamper, you supplied all the rules for feral cats. A special thanks to LeAnn for spending so much time enhancing my simple words.

And to my husband who sticks with me, not only through the books, but the dirty dishes as well.

Prologue

Despite all the magic we had embedded into White Feather's house when we rebuilt it, the perimeter of his property—now our property—was sadly lacking in earth wards. Transplanting desert sage and sweet grasses in specific spots would not only keep us safer, it would be a ready supply of ingredients for many a spell. Granny Ruth had also offered to provide us with some kick-ass spiders.

Thinking of the spiders sent a creepy chill down my back, but I wasn't about to turn down her offer. They wouldn't be delivered until after I had applied my share of the protection magic anyway. I remained knee-deep in sand and sage, working in the dimming evening light. As I lowered the largest sage into the hole, a voice from behind me hissed, "Adriel."

The unexpected interruption sent the desert herb sailing behind me as I twisted to meet the threat. Still on my knees, I spun around, fell backwards into the hole I had just dug, and raised my silver. My fingers were wrapped around a lame hand shovel, which offered no protection at all.

My heart sputtered and a disgruntled sigh puffed out as I realized the threat was only Lynx. "Must you sneak up on me?" Even though Mother Earth communicated with me almost as well as the breezes did with White Feather, Lynx was a special cat. He was more an extension of earth magic than a foreign entity, so Mother Earth felt no need to mention when he was skulking about.

"How was I to know you weren't paying attention to your surroundings? I came over to tell you that Roberto needs a meet." He offered me a hand up.

Since my bottom was squarely planted in the hole, I had no choice but to accept his help. He was strong enough to nearly lift me to my feet with just one skinny arm. I'd known Lynx since he was a hungry alley cat scrounging food from garbage cans. All muscles and sinew then, he was even stronger now that he was better fed and leaving his teen years behind him. While he might look like a piece of scrap blown in with the tumbleweeds, his eyes flashed intelligence, and his lithe movements were faster and smoother than those of a normal human.

"Roberto, the deaf kid, wants a meet?" I stuffed strands of my long dark hair back into my ponytail.

Lynx handed me the sage that had missed him completely when I threw it in defense. "You know any other Roberto?"

This was Santa Fe, New Mexico. I could think of four without even trying. "Not that are deaf."

"He's not deaf when he's in a graveyard talking to ghosts, which is why he needs a meet. He has a message from Martin."

This evening just got better and better. "Martin? Martin isn't in a graveyard!"

Lynx shrugged. "He's dead, which means Roberto can talk to him. I mentioned Martin to Roberto after our visit to Fairview Cemetery a few weeks ago. Some of the dudes hanging around that place are flakes. The kid could use better company, you know?"

My eyes bulged. If Lynx thought Martin was better company than the ghosts Roberto had been communicating with in Fairview Cemetery, the kid was in more trouble than I could rectify. Of course, Roberto talked to dead people, so how much assistance could I possibly be on my best day? His ears were deaf to the sounds of this world, but not to those communicating from the other side. He spent a lot of time in cemeteries, which was where I had originally met him.

"Our *visit* to the cemetery?" I repeated, eyes narrowing. It had been a hell of a lot more than a visit. Leave it to Lynx to act as if nearly being swallowed out of existence without benefit of dying was mere social happenstance.

"Wants to meet tonight. Midnight. Tent Rock," he said.

"What is it with you and night meets! Martin can talk to me during the day. We'd be insane to hike around those rocks at night." And I'd been avoiding Tent Rock because Martin was haunting the place. Sure, earth magic was strong there. But who wanted to have Martin peering over your shoulder when practicing a spell or gathering magic? He'd been a drunk, flirtatious, covered-in-dirt old man in life. He hadn't bothered to leave most of his bad habits behind when he died.

"Martin's in some kind of trouble. Roberto says he can only appear at night and even that is getting more difficult."

My mouth gaped open, and I stared at Lynx in disbelief.

He shrugged. "I know, I know, but who else was he gonna ask?"

* * *

Earth witches did not have any power over the dead, on behalf of the dead or even communicating with the dead, as far as I knew. There was no earthly reason that I should have ever seen a ghost, but it had happened more than once. The first one I encountered hadn't really communicated with me; she'd either been in too much pain or was too far gone.

Martin had been an earth witch in life, and I'd always assumed that the reason he'd been able to give me a ghostly message once before was because we shared a level of common magic. That was more than I had wanted to share with Martin. My feelings on the matter hadn't changed just because he was dead.

If Lynx thought I was leaving White Feather behind on this insane adventure, he had another think coming.

"I wonder what Martin wants to talk to me about," I muttered as White Feather and I climbed the beginning of the trail into Tent Rock. I wasn't sure whether to be happy about the full moon or not. The moon would automatically call more magic into any situation, and it also lent more light. With ghosts, however, magic and light could be a help, a hindrance, or not matter a whit. "Couldn't Martin have just had Roberto ask me whatever he needed to know?"

"Apparently not. And since you've been avoiding Tent Rock, Martin had to use an intermediary to reach you."

"Hmph." White Feather was probably correct about that part.

I knew where Martin would appear because I'd had more than my fair share of trouble in the bowl-shaped indention halfway up the trail. The magic was so strong there, a normal could have felt it. It wasn't any problem for someone like Lynx to sense it, and it was a natural spot for Roberto to have found Martin.

I heard them talking as we ducked under the overhanging rock and rounded the bend. As I edged slowly around the walled canyon into the side clearing, it took me a second to realize I was hearing Roberto clearly as he asked Martin a question. Roberto, being deaf, never enunciated clearly. Martin had never slurred his words, even when drunk, but tonight, it was Martin's voice that sounded as though he were talking under water.

I stopped so abruptly that White Feather nearly knocked me down.

Roberto was a dark shadow four feet off the side of the trail. Lynx stood more in the open, but he'd promised to be in plain sight if the meet was still on and safe. The glowing wisp of fog between the two of them was not shaped like a human.

This meet didn't look safe to me. When Martin had appeared before, his features were clearly defined, albeit transparent.

If the wisp of fog hadn't replied when Roberto spoke, I'd not have believed it was Martin at all.

"He's in trouble." Lynx kept his attention on the ghost as he addressed us.

"Roberto or Martin?" I asked.

Lynx cut his eyes to me. His pupils glowed yellow. He had changed to cat eyes either because he was nervous or so he could see better in the dark.

"Martin, not me," Roberto answered my question. "He can't ghost here properly anymore. It's been deteriorating over the last week." His hands flew as he signed what he was saying.

Lynx started to repeat what Roberto had just said, but I cut him off. "Got it."

White Feather touched my arm. "I didn't."

Well, now, that was disturbing. Since White Feather wasn't a threat, I kept my gaze on Martin. He was talking again or attempting to.

"Baalance. Wrooong." The rest of what he said was too garbled for me, but Roberto had been at this longer, and it was his gift.

"There are other things crossing," he translated. "He doesn't want to be destroyed by them. The creatures come from—" He stopped and rubbed his forehead. "I can't understand that part. He's tried to tell me before, but I don't know what he's saying. Something about the dark where magic doesn't exist." His hands went up in the universal shrug.

The mist swirled closer to me. I held my ground, but only because White Feather was at my back. As it was, I leaned against him, trying to stay out of reach of the unearthly glowing strands of fog.

Martin's eyes were not really recognizable; they were pits of emotion. There was no pupil, no face around them, just sparks that somehow translated to panic. "Soooleessheeell."

"Shoeless?" Being without shoes hadn't bothered Martin when he was alive. At this point, he didn't even have feet! From a barely discernible waist on down was nothing but a gray mist.

"Soooool…Lessss."

Then I got it. "Soulless. Okay, Martin, the things are soulless, but what do you want me to do about it? I'm not dying just to pull your ass out of the fire!"

For a second, the eyes laughed at me. The spark went from lightning white to a swirl of fog.

Roberto watched me as he talked rapidly and signed at the same time. Lynx followed his hands, but I had no trouble with his words. "Martin says he knows how to stay safe, but a girl is trapped In Between with him, and she doesn't belong there. He thought he could help her back over, but he's weakening. He's worried she will get stuck there."

"What girl?" I struggled to stay focused on the problem rather than screech at Martin for dragging me into a mess, one that I didn't understand and probably couldn't fix. "Does she have a soul?" I was not about to bring anyone back here without a soul. Wouldn't that be like rescuing a vampire? Or was that like creating one? No…

Thankfully Martin interrupted before my mind walked off any deeper into crazy. Roberto translated Martin's blur of words. "Soul, yes, she has one, but she's still alive on this side and her soul needs to come back here. She can see the—" Roberto shrugged again.

There were a million questions, but from the way the wisps were starting to separate, I didn't need to be told we were out of time. "Martin, we can look for the girl on this side, and maybe we can help, but why did you call me here?"

"The bloodstone." It was Roberto who answered since Martin was now nothing more than an arm attached to a fast-fading light that might have been his chest. "He thinks he can use the bloodstone's energy to help her."

I didn't generally carry the green and red stone around, but the last time I had talked to Martin, he had felt me using the bloodstone here. In short, I wasn't likely to ever come to Tent Rock without it.

Bloodstone, or heliotrope, carried natural powers for healing, especially of blood or circulation. It also aligned and healed a person's energy. Its lesser known use included an ability to call storms and hold the power of the wind. Wind magic had the power to carry messages into the past or future because wind had been there before and could go anywhere without the check of time. Maybe heliotrope had some power in the realm of the dead.

The particular stone Martin asked for was one he had harvested from Mother Earth when he was still alive. It held Martin's magic, my magic, White Feather's magic and my best friend's water witching magic.

Only a fool would give up an object of such power, but it was out of my backpack and on my palm without hesitation. Martin may have been an obnoxious drunk while alive and a pest after he died, but he had given me the stone without strings attached, and later he had given his life to save us.

"I give this without restraint, freely—"

Martin's shriek split my oath. I nearly dropped the stone to cover my ears. White Feather shifted the breeze in an instinctive reaction to save us from danger even though the peril seemed to be limited to a caterwauling meant to serenade a banshee. My ears rang in protest.

Roberto said, "He says I can give him the stone because I can reach across. But it needs your earth magic to push through the connection so don't negate that with the freely given spell words."

"Since I have no idea how to give it to him, I'm glad you do." I turned over the stone. White Feather moved from behind to beside me, barely restraining himself from protectively elbowing me out of the way. I saw his mouth move, but couldn't hear the words.

Maybe my sudden deafness was due to the ringing in my ears, but that made no sense because I had no trouble hearing Roberto when he yelled, "Hey, wait!"

Martin shouted back. They both had a hand on the stone. Martin's energy might be weak, but it certainly wasn't dead yet. Where he touched the stone, his hand was gray and nearly solid.

"Leggo!" Roberto screamed. His fingers turned an odd gray color, drained of blood.

Martin wailed in response, a horrific sound that not only echoed, it knocked rocks loose.

Roberto bellowed back, jerking his hand.

Lynx grabbed Roberto's free arm and pulled, but the mist snaked up

Roberto's graying arm like a giant glow worm intent on devouring dinner. Inch by inch, it sucked Roberto into Martin's world. He was turning into a corpse before our eyes.

"Uh, Martin…"

Eyes rolled across the fog. "Eneergy…feed earth."

"Unless you want someone else to join you who doesn't belong there, let him go," I shouted.

White Feather sent a stiff breeze into the fog that was Martin, but the wind just crossed through him as though he wasn't there.

I reached for the stone, anchoring myself to Mother Earth. White Feather knew the second I grounded, and he grabbed me around the waist. If he yelled instructions, I couldn't hear them. In this strange place, warped with the magic that Roberto used, I could hear Martin more clearly than my living friends.

As soon as my magic touched the stone, I saw Martin clearly. He was gray. Everything was gray except the pulsing green and red of the bloodstone. His dead fingers were wrapped around it, but Roberto's hand was still stuck to it.

"Let it go," I commanded.

"I can't," Martin replied. His eyes were no longer sparks. They were just transparent gray that held a human panic and a sadness that hadn't been there when I last saw him.

My magic pulsed against the bloodstone. No way would I physically touch it. I could feel White Feather, his strong arms holding onto me.

Could I call the bloodstone back? Martin had called it across. His earth magic was stronger than mine…well, it might have been in life. Mine would be the stronger now.

There were no tools to use here. Though I could still feel my earth magic, Martin was right. The place where Martin now resided pulled at the stone, at me, at Roberto. It pulled at Life.

It could have the stone and what it held, freely given, but it couldn't have Roberto. He didn't belong there and neither did I.

I had learned to manipulate pieces of Mother Earth, but I wasn't proficient and had only practiced with silver. "Bloodstone." I called the stone anyway. Blood was the tie to human life. There was no need for blood in Martin's colorless place, especially Roberto's blood.

The crimson specks of the bloodstone answered, responding to my pull, shifting forward, like to like. The drops of bright red swelled under Roberto's fingers. I reached out and gingerly touched his shoulder, a part of him that hadn't yet turned ashen.

With a sucking, popping crack, the red separated from the green. I pulled harder, trying to draw the red specks to us, to Roberto, to earth.

A gray blob rose up behind Martin, a mass I had thought was a rock or just another shadow. As I pulled, Martin came forward, suspended halfway between his world and mine. With the draw of magic, his arm glowed and radiated ever closer to Roberto's shoulder and my hand.

The gray apparition darted forward. My grunt of warning came too late.

The shape collided with Martin. As it touched his shoulder, it turned into a hand. The blob resolved itself into a woman. She was as colorless as he, but there was an odd iridescent shimmer about her. Snippets of energy occasionally pulsed across her, relieving the unrelenting gray.

"It's the girl!" Lynx shouted.

As she knocked into Martin, he flew backwards, still grasping the stone.

The force of his pull would have drawn me and my magic forward if not for White Feather's strong hold. With a muffled plea, I reached my free hand to White Feather's arm around my waist. Our rings touched and sparked, providing a sudden influx of life magic that was more than enough to break the hold of the gray. I clung to him and kept my grounding to earth, tugging at Roberto and the bloodstone with everything I had in me.

The woman's eyes burned straight through me, a flash of blue, just before a maelstrom of colors burst across the dead landscape, blinding me. I lost my grip on Roberto and fell back so fast, there was no time to brace myself for the impact.

I couldn't be certain whether I'd been sucked in or pushed out until White Feather groaned underneath me.

"What the hell was that?" he muttered, spitting sand.

I blinked, wondering just how hard I'd hit my head. Everything around me was a mix of dark shapes looming, waiting to attack.

No, wait. Like fools we were running around Tent Rock at midnight. I tried rubbing my eyes, but other than grinding sand into my skin, it accomplished nothing.

"Dead witches are the worst," Lynx said right before dropping a whimpering Roberto next to us.

"Do you have a light?" I demanded.

"What for?"

"Lynx, not everyone can see as well as you do in the dark. Or in the light for that matter."

"Light will just draw attention to this mess."

White Feather turned on his flashlight. Roberto was shaking like a leaf. He stared at me in horrified silence as though the situation were all my fault.

"You okay?" I sat up and felt for my own head. Sand coated me from head to toe. Being washed in desert must be a prerequisite of the magic here.

Roberto stared down at his hand. I turned it to face the light. He said something, but the magic had shut down, whatever kind it was he wielded. I could no longer interpret his words.

Lynx tilted his head, and asked, "What happened to the rest of the stone?"

I picked up the nugget from Roberto's palm. "Martin has it. Only the red part crossed back with us. There isn't a hint of green left in the piece."

Roberto nodded. He found the strength to stand and began signing frantically at Lynx.

White Feather said to me, "Can you hear me at all?"

I nodded. "Yeah. Martin's gone. I couldn't hear you while Roberto was holding open the link. He included me somehow."

"That must be why you ignored my suggestion that you not go after the bloodstone."

"Probably," I hedged.

"And the reason you ignored me when I told you to stop pulling on the stone."

"How did you know I was pulling on it?" We both stood and brushed uselessly at the sand.

He grunted. "I could push wind into it, but not pull it back. I could feel you there as if I were pushing wind at you. You weren't listening to me."

I leaned over and picked up my backpack. "Thanks for holding on to me."

He reeled me in close. Lips against mine, he said, "Always."

Lynx said, "Roberto wants to know if you can find the girl."

White Feather sighed.

"Good question," I replied. "I don't think we can find her tonight." Since I hadn't recognized her washed-out features and had no idea how to bring her back across if we found her, I had a bad premonition that locating her was only going to be the beginning of our problems. "Maybe now that Martin has the stone, she'll be fine."

Roberto signed something, but Lynx was too busy staring where the ghosts had been to bother translating. "We'll need to find her to be certain." His ears swiveled once, hearing things only a cat could hear. "I wonder who she is and how she got stuck there."

No way to know right now. She hadn't left a calling card. Martin wouldn't have the energy to reappear and I didn't want to be here if he did.

I had no way to know that Lynx and Roberto would keep looking without us. Only a fool would delve into something so dangerous.

Chapter 1 - Shadow

When I first died, thoughts of revenge consumed me. I knew how it happened, but had to guess at the why. The guy who killed me hadn't paid for the crime. Not that I knew whether or not he had been arrested for my death, because I was too busy trying to survive In Between. No matter. He had not paid the correct price including change—because death was the ultimate price.

Yeah, it's like you've heard. Some people cross over completely. I see them sometimes. They slide through in a daze, not seeing, not knowing where they are. Others stare right at me and nod, as though we're passing on a street. Some of them look right through me like the ghost that I am.

But there are other people here too, as well as other creatures: spirits, monsters, ghouls, imps and even demons. The demons don't belong here. They spend all their time plotting how to cross through In Between to reach the world of the living. Most of them get spit back so fast it causes a weird bending in the bubble, one that burns them and everything around them. The blue-white flame either ends the horned beasts or sends them back where they came from.

It's safer to avoid the edges of In Between, even the one leading to my old haunting ground, pun intended. For some reason, at that edge, I can usually peer through the opaque flesh of the barrier right into the slightly distorted view of my former world. I can see where I used to exist and where I'd much rather be.

Spirits and demons can sometimes force open those edges, and I didn't want to be where I was right now because a demon was busily cutting through the weave.

I held myself as still as only a ghost can be, but even in In Between there are drafts.

This demon wasn't close to humanoid; it was of the young, not very powerful variety, but old enough that fire licked the edges of its form. When demons lacked power, they were harder to see in the gray of In Between because instead of bright demon-red or lots of flames, they were more of a curdled dried blood color with a black shadow radiating outward.

This one was pushing at the weave, scratching along the surface with sharp claws, trying to puncture the barrier separating us from the world of the living. I couldn't decide whether to remain frozen or float backwards. If it detected me I'd be toast, but if it broke through the edge with me this close, the backlash would sear right through me.

I gathered myself downward into a crouch, determined to be nothing more than my name suggests. I have no memory of my living name, but

Shadow fits the ghost that I have become.

Ghosts don't sweat, but we get the shakes. The tremors ate at my concentration. *How long did I have to escape?*

The demon peeled back another layer of foggy fabric separating In Between from the living world. He gurgled with delight and then let loose a screeched pitch that sounded like raw metal scraping on asphalt. He dug his claws in again, drooling liberally. His fetid breath was a rotting odor so foul, it was a good thing ghosts didn't need to breathe.

I floated to the right, hoping to slide outside his peripheral vision. How the beast was able to tear away layers as thick as pig fat and at least as stubborn as alligator skin was beyond me, but I'd seen the results and been too close to the backlash once before. The damage nearly killed me. I had drifted aimlessly, barely able to move, trying not to hurt for at least a week. If Martin hadn't found me and dragged me to a safe place...I didn't want to think about what monster might have claimed me for a snack.

Breathing did nothing for my survival, and it wasn't the fastest way to move either, but it was my best choice now. Sucking in air and pushing it back out might gain the attention of the demon because breathing belonged to the world of the living, and demons fed on anything with life—or even those that had once been alive.

Despite the danger, I puffed myself backward, stealthy as a ghost.

The edges of this demon were dark, especially around the knobs on the head. The slobbering beast was obviously very hungry. Hopefully it was inexperienced enough to ignore its surroundings in favor of digging and tearing at the fabric of the living world.

By my third breath, I had traveled about six feet. And by my third breath, the thin seam the demon was tearing at shone with colors other than gray. There were only a few more layers between it and the living. If the demon was strong enough, he might pop through without peeling further.

I breathed harder and faster, even though it might get me noticed.

The demon discarded strips of fog behind him like a gravedigger depositing soil.

My eyes remained glued to the seam, not only because I wondered how much time was left for my getaway, but because I too was drawn to the world of the living. My hunger wasn't the same as that of the demon, but there was still curiosity, envy and loneliness.

Half my brain was hoping for a glimpse of life, the other half was gibbering senselessly about escaping. Amid the expanding light behind the edge, I finally glimpsed a washing machine. Piles of sheets in a large commercial laundry hamper waited next to it.

That figures. You spend all your days hungering for the joy and excitement of life, and you get the laundry day from hell, complete with a demon drooling over a few sheets because they happened to be spattered with blood. I absently wondered if the demon would lick up the dots and bloody blobs. Maybe the sheets wouldn't even need washing after the demon was done with them.

Thankfully, there were no people visible through the faint layers. If a demon was involved and a human was waiting, it was almost always an idiot attempting a demon binding. The power from that sort of thing could suck half of In Between into oblivion, or so Martin claimed.

Since I was already dead, I didn't know what would happen if I were sucked into a locked pentagram with a demon, but I wasn't anxious to find out what kind of pain would result.

Just as the blue behind the layer lightened to daylight, a short woman with gray hair trundled into the laundry room with another bin full of dirty sheets.

The demon bounced up and down as if he'd hit the jackpot.

His focus gave me the opportunity to swoosh another three feet away.

Completely unsuspecting, the lady tossed a bundle of laundry inside one of the washers. The edge of one sheet snagged under the black smock apron she wore, but she ignored it and started the water flowing.

The demon howled. Maybe he had intended to lick all the soiled sheets, bloody or not.

The woman twitched and turned to look behind her, but her eyes roved straight past the demon.

The humpbacked monster gave a gleeful chortle and slowly dug a single talon into the last layer of weave as though he were anticipating the feel of her flesh.

It might have been the water rushing into the washer, or it could have been the demon's foul presence, but the washer in front of the lady began to vibrate. With one work-worn hand she shoved the dangling edge of the sheet into the washer.

The demon sliced into the weave.

I blew out every ounce of air in my ghostly lungs and hit the fog at a dead run.

The sound of the blast hit me first. The white heat took too little time to catch up.

Chapter 2

The backlash from the explosion rolled me like a ball and threatened to scatter me like soot. The torn edges of In Between ballooned away from the blast, roaring with the sound of a thousand winds. Those pieces were my friends, blocking some of the dangerous debris as the demon was rejected and summarily slapped backwards.

Of course, the same thing that saved me might kill me. Anytime I was forced too close to the living world, I relived my death, that moment of shocking, mind-numbing pain when I looked down and I wasn't anymore. Throbbing pangs radiated from every body part as if sharp sand flowed through my fingers. The ice was a cold that cut. As the hurt melted, nothing remained but sloshing gray.

I started swimming through it, much as I had that first time. The fog this close to the border was in strips, interlaced like woven cloth, entrapping me as the pieces strove to weave themselves back together.

I sucked in air as though breathing, but this time it was in search of the damp smell of In Between. The taint of anything burning would be my only warning if I swam too close to a certain fool demon who had just attempted a trick without enough power to pull it off.

My essence fought to stay in one piece as the torn steely bands wove themselves tighter, heedless of the fact that my misty body parts might be tangled among them. Flowing around the weave required changing shape, concentration and something else, something that was the nature of being a ghost. My soul kept me linked together, but when your eyeballs are squished into a thin rope and sideways, you lose a lot of perspective. If I wasn't careful, I could accidentally leave pieces behind.

Martin had recovered the missing pieces that first time.

My head snaked into one flat piece. That shape didn't bother me at all so long as my eyes were in place, returning my ability to see straight. I searched out corners that might hold any color other than gray.

"Crap!" I was still too close to the edge. In the shifting weave, a room became remarkably visible. The view was every bit as sharp as when the weave thinned because someone was about to die. There was no pain, so I hadn't breached the border, but the pressure was building.

I stared hungrily; I couldn't resist. Maybe I wasn't even as close as I had initially thought because the walls were grayish and the light was dim. But, no. The room actually was drab. It appeared to be some sort of medical facility with white sheets, stark walls and a bed with a pink bedspread instead of boring white. A shelf along the wall was full of flowers, a teddy bear, a stoneware pitcher and two rocks.

A dark-skinned girl with braids sat on the bed, her legs crossed and a fierce collection of wrinkles slanting across her lips and forehead. She was maybe eight or ten years old.

She stuck her tongue out at me.

I was surprised, but from the way she stared right at me, it was obvious she could see me.

"Go away, stupid ghost."

A woman came from around the cloth partition. She held a notepad and pen, but looked up and gave me a half smile of acknowledgment. *Both* of them could see me!

"Everyone thinks it would be so neat to be like a cartoon, seeing ghosts or zapping people with lasers, talking to animals, being cool. It's stupid. Useless." The little girl wrapped her arms around her knees and rocked back and forth on the edge of the pink bedspread. "Aunt Brenda, make it go away."

Her aunt smoothed a hand across the girl's head. "You need to learn to separate your feelings from theirs. Or are you supposing you can smoke that nonsense your older brother does and that will help you ignore it?"

The girl pulled back from her knees in surprise. "I didn't say I was going to smoke drugs!"

Aunt Brenda rewarded her with a small smile. "I know. But people do. Sometimes even after they get to be my age when they should know better. They never learned to deal with it. It doesn't matter if you're like your ma and can feel what is happening miles away to someone you love or if you're like me and you can see the ghosts."

Rock, back and forth.

I felt like a spy. But the girl and her aunt could see me. They had looked right at me and done everything except say hello and invite me for tea.

"Why do they come here?"

Aunt Brenda turned to me. "Do you know why you're here?"

I shook my head. I raised both hands and shrugged what would have been my shoulders.

"You will figure it out. You ghosts show up a few times. Then you ask."

"Ask what?" When I spoke, the curtains moved as though there was a breeze, but the window was closed.

The aunt looked back at the girl. "Then you and me, Espy, we decide whether we can help or not."

"Why do we have to help?" The girl asked the question floating in my own brain.

The aunt reached out a hand in my direction, fingers splayed. She didn't touch me; she couldn't and even so, she wasn't close enough.

"Sometimes we are the ones who need help from the other side. So when they ask a favor of us, we try to help."

Roberto, Martin's friend, was like Espy, the little girl. Roberto could not only see us, but talk to us and hear our answers. The girl was able to understand me perfectly. The aunt I wasn't so sure about, but when Roberto had wielded his magic, everyone near Roberto seemed better able to understand Martin and me.

Still, for me to see them this clearly...I panicked. The edge was thin here, probably because the demon had just tried to force himself through nearby.

I swam backwards as fast as my gray could paddle. Predictably, I hit the wall. The woven fog had already started to close with me almost embedded on neither side. I wasn't some dumb newbie. I knew that when you hit the wall, you bounce. When you bounce you go backwards, right into the firm line that you are not allowed to cross.

The scream peeled back my face. Oddly, I heard the aunt's pen drop to the concrete floor.

Espy grimaced as though hit by an echo of my pain as I was bounced backwards and away. Something about her sparked a memory of another little girl holding my hand and laughing up at me as I showed her how to twirl a pretty baton, but the thought disintegrated with the rest of me as the weave sliced me to pieces.

Chapter 3

By the time I wafted away from the weave, I was in bad shape. Several parts of me were bruised. Ghosts don't bleed, but we leak. Don't ask me; I don't know much besides the fact that it's painful, and if a ghost leaks too much, she isn't anymore.

The structures In Between are mostly what we make of them. A ghost shelter looks a lot like a cairn, little more than a collection of stones where we can hide. Mine was more of a hillside cave, because Martin had been the one to rescue me after my first accident, and he knew all the best spots In Between.

I pulled myself inside my shelter, feeling fortunate the weave hadn't spit me out into an unfamiliar area. No one knew how big the bubble was because it was elastic, ever-changing and had a wicked boomerang. I'd been lost plenty of times before, and it was the last thing I needed when hurt.

Like lumpy dough, I oozed onto a flat rock that served as a chair, pressing the gray leaks to staunch the flow as I tried to hold myself together. The fog drizzled a misty rain, but once I was inside my protective shelter, it no longer threatened to wash me away.

Rain was good in that things wouldn't be able to smell and follow me, but bad in that I was chilled. Worse than that, emotional stress caused the fog to echo back my feelings, magnifying them. That left me increasingly miserable by the second.

I wallowed inside the gray blob that was the jacket I had died in, but as I spread thin, I repeatedly had to reel in parts of myself. I rarely ever had feet, but usually had legs.

Tired, I curled into my favorite spot and dozed, wishing I were alive, yearning for the small comfort of a cup of hot cocoa or a friend.

* * *

Martin and Troy were my best friends In Between. Troy was younger than me by six years when he crossed; a car accident that he remembered all too well. He still resembled the healthy seventeen-year-old football player he had been, albeit his best color was now gray. His jeans, jock jacket and t-shirt were as casual as my own denim jacket and jeans. It didn't matter what we wore anyway. More than half the time we were faces with unformed limbs.

Troy most likely befriended me out of pity. Like another bit of the roadkill he collected, comforted and protected, he mentored me. As I described my latest ordeal to him, I certainly felt like roadkill.

"Man, Shadow, what is it with you and demons?" He hovered near the rock that served as a table inside my cave. I stayed in the corner so he didn't see the full extent of my latest injuries. We had no need to eat, but we did need energy. Much of it came from slashes of quick light that passed through In Between, but Troy had a habit of bringing bits from the living world; a leaf, grass, roadkill that wasn't quite dead or other animals that were more than happy to breathe their last bits of life on us before becoming another of Troy's numerous ghost pets.

He set a smear of mud on the table.

"Did you harvest that from a roadkill?" A bright green blade of grass was embedded in the mud. I needed energy more now than usual, but was loathe to use this particular piece because of its likely origin.

"That's the easiest way."

"Gross." I stared hungrily at the clump of mud, wondering if a ghost could catch a disease from smeared raccoon parts. The latest roadkill ghost, said raccoon, stared up at me and made a chattering noise.

It took a few days of the animals being In Between before I could understand them. Without Troy's tutelage, I'd never have grasped the concept at all.

"I figured you wouldn't care for it." Troy grinned, and from his gray palm produced two juniper needles. "These came from the tree where I brought Coon through. Untouched by any critters unless a bird pooped on them before they fell through."

Feeling starved, I pushed the best arm I could form towards the pine needles.

He obliged me by dropping them into what would have been my hand had I pulled off forming one.

The pine was still warm, in a living sense, not a heat sense. "Wow! Thank you." Anything that came from the real world, even if it had been plucked, harvested or died, held some amount of energy. The needles were sharp, tangy and if not alive, they had life energy. It soaked into me, helping heal the throbbing leaks.

"How is Coon doing?" I asked when I finally felt able. Raccoons were all addressed as "Coon," but the intended one seemed to answer when Troy spoke to him. Out of respect, I directed my question at both Troy and Coon; Troy because his answer would make sense, and at Coon to avoid insulting him.

Coon gargled, clicked and reared up on his hind feet. They weren't words, but the concept was conveyed. "Got smashed, huh? Stinks."

Troy smiled. "He's still upset about it. Claims he was about to convince a Miss Coon to mate."

Coon made more noises, and he looked very sulky indeed. Whatever he said was too complicated for my limited ability to understand. Coon's earthly desires would fade soon. Most of the animals only stayed In Between for a few days, a couple of months at most. For some unexplained reason, three of his pets had remained with Troy since his arrival.

I had the vaguest living memory of riding a red roan, but like In Between, the fragment was little more than mist. The galloping freedom I envisioned was probably nothing more than me transferring the feeling of ghostly floating onto a living activity.

"So what is it with you and demons?" Troy repeated, interrupting my reverie. "I've only encountered three and believe me, I've been here a lot longer than you."

"And two of those were since I arrived," I replied. "You think all these demons are my fault?" I was half kidding and certainly didn't want any link with demons. They were notoriously dangerous, feeding on ghosts, spirits and humans—the live ones, the dead ones, they weren't particular.

Troy nodded. "You're right, it has been in the last couple of months, but at least one of those demons was the same one you saw when you didn't know how to get the hell out of Dodge."

"Thanks." I said it again, although he hadn't been fishing for gratitude. My gray shivered with the memory. The demon had been an older one with big, ugly horns, a forked tail and roiling black mixed with the bright red of molten rock. Troy had had only a millisecond to send in the dogs—and the 'coons, skunks and other animal distractions, saving us both.

"Where's Spook?"

"Out sniffing around. Keeping watch."

"For a three-legged dog, he works hard." And it was my fault he had three legs because he had lost one of his back legs to the demon when he jumped between us, allowing me time to escape. Sadly, what that demon touched could not be recovered.

"He's always been a busy dog."

"He doesn't like me."

"You've said that before." Troy grinned. "Truth is, I don't think he likes women, but that must be something that happened dirt-side. None of the women here have been mean to him."

I snorted, which for a ghost was more of a moaning groan. "As if you'd allow anyone to mistreat your buddies."

"Including you." He reached out and grazed his hand along what would have been my chin. Most ghosts didn't bother to touch because of the unsettling lack of a physical barrier. It was just a brush of emotion, much worse—or better—than a living touch.

"I don't have much to offer you," I said. "I haven't collected a darn thing that has fallen through. I was out foraging this morning when the demon sent me scurrying."

"Are you sure it wasn't an imp?"

I shrugged. "There's not much difference."

"Yes, there is. Imps are usually on errands. Demons are mostly plotting to go across and stay. I asked Cinderspark about it."

"That's interesting. What does she think about all the demons?"

Troy shrugged. "I didn't ask her. Maybe we should though. Ever since we fought off that demon, I've felt drained and tired. If demons or imps are attempting to cross, that could mean some are making it all the way dirt-side."

Troy had warned me that even though a demon was dirt-side, I wasn't safe from it. They could see me and reach right through the veil. I was positive I did not want to die the remainder of the way by being pulled back through the weave and letting a demon harvest the pain of my death. I wasn't that generous.

"Since Cinderspark goes back and forth, maybe she'll know something," I agreed. One day I hoped to be brave enough to ask Cinderspark if she could find out anything about the living woman I had been. So far, every time I had had the opportunity, I stifled the urge. I wasn't sure if I was hiding my past from her or myself.

Chapter 4

Cinderspark was cute as a button and about five inches tall if you included her wings. She was probably the equivalent of a nine-year-old human. I didn't remember seeing a single fairy when alive, but Troy and Cinderspark seemed to have come from a slightly different world than mine anyway. At the very least, we'd left during different times because things he talked about seemed futuristic to me.

Fairy or no, I was pretty certain Cinderspark wasn't supposed to visit In Between. But how does a ghost tell a fairy child what to do? We couldn't threaten to rat her out to her parents unless her parents visited In Between, and I certainly hadn't seen them.

After devouring the treats Troy supplied we set out, using a few relatively stable landmarks to guide us to the ghostly limbs of the ancient tree Troy called home. Spook, his three-legged dog, bounded ahead, always happy to check the terrain.

Troy's tree was the only place we ever saw Cinderspark. No one knew why the portal existed, but it must have had something to do with Troy because the tree was where he guided the roadkill through from dirt-side. The juniper on this side was devoid of any living material, as were all the trees here. It was a sad, hunched over thing, split in the middle, gray as my own being. One side resembled driftwood, shiny and smooth. The other was dull gray like the rest of In Between.

Once we were close to the tree, the weave and even the snaps of Troy's jeans became clearly visible. There was even the slightest taint of color to him. His face went from ghostly transparent to an almost solid and handsome young man. His hair took shape, ruffling in the breeze. Every so often, he'd reach up and pat it down.

My own hair, when I wasn't a completely bald-looking rounded ghost-blob, did not sway in the wind. My head and face were shaped, especially when I concentrated on the task, but nothing about this location caused my hair to dance with life.

Troy's cave was only a few feet from the limbs of the juniper. It was better hidden than mine and underground rather than tucked into a hillside. A ghost squirrel popped out of the shelter to greet us.

Spook waited patiently with us for Squirrel to report.

"There's a death happening over that way," Troy said, pointing into the gray abyss.

I had understood Squirrel's news. The bobbing critter knew how to convey death emotion, but that was an easy one for any of us.

"What do you think? Should we investigate?" Troy stared out across the shapeless landscape.

Not all deaths drew me. Violent murders, especially multiple murders, elicited no empathy from me even though I had been murdered. I couldn't pinpoint why this one drew me, but when I concentrated, the taint of an illness and a stark yearning for home washed over me. "Yeah, let's check it out."

Deaths were easy to find. There was always an opening in the weave as the spirit or soul crossed over. Sometimes the person crossed all at once, but most of the time it was like a slow leak, trickling through the weave gradually.

Maybe focusing on it made the bubble flow in our direction because as soon as we headed toward the death, the draw increased. We were almost there when I spotted Amy rolling in from another direction.

If I were still alive, I'd have sighed in exasperation. Since breath wasn't necessary anymore, I didn't bother, but a peek at Troy told me that he had noticed her. My focus had been tuned to the death, but Troy was watching Amy with open longing.

I failed to comprehend the attraction. Maybe it was because Amy still sported much of her earthly form, and it was a young and pretty one. Like Troy when he was near the tree, her hair blew in the breeze, and her delicate features were almost always perfectly formed, right down to a pert nose and jewelry that should have sparkled. The large gem on one hand was colorless here, but now and then her delicate chain necklace and dangle earrings seemed to glint gold.

I had never seen her abandon her concentration enough to lose her silhouette. Maybe it was her youth or maybe it had something to do with the way she died. It could be that the rest of us were lazy, me in particular. I simply lacked the initiative to hold my form very often. Why bother?

I clutched the pine needles Troy had given me and wished we'd found Cinderspark. Her fairy dust always made me forget that I was fading into the fog, even if the vitality didn't last. I concentrated on my features now, knowing how to arrange all the pieces.

When I glanced again at Troy, it was obvious my effort was wasted.

Amy reached for his hand. Troy smiled and clasped ghost fingers in hers.

If you think life isn't fair, wait until you die. It ain't no chocolate milkshake with real ice cream here either.

Rather than watch Troy and Amy revel in their moment of happiness, I let the death divert my focus. My first glimpse was a shock. He was young, healthy...*strong*...except something was eating away at him.

His breathing came in gasps. Each release of air pushed the string of his essence through the weave. Then, slowly, he'd take another and the string of gray would be sucked back. But not very far. Not enough to save him.

"He's really sick," I said.

Instead of focusing on the death in front of us, Troy stared off into the distance. "Another one. Close too."

Amy hovered at Troy's other side. There was no point in hiding my chagrin; she had eyes only for Troy. She still clutched his hand, making me shiver. Touch here was so personal. Troy never flinched away from her, though.

I glanced back at Kyle, the guy across the weave. Uh-oh. I knew his name. That was bad. Most of him was already across the line if his name was here. I still didn't know my own name, and no one else had figured it out either. Usually, as a person's essence came across, the bits and pieces were accessible to us. No one knew why my name hadn't come with me.

Kyle was alone. From the impersonal bed, dresser and television, it was obviously a low-end hotel room. Strange. There was a phone on the table near the bedside and a cell phone on the desk. Why didn't he call someone?

We waited.

Stupid though it was, I wished I could reach through the weave and dial 911. There was hope yet, though. He rallied to almost full consciousness, breathing stronger, pulling his lifeline back. His eyes opened, but they were feverish. He looked right at the weave. There was no way to know whether he saw us there, watching, waiting.

When he sat up, I folded my hands in prayer. *Call someone.* I chanted the words even though he wouldn't hear them.

Instead of reaching for the phone, he stumbled to the end of the room and stared at a large black guitar case.

Were there drugs in there that could help him? What was he doing? I didn't like him wasting all this time.

Martin suddenly hovered at my side, doing some chanting of his own. Martin showing up meant the life beacon was still very strong on our side.

I checked. The thread of life was thinner here now that Kyle was awake, but it was still here.

Call someone.

He unlatched the tall case and rubbed his hand along the grain. When he touched the instrument, it connected to his lifeline, and all at once I knew what had happened.

He had fallen off the stage. His head had slammed against the edge of the stage, hard. Someone must have brought him to the hotel thinking he would recover...uh-oh.

I looked at Martin, hoping for reassurance, but he just chanted steadily. He wasn't your average ghost. He was calmer than most of us, peaceful unless he was angry. Most of the time Martin resembled a disembodied genie, minus the headpiece. He was all sculpted chest with nothing but smoke below the waist. I'd only seen him fully formed a couple of times, and he was buck naked then. When we first met I thought he was young because he showed no signs of wrinkles, but after getting to know him, I realized he had died older, maybe at sixty or seventy.

The musician's lifeline, now that I knew what to look for, showed the bleeding. It was too late for him to figure it out. He had already stumbled back to the edge of the bed, sweating, holding his guitar case and staring at the cell phone.

But I had seen too much to hold out hope.

He reached for the cell, nearly toppling over. He lay back down, the guitar clutched in one hand as though he were about to take it out of the case.

He never placed the call.

Maybe I only felt the ones who died before their time. I'd like to think my clock hadn't run out and that maybe I'd actually still had some purpose. I was still angry that my time dirt-side had been cut so short. Kyle was angry too.

There were four of us nearby when he and his grief hit the airwaves in the gray.

Martin was there, still singing in his monotone way. He never had answers to the "why?" of things, but he was there. I don't remember him being around when I crossed, but anytime I lingered too close to that memory it burned.

"This can't happen," Kyle said, holding a ghostly guitar case against his chest. "My wife—"

"Can't ever be ready." Martin laid a hand on what would have been Kyle's shoulder.

I knew that touch. It wasn't the same as if we were alive, but Kyle would feel it.

He stared at the ghostly hand before he screamed.

That first touch was as eerie as being touched by a ghost when you were still living. Cold. Dead. Nothing but pure emotion because that was all we had left.

Martin stepped back, chanting again. "You weren't ready, but you'll accept it in time."

I scanned the gray for Troy, but he had already gone. I searched the direction where he had pointed at the other death, but fog breezed back at me. I felt no pull. Of course, with Kyle still wailing in front of me, he was capable of blocking a lot of emotion, including a death, for a long time.

"I'm not sick anymore!" The shout went nowhere, dissipating into the ether. "I feel better. I do!"

"The injuries go away," I explained.

He must not have realized I was standing there until I spoke.

Sometimes the gray was like that. It took a while to discern shapes when you were used to color.

Kyle's face was streaked with very real tears. If I touched them, because they were of life, they would probably provide energy, but I wasn't that desperate. Thankfully Troy had brought the juniper needles.

"*My wife needs me.* I need to get home! I told them to take me home, but they didn't want to drive all that way!"

"So go home."

It was not instantaneous, but his sobs choked back. "How?"

"It won't be the same," I warned. "You're In Between. You're stuck in this realm, but you can visit." I waved my hand at the dead body, his dead body across the curtain. "You can't cross again. You can't cross anywhere until..." I hung my head. "There are other curtains. Eventually you will cross through one of them. But not that one."

It took a long time for him to speak. He finally released the neck of the guitar case and held it by the handle. "Show me how to go to them."

It was good that he had decided to make the journey. The hounds were howling off in the distance, but of course they had already smelled his emotion. Grief like Kyle's would attract all kinds of monsters if he stood here long enough. Even without a plan, we'd have had to get him moving.

"It's a little like surfing," I said. "You float along, but you do have to paddle."

Luckily, learning wasn't that difficult. Pushing against the gray was something you wanted to do instinctively the minute you arrived.

I gave a nod to Martin, silently agreeing I would help this time.

Martin drifted off, still muttering in half song.

As Kyle and I floated, I urged him to listen, describing the hounds and how they would chew him up if they ever caught him. He didn't care now, but if he saw them later, he'd change his mind.

I surveyed our surroundings constantly, waiting to glimpse the drip from a twisted fang or the glow of red from unfriendly eyes. The hellish dogs were still far off, but the fog always had shapes, and I was very worried about what those shapes might turn out to be. We weren't running, but the memory of the heat and stink of monster breath kept me firing questions at Kyle. I had to figure out as quickly as possible how to follow his memories to the place he wanted to go.

When he told me about his unborn child, I knew we were in deep trouble. That kind of grief brought us right up against water. The second he spoke of the child, we hit the bank.

"Oh shit, Kyle."

The mermaids stretched across the rocks just offshore weren't there to see us safely across either. We needed to burrow underground and quickly.

Chapter 5

Water was a random appearance In Between. As far as I knew, no one here actually drank the stuff. Bodies of water seemed to be some sort of portal, but if anyone understood how they worked, no one had bothered to explain it to me. I wasn't about to cross this sudden lake with mermaids sitting there beckoning. This was the closest I'd ever been to the fish ladies. It was more than close enough.

"She looks like Paula, my wife," Kyle murmured.

Instead of searching for shelter, he was staring at the nearest mermaid. "They probably *all* do, Kyle. We need to get out of here." The hounds were quiet behind us. That didn't mean they weren't there. If we were really lucky, they had stopped or even stayed near the other death. But silence from the hounds wasn't a guarantee that they weren't stalking us. Even if they weren't, as the mermaids proved, there were other things out there that were hungry for grief.

"Is Paula on this side too?"

Impatiently, I shot back, "That mermaid doesn't look pregnant to me. I'm guessing that means it's a charade to draw you closer. And then guess what will happen?"

He finally shifted his attention to me.

"Gobble, gobble, time for mermaid dinner." There were rocks a ways off on our right. We could probably shelter there. If the hounds found us holed up, eventually they'd tire of waiting, or if they were hungry enough, they could battle it out with the mermaids.

"You're right, she doesn't look pregnant," Kyle said.

"You're dead, Kyle. Your wife isn't. If you want to see her again, I'd suggest you stay away from creatures that look anything like her, especially if that shape is gray." The mermaids did have flashes of green to them, but it was monster green—a blackish dank algae green. Even from here, the stuff had a smothering quality to it.

Seeing someone who resembled his wife had calmed him. Had I seen someone I knew...but initially, I only had one memory, and it was of the guy who killed me. Later, memories of people had leaked into my consciousness. I was pretty sure one of them was my sister, but oddly, my emotions remained distant as though I was accustomed to keeping her a secret. That made no sense to me, and no matter who she might be, there was no name or face to complete the memory.

"It's not my wife," Kyle said slowly. "How strange."

"Come on, Kyle, we have to hide." I hated to do it, but I reached out to tug at his arm. Neither of us was solid, but contact was contact, and it had a force. I pulled gently, grinding my non-teeth against the rage and pain that radiated from him. That sort of thing could echo back through me, and if we accidentally created a loop it would magnify our emotions. We could attract every monster In Between in a hurry.

Kyle yanked his arm away. "Don't do that. It hurts."

"I know. But not as bad as it will if she takes a bite out of you."

The slimy mermaid glided forward and draped herself over another rock, one that was much closer to us. She smiled.

I don't know what Kyle saw, but her saber-toothed fangs were more than enough for me. I pedaled my ghost feet as fast as they could take me, barely caring if Kyle followed this time. As soon as I reached the rocky alcove, I thinned my head and inspected the largest crevice.

Kyle was waiting behind me when I oozed back out of the cairn. "It's empty." I opened my mouth to describe how he needed to squish himself through, when laser spots of red blurred behind him. "I hope you feel skinny," I squeaked. "You're gonna have to compress and blow yourself in faster than a tornado."

He glanced back to where my eyes were focused.

"Go," I said, not waiting to see if he listened. I rolled sideways, dodging away from him. There were other crevices. It was best if we didn't stand together, and I was more experienced than he at gathering, thinning and dodging.

Unfortunately for him, the two-headed hound didn't even spare me a sniff. It knew grief when it smelled it. Like a distorted smile, it peeled black lips back and loosed two howls of triumph.

In desperation, I threw the rock I had hidden in my hand, propelling it through the fog. Emotion had power here.

The missile hit the hound square in one open mouth.

Already thin, except for the rock-throwing hand, I slithered through the boulders, nothing but smoke. I focused on working my way through crevices back to where I had left Kyle. If I arrived in time, maybe I could help yank him through.

It took a while to pull myself back together. There wasn't enough open space in the rocks for me to keep all the parts where they belonged, but close enough.

My eyes swiveled, but there was no Kyle.

"Kyle?" The hounds were still baying, but the sounds had retreated a ways. No way could they have devoured him that quickly, not all of him!

I squeezed my eye through a crack, slowly letting it swivel and check before squishing the rest of my head through the crevice.

The two-headed hellhounds had gathered in force. There had to be fifty of them, slathering, drooling, and yelping. Those in the rear were growling, threatening their own.

Kyle was in the water. Correction. He was on the water. I had never attempted to float on water or walk on it either. Things In Between were solid enough in their own way, although the rules were often different and dangerous.

I sucked myself back inside the shelter and slid over to a spot with a better angle.

Once I squeezed through, I could see that Kyle was actually balancing on his guitar case. The hounds were not pleased. Two or three of them ventured haunch deep into the waves.

A mermaid was not far off.

"Kyle!" Damn fool. I had no idea what to do. If only I had Troy's animals to create a distraction. I could ooze through the rocks all day, but there were hounds between Kyle and me. The mermaid's ravenous smile hadn't gotten any less toothy. She flicked her tail, slapping against the water hard enough that the splash resonated over the noise of the hounds.

Waves from her lashing tail radiated out and then bunched in a rather alarming cascade directed at Kyle. He kept his eyes trained on the water rather than the hounds or the mermaid.

Damned impressive for a first-day ghost. With arms out, he balanced precariously on the guitar case as it rocked back and forth.

A larger wave erupted, and I clutched my ghost hands together, wishing for a fishing rod, a spear, anything to help out. My arm drew back automatically, fixated on throwing a weapon I didn't hold.

Kyle managed the wave, if barely. Before relief had a chance to set in, the sudden lack of motion after the swell knocked him right off.

"Oh, Kyle, no!" He was done for.

His head didn't stay under for more than a second. With an impressive heave, he launched himself back onto the case like a professional surfer. Neither the mermaid nor the hounds had time to make a decisive maneuver in his direction.

The mermaids were probably the more dangerous, but they weren't anxious to venture any closer to the canines. And the hounds didn't like the water.

Kyle crouched on his perch, waiting, watching and dripping.

I shivered. A sense of helplessness settled across my shoulders, drawing the double noses of a hellhound or two. I clamped down. Kyle had inadvertently done himself the biggest favor of all by allowing himself to be distracted by the mermaid and beastly dogs. The pain he had been radiating was compressed as he concentrated on survival.

The canines at the back of the pack sniffed the air expectantly again, but my emotions were now tightly cloaked.

Another mermaid drifted to the opposite side of Kyle.

"Crap." Those babes could swim. It didn't take me long to figure out their plan. They started bobbing about, using their tails to create a new series of waves. Gentle, unrelenting ripples, not ones large enough to capsize him, but undulations that drew him out toward open water, away from the hounds.

Kyle dropped and paddled. He didn't have much substance, and he lost ground, but not quickly.

The hounds recognized a losing battle when they saw one. They shuffled out of the water and offered Kyle plenty of room, a clear invitation for him to come ashore.

Annihilation by mermaid monster or disintegration by dripping canine fangs. Some great options there.

A larger wave rocked Kyle. It hadn't come from the mermaids, either.

"Paddle!" The disturbance under the water was nothing more than a large shadow to me, but it had to be something that frightened the mermaids because one minute the bathing beauties were there, the next, nothing but a ripple and empty rocks.

Their sudden disappearance did nothing to soothe my nerves. My eyes shifted from the hounds to the waves.

In the far-off distance, a violin sounded a discordant shriek, but it cut off so suddenly I wondered if I had imagined it.

Kyle paddled furiously, closing in on the shore again before standing on his case.

One of the devil dogs stepped my way, his red eyes honing in on me. The orbs were rimmed with a black so deep, it promised to unravel me.

I ducked back inside the rock. The hound edged closer, but we both knew I was safe.

Ripples of water threatened to send Kyle into the jaws of the hounds, but he adeptly controlled where he wanted to be while keeping an eye on the open water.

The lead canine put a paw in the water, lifted and sniffed at it with both heads. He backed out of the lake with a yelp. Whatever he smelled had him turning tail and loping off into the gray.

Few of the devil dogs followed their leader. They were too hungry.

Kyle didn't know that the hellhounds' patience was limited, but since he had nowhere else to go, he stayed put. If I had been out there with him, I could have told him how to draw his grief inside, how to be small, invisible and nonexistent.

He must have figured it out, or he was so scared he went numb. Maybe sharks similar to those in the real world were out there in the water. Whatever the reason, Kyle barely moved on his board. He stayed down where he could paddle if he needed to, but he held very, very still.

* * *

The gray had taken on what passed for darkness before the last of the hounds faded into the nighttime ether. I poked my head further outside the boulders and then oozed the rest of me out slowly, making sure I didn't draw any attention.

Kyle's grief was still a powerful beacon. In the distance, a square dance fiddle frantically played out of tune. The music was an ominous warning, each bar ending in sour notes.

The mermaids hadn't returned, possibly because whatever lurked under the water still waited. It was as safe as it was ever going to get. I called out, "Swim in. Stay cold. Don't think too much and don't feel. We don't need anything else sensing us."

The freezing burn of what we are is painful, but it was possible to keep the grief locked inside where it wouldn't attract the monsters.

Kyle stared at me, not paddling. I knew what he was thinking.

"You can come back here and dive in any time. You probably ought to at least say goodbye to your wife first."

He jolted half upright as though I had smacked him.

"Keep the pain contained," I reminded him. Sound traveled across the water and so did our emotions. "Come in as quickly as you can."

He stepped off the board and swished through the water. It was good to know that if I ever needed to, swimming was a possibility.

The grating music of the fiddle intensified. The pounding of hooves, a sound that should have been impossible with the muted fog of In Between, danced a horrific offbeat to the notes shrieking across rusty metal strings. Sparks of flame cut through the gray here and there, promising we were out of time. The only entity here that controlled fire was a demon.

Kyle's limbs jerked with the broken melody, which wasn't all bad because he swam faster. He contained himself too, but only because exhaustion had no doubt set in.

Chapter 6

Training someone to survive even their first day or two In Between was like digging a grave in weather that varied from a drizzling rain to ice cold sleet. Even without touching Kyle, the wave of his emotions smacked me with ice needles more often than not, but it didn't matter. We had to run and run fast. I ignored his stress and kept us forging forward.

The demon may have been attracted to the area by Kyle's grief, but with us floating away at full speed and hellhounds and mermaids contributing to the confusion, the scent of agony had to be dissipating. My emotions were tucked so tight not even I could find them.

After the sparks from hungry flames disappeared into the murk behind us, we still didn't slow down.

When we were finally far enough away that the evil fiddle had faded to silence, we rested in a state nearer a coma than ghost.

The final leg of the journey exhausted me every bit as much as it hurt him, because hunting down the place in the weave where he could see his wife involved a lot of stopping to hide.

When we finally found the right location, I tried to stop him from crashing into the barrier, but I wasn't fast enough. "Kyle!"

He threw himself forward in despair.

I sighed and spit out instructions. The weave wasn't as thin here as it would have been had he died near his home. Luckily his link to his wife and the baby was strong enough that he could see them.

I talked, following a ritual we had for all newcomers. It was a waste of time, but I provided all the helpful hints for finding a shelter, surviving, and explained how he could find me later.

He didn't care. I knew he wouldn't. But I had no more left to give, and there was no point in staying. He'd swim against the weave, trying to break through; we all did. He'd probably see his own funeral from some half-stuck position in the weave if he didn't splinter himself into tiny fragments. Eventually, he'd figure out how to float back together.

Slashed by the weave, his pain radiated along the edges of In Between instead of out into the gray where predators were more likely to hear or smell him. The line between worlds would help contain his emotions even as the weave threatened to destroy him. He may well be discovered and eaten, but there was nothing else to be done right now.

On the way back to my shelter I discovered Martin plucking bits of lichen from a rock. Or, since it was Martin, perhaps they were dead worms. No matter. If they had a spark of life, they would provide energy.

He broke out of his tuneless hum to ask after Kyle. "Get him settled?"

"Settled? Is that what this is?" I plopped down next to Martin's hovering head and told him about the water, the hounds, and the mermaids. "Kyle is lucky he made it out of there."

"You saw the River Styx? That could be another sign."

"What are you talking about?"

"The River Styx. In Greek Mythology, it leads to the portal of hell. Of course, that isn't the only river. The River Styx is actually a convergence of waterways, which implies there are other portals."

"Yes, I've heard of Styx, but we were at a lake. Although since it had mermaids maybe it was an ocean."

"The myths are riddles. They often leave out the most pertinent information." Martin chuckled. "Imagine those who didn't know a coin was required to cross the River Styx. Those people had no way to pay for passage and had to wander the shores...or worse."

The myths weren't the only thing that left out information. Martin was already several feet away and drifting fast. "Where are you going?"

"To the river, of course. Can't let something like that go by without inspecting it."

Figures. I describe a dangerous body of water filled with creatures likely to eat him, and he acted like it was a tourist attraction. I hadn't even told him where it was located. Not that location was all that meaningful here. Martin would either stumble across it or he wouldn't.

By the time I made it back to my own shelter, my form was as faded and distorted as if I had spent a week fighting the weave.

Troy was waiting for me just inside the cave, looking as bad as I felt. Whoever he had witnessed coming across must have required his help and a lot of energy.

Spook sat very close to Troy, guarding him fiercely. If that dog had been able to, he'd have merged his energy with Troy. I only wished I had something to offer him, but there hadn't been much to harvest on my way back. The one or two sparks I'd seen had gone out instantly when I picked them up. They were so small, my ghost absorbed them like sugar dissolving in water.

"I think we should find Cinderspark," Troy said.

"I know. Why did you wait for me instead of looking for her?" I was perplexed. Troy was the best at finding her and he was comfortable doing his own thing. "I'd have come looking for you sooner or later," I told him.

Troy kept his head down, too tired to lift it. "I dunno. It's what we were doing before we heard the call, and your place was closest after we were done watching the soul cross over."

We sat, unmoving for a span of ghostly time. Whether it was a day, an hour or minutes didn't matter. It was a form of rest and meditation. We didn't need sleep, and we didn't generate any real energy without an outside source, but it still helped.

Getting to his tree took longer than usual because we were both drained. Spook stayed close instead of testing the gray ahead. He walked between us, but it was impossible to say if he was offering me support or keeping me away from Troy. It wasn't like I ever hung on Troy like Amy did. Even if we touched accidentally, I was always careful not to drain energy. I wasn't some demon or ghoul feeding off of anything and everything.

The route we followed was familiar, which was both good and bad. While we could reach the tree faster, we weren't likely to spot any energy unless we detoured close to the edges where something might have drifted through.

"Was the other death bad?" I asked.

Troy nodded. "It was awful, a little girl hit by a drunk driver. Thankfully, Martin showed up. He took care of her."

"Oh, that is bad." I was silent for a bit, contemplating. "I'm glad Martin was there." But if Martin had been the one to help with the crossing, it begged the question of why Troy was so feathered out and weak.

Instead of offering an explanation, all he said was, "I was glad he showed up too."

When we arrived at the juniper, he said, "I'm going to cross."

"Now? Troy, you don't look so good."

"I don't think I can wait for Cinderspark."

Stress caused my face to thin. "What do I do? What if you get stuck? I can't cross! You know I can't!" Panic made my legs scrunch up into my chest cavity until I was a head sitting on a ball of foamy gray. The tree was his entry point, but go across? "It can't be safe!"

"The animals do it. I've done it before. It'll be okay."

There was something special about the animals he helped. They were a merging of both sides, not just ordinary ghosts. Well, some were, but those were the ones that faded the quickest. The others stayed around Troy, keeping him company.

Before I could protest further, he said, "I was in a car accident. Maybe that's why the little girl's death hit me so hard."

"What? That doesn't make sense." Watching someone die was hard, but I'd never been drained by a death. Then again, who was I to argue with Troy? When a child crossed over it was always more difficult. Children had so much life. They were huge, multicolored beacons, beautiful and precious lights. No matter how they came through, it was horribly sad. "What do you want me to do?"

"Nothing. Just be my backup. If it goes well, I'll return with some energy. If it doesn't...well, it will be fine. I'm sure of it."

I followed far enough to watch his tired form as he approached his tree. Going to the other side could kill him. Even an attempt had to be painful, whether or not he was somehow attached to this portal.

When he touched the juniper, color burst out in a star pattern. His jeans suddenly turned a light blue, his hair darkened, and his high school football jacket glowed briefly before he was gone.

I held my breath, watching. Then I remembered I was supposed to be his backup. Color meant energy. If anything had noticed, trouble would arrive in a flash. The hounds weren't likely to be attracted, especially by something so instantaneous and lacking in emotion, but there were other creatures to be feared In Between.

I edged closer to the gray branches and like Spook, began to inspect the surrounding boulders and shapes.

The flash of color had been brief. We probably weren't in any more danger than usual.

Unable to help myself, I drifted next to the tree. There was no feeling of the edge of the bubble, no pressure, no weave. Close to the edge, the fog was always thick enough to see and feel. Here there was just a split trunk and gray limbs.

I put my hand out, but when it came in contact with the foggy bark, I remained as gray as ever. I was more transparent than usual, but I was tired and had no reserves.

The tree did not emit any energy. Its jagged, bent form easily blended with the surroundings. The driftwood side was shiny, and the sheen made it appear damp.

It was natural to want to run my hand along that smoothness, and for a moment, I forgot myself. I forgot that I couldn't "feel" things like a living person. We ghosts could surround or push objects, but there was rarely real tactile feedback.

Surprisingly, the driftwood felt slick, but not slimy. There was a warmth to it that was not gray. Although my hand remained ghost, the colors around me darkened. Looking behind me, everything was gray. Peering down at the driftwood, I could see sparks like stars.

The darkness inside the tree was not unlike night. It smelled different too, now that I was touching the trunk. The tree held the rich scent of earth, something other than the gray of In Between.

I realized that the portal had remained open when Troy crossed. It probably wouldn't close until he returned.

The colorless world was behind me, which meant there was something different in front of me. Warily, I stepped into the darkness, wondering if I'd be able to escape.

Well, you only live once, but you can die many times, many different ways. I stepped again, following Troy into the tree even though he had to be far ahead of me.

Chapter 7

The darkness inside the trunk of the juniper was nothing like the weave. I drifted through the breezy blackness, very leery about what might be here. There was light ahead; probably the living world. I checked behind me to make sure the gray opening was still in sight. There was no need to be completely stupid.

There were rocks scattered alongside a path, mostly small pebbles resting on darker ground or tree roots. The area was more a tunnel than empty space, but if there was a ceiling, I couldn't discern it.

The light source, when I reached it, was not the world of the living. It was a river. The beam of brightness flowed in and around roots, not radiating very far into the darkness. Streams of varying colors splashed along, with power surging like a heartbeat. The electricity rippled across my gray. The energy reminded me of Cinderspark's wings; colors, light as air, pulsing in a steady stream.

Had I not thought of her then, I may not have seen her. She matched the mixing dance of light exactly, flickering in time with a silent music. She was color, but she was an unmoving pattern against the flow behind her.

Cinderspark was always a huge beacon of brightness. Being In Between had to be unnatural for her because she retained her youth, her beauty and her aliveness. When she flew, sparkles bounced off of her, and bluish-green swirls followed her like moving lights in a photograph. The sparks, if I caught them, would feed me. Troy called them fairy dust.

"Cinderspark?"

"What are you doing here?" Cinderspark's wings reflected her namesake, shooting tiny bits of fairy dust in multiple directions. She was angry.

"I followed Troy. He came to visit dirt-side."

Cinderspark frowned mightily. "If he came here searching for me, you can tell him I won't be visiting anymore."

"Oh no! Did you get in trouble?" Disappointment radiated from me. I quickly gathered it back.

Cinderspark sniffed, waving at the wisp of emotion that floated close to her. "No."

"Oh, Cinder. He's going to miss you. Me too," I said. "He went dirt-side to ask you about the number of demons we've seen lately."

Her wings stilled, but she didn't fall. "Troy is different now. Something is wrong." She fluttered back and forth, pacing. "The thing is, he's there now, waiting as if he's expecting roadkill. He used to only show up when there was roadkill, helping the animals across. But lately it's as if he can't tell when there is roadkill and when there isn't. It's all wrong!"

"What's wrong? What is this place?" I asked. "Does this river belong to the fairies?"

Cinderspark giggled. The joy of it hit me gently. She shared it with no thought, and it required no effort on my part to gather it. Like a drink of water, it quenched.

"No, silly. It's just a ley line. This one is much more accessible than most, because of," she looked guiltily upward, into the dark. "Well, because of Troy."

"Oh."

"If he knows about the demons, why is he—" she stopped. "Have you seen the demons too?"

I nodded. "The last one I saw didn't make it through. About two day cycles ago, maybe three. We were coming to ask you about it when we were called to help someone come across."

Cinderspark stopped her fluttering again. She plopped on a rock that jutted out from the side of the cavern. "Troy used to help a lot of people across. He still helps the animals, but he doesn't have the energy to do it properly most of the time. I thought I could help him."

"You do help! Your energy is very special!" I spread my ghostly hands. There were no proper words for what Cinderspark provided.

Cinderspark shook her head. "I want to ask my mom what has happened to Troy, but if I did, she'd be very upset with me."

"Because she'd find out you come here and forbid you to return?"

Cinderspark nodded. "Troy's problem isn't exactly a demon mark, but he's been marked. If I continue to give him energy, that mark will eventually lead to me. That's the way it is with a demon mark, or even a fairy mark for that matter. But his mark isn't a demon mark, not precisely." Her words tumbled out so rapidly, it was hard to assimilate the information.

"Demon mark?" Her words sent a chill through me that was colder than the ice of another ghost.

She bobbed up and down. "I don't know exactly what it is! That's the problem. What if...what if it's just a demon type that I haven't seen? I can see the mark. I didn't really notice it at first, but now it's growing."

"Oh, no."

She nodded, flying every which way so quickly, I stopped trying to track her. "It's true!"

"I believe you." I stared into the swirls of the river, the ley line. Guilt consumed me. "He rescued me from a demon. He must have gotten hurt or marked. I had no idea."

Cinderspark shook her head, sparks flying. "No. That isn't how a mark happens. It's not a battle scar. It has to be accepted for the binding to take place. Uh-oh. I have to go." And she did.

In the blink of an eye, I was left alone with only the glow from the ley line running through the rock. Given Cinderspark's sudden exit, I gathered myself into a tight ball and drifted back towards In Between. There was no point to further exploration. Waiting around to see whatever it was that scared Cinderspark would be worse than foolhardy.

* * *

I didn't have any experience with fairies, demons, demon marks or magic of any sort before I died. Turns out, In Between lacked libraries or the internet. Maybe I should try to contact someone dirt-side and see if they'd run a quick Google search for me. Of course, there was the small problem that even on the side of the living, there was probably only a handful of people who would know anything about demon marks.

When stumped, I usually asked Troy questions because he'd been here longer than me, but in this case, it didn't seem like a great idea. Maybe Martin would be able to help me.

I waited outside the juniper while sorting my options, pretending to be Troy's backup, pretending I hadn't just infringed on his territory.

When he finally slipped out of the trunk, he was filled with energy, virtually bursting with life, except that he was still dead. I studied him meticulously from head to toe while he was still close to the tree, where colors were most visible. Since he wore a school jacket and jeans, there wasn't much flesh visible. Then again, as ghosts, maybe a demon mark didn't have to be on his flesh. His face and neck were clearly formed as he approached. There were no weird, detectable marks.

"I couldn't find her." His voice was strong now, barely ghosting at the edges.

I didn't answer. My attention was completely focused on examining every piece of hair, every bit of visible flesh, including his ears. He hadn't worn earrings; there was nothing there but gray ear. The jacket looked like any high school jock jacket. Embarrassed, I forced myself to inspect his legs, all the way to his shoes. He was nicely built. Right now he glowed.

I sighed in defeat. I wouldn't know a demon mark if it floated in front of my face.

Noticing my preoccupation, he asked, "You okay?" His eyebrows were raised.

Who could blame him. I'd been fixated on him like some kind of lovelorn groupie. "Fine. I, uhm, found some leaves that must have floated through."

"That's good. There wasn't much to bring back. There was no roadkill either, but I managed some blades of grass."

"You keep them. You tire so easily lately. You might need them later on."

I stared at the blades clutched in his hand.

He nodded. "You're right. I don't know why, but the energy doesn't last long anymore. Maybe it's because I've made my peace topside. It isn't as easy to slide through anymore, and I don't feel the call like I used to." He slipped his hand into his jacket pocket.

"What changed?" My heart beat faster. Maybe he knew what had happened.

"I said goodbye to my parents."

That didn't sound right. "What?"

He nodded. "I made my peace with them. I let them know it was okay that I had moved on. But that was a while ago. A new sapling started growing in place of the huge tree that the vehicle crashed into. The new growth is causing the opening here to narrow, and there just isn't as much energy available."

But Cinderspark had said he was marked. "Did you see anyone else? Was there anything bad there?"

He focused on me then, instead of staring into the gray. "No. I guess I forgave the people responsible. They kidnapped Cinderspark because they thought she could spin gold. I helped her escape. That's how we became such great friends, but she's been around less frequently lately. It's like I insulted her or she's afraid of me for some reason, but that doesn't make sense."

I had to tell him what Cinderspark had said, even though it meant confessing I'd invaded his privacy. Why hadn't Cinderspark told him the truth? Maybe I could avoid the whole truth. "She came through while you were in there."

He blinked and his form wavered in surprise. "She did?"

"Troy, she is afraid, but not of you, but *for* you. She said you were marked by something." I gave him as much detail as Cinderspark had given me without admitting I'd gone into the tree. I felt like a burglar who had taken his secret stash with no ability to return it. I owed him the truth, but wasn't brave enough to admit my transgression. If the energy here was fading, I'd just pillaged some of the last dredges. "She wants to help, but she's very afraid of the mark, whatever it is."

Troy shook his head. "I can't put her in any danger." He pulled his hands out of his pockets and clenched his fists before shoving them back in. His fingers were their normal gray, although one hand was less formed than the other. That could easily be the whim of In Between or lack of concentration.

"Can you see anything? Any mark at all?" he demanded.

I shook my head. "I don't see anything unusual, but I don't know what to look for, and she didn't have time to tell me!"

"Maybe I can figure it out."

"We have to figure it out! The way she described it made it sound like it was a mark that would draw a demon, or whatever marked you, right to you."

"No, not we, not anymore. If Cinderspark is avoiding me, I should be avoiding everyone."

Cold fear filled me again, and it had to be worse for him. Loneliness might be just as bad for some people still alive, but I doubted it was as screamingly miserable as it was here. People talk about cold spots, well, wait until you're on this end. Those spots reach the land of the living because the kind of pain that comes from being a lonely ghost can't be stopped by a murky curtain. You walk near a lonely ghost, and you'd have to be a serial killer to miss the vibe. It's a physical pain that, since I'm dead, shouldn't be felt anymore, but the hurt is real.

Troy raised one hand halfheartedly and began to drift away.

"Troy, you can't tackle this by yourself!"

Spook came around the tree then, barking. He was having none of Troy's nonsense. He took his spot, trailing after Troy, leaving me standing next to a juniper that wasn't mine and with worry that had nowhere else to go.

Chapter 8

I floated slowly towards home, searching for Martin. He was the only one I knew who might have a clue about demon marks. He seemed to take great pride in knowledge of obscure facts. Either that or he just enjoyed babbling nonsense while pretending to be erudite.

As the gray drifted around me, I felt a tug to the edge. From the beckoning light, I knew it wasn't a death. There was still a whisper of a gentle life breeze, the brush more like the magic of Troy's tree than the opening of the weave to let in a soul.

It rarely paid to be curious In Between. But energy was energy and who really knew all the reasons a link to the other side might exist? Truth was, I was a moth to a flame where the living side was concerned even though other, more dangerous things were attracted there as well.

Before I could puff myself closer, a darker gray on gray froze me on the spot. Ghouls lacked the red eyes of demons and hellhounds. Once you were too close, there was nothing but a sucking blackness that would absorb you before you could escape.

I guardedly watched the shape as I paddled away in the opposite direction as fast as my blob could bobble. If weapons had been available here, I'd happily float around in full Rambo gear. Too bad shotguns never came through. Then again, there were far more dangerous creatures here than myself. With my luck they'd control all the guns. But even something simple would be better than nothing. My hands clenched as though with the memory of holding a weapon of some sort, but it was the ghost of a ghost, an instinct more than a recollection.

The blotch of gray didn't follow me, but the moan of misery did. Ah, a spirit then. Other than coating me with sadness, it couldn't actually do any harm. Martin said the spirits were very old ghosts who had never moved on, either because they hadn't made their peace or they had gone bad. They tried to take over other ghosts, but had no power to do so.

I had no idea what he meant about going bad. Did ghosts spoil like meat left sitting out? Did we go rancid if left in the gray too long?

The dark shadow drifted away from the tug; the call from dirt-side wasn't a death so the spirit couldn't wallow. It fed on misery the way most of us ghosts subsisted on discarded life energy.

I resumed hunting the pull along the edge. The scent of life was easy to follow once you were in the current because the edge accommodated, shifting.

The walls that came into focus were the same blank concrete as the other hospital rooms, but there was no patient this time. The dead guy caught my attention first because his energy was similar to my own, borrowed; not that of a living soul. He was in blue nursing scrubs, standing across the room from Martin's two friends. Roberto was the short Hispanic guy who had talked to us and given Martin the bloodstone. The other guy had to be Lynx because the ghostly image of a cat with long tufted ears hovered around his face. While his eyes shifted between the yellow glow of a cat and those of a human, both were filled with the spark of life.

"Martin says the girl doesn't belong there. We need to find her body here and call her back. I thought you could cross because you're already dead. You could ask her questions to help us locate her on this side," the cat said. "Why wouldn't it work?"

The dead man in nursing smocks had a ghostly image of his own. The image around him was a humanoid shape, but leathery as though mummified. The human form had hair neatly tied into a ponytail. In the ghost image, his head was rippled black skin with short, shiny hair so tight across a bony skull, it was nearly invisible. His bat ears were enormous, and I couldn't tell if the wings across his back went with the human form or the other creature because they seemed to belong to both. Part of one wing was missing, and the human was minus most of one arm.

"There is no way I can cross." The dead man's voice was elegant but clipped, matching his cold black stare. Since he was dead, he could probably cross easily. Of course, once he was In Between, I doubted he could find his way back over to the side of the living. Even with the gentle winds crossing the open weave right now, the weave encouraged me to stay away. It wasn't yet painful, but the pressure was a headache building across every part of me.

Roberto's voice was the easiest to understand. Like the cat, his hair was black or close to it, but his was longer, instead of a buzz cut. The thick part on top stood nearly straight up from the breezes crossing into the weave. "What's your name?" he asked me. Unlike the others, his pleasant tenor came right through to In Between as if he were standing in both places at once. He was easily able to see me, just like when Martin had spoken to him.

"I don't know," I answered. "Everyone calls me Shadow."

"Roberto," he introduced himself. "That's Lynx and Patrick." He pointed to the cat and then the dead guy.

"Patrick can cross, but once here, I doubt he could cross back," I told Roberto.

There might have been a flicker of surprise in the dead guy's eyes. He gave me a nod of either welcome or acknowledgment. "Is that so?"

The cat half hissed, but sounded more excited than angry. "When Roberto does his thing, it's as if there is a window. She found us!"

I had been drawn here, much like other places in the hospital. "Why are you looking for me?"

"We saw you with Martin when you helped tear him away from

Roberto. Saved both their asses, if you ask me. Martin said we need to locate you on this side. Patrick is a vamp so we figured since he was dead, he could cross and ask you questions without it killing him." A Cheshire grin stretched across both the ghost cat and the human face. While there was no sound of laughter, there might have been a ghostly purr.

My attention flicked to Patrick. I hadn't believed in vampires when I was alive. Now, it wasn't even a slight stretch. "A vampire? You use the energy from blood as your own life energy source."

"That's what I said," the cat agreed. "He's a vamp." His human eyes flashed yellow again.

I wanted to reach out and touch that energy. It sparked like fresh green leaves, like the earth energy Martin had brought back the last time he had talked to them. Lynx was beautiful, his face full of shifting shadows; even the human side of him seemed to dance in the low light, drifting between rays so that he was somehow partly camouflaged. His glowing eyes matched the taut energy bundled inside his body.

I had never possessed that much life energy even when alive.

"Do you know where you lived? The names of any relatives? How long have you been stuck where you are now?" Roberto shot questions out quickly, and I realized he was tiring. The weave drew closer, but the pressure level wasn't any worse. The dangerous edges would remain that way, hovering, until it snapped closed. If it happened suddenly enough, the steel fabric would shatter me into so many pieces I'd never recover.

I slid away, ever so carefully. A wisp of my arm brushed against a greedy edge of weave and the pain rocked me dangerously close to a different part of the grasping bands. "I don't know the answers to any of that. And time is not the same here." My voice squeaked with pain.

"Go! Hurry," Roberto yelled.

The cat tossed something at me. Instinctively, I reached for it, although, of course, it could not cross the barrier. Except it did.

"How we gonna find out who she is if she doesn't know herself?" the cat wondered, all trace of happy purr gone.

"That's not a problem." The vamp's voice was fading, but his words were still clear. "I don't know who she is, but I do know where her body is on this side."

The weave slammed shut, slapping me backwards like a piece of gray litter tumbling onto the landscape. My hand clutched the bundle of woven weeds and fur. I wasn't going to lose it, no matter what.

Chapter 9

If I could have held near the edge, I would have stayed, pain and impending doom notwithstanding. The vamp knew where I was? Why did he know and I didn't? A second or two longer, and he might have told me. Not that it would have mattered. I couldn't go there. But if a vampire knew where my body was, did that mean I was a vampire somewhere on the side of the living?

No. I was here. The vamp existed on the side of the living. He must imbibe from the living to be able to remain there. He was dead. I was dead, but I was In Between. Sucking nutrients from pine needles and shafts of light that leaked into In Between didn't make me a vampire.

There were ghouls that ate the living or the dead; anything for souls or bits of life. They were like the hellhounds, but faster. Shoot, most everything except the roadkill and a few human souls ate everything and anything In Between. The mermaids weren't the types you invited over for coffee or tea. Not that I'd actually witnessed them eat anyone, but those teeth weren't for gnawing down trees like a beaver.

I frowned, holding my arm where it had been slashed by the weave. My essence was leaking, and I was drained again, but the packet the cat had thrown me was full of energy. How had it made it across? Why had he thrown it, anyway?

The braid smelled of him, of earth, of magic. Before In Between, I hadn't known about magic, but now having met Cinderspark and the others, there was no doubt it existed. This braid was plant energy, human energy and a unique spark. I breathed it in again. Clean. Earthy. Electric. There was a small pebble woven through its silky length. A hole in the center of the bead allowed the braid to run through it. One darker gray spot had dripped across the pebble, and I wondered if it was the same earth Martin had requested—a bloodstone.

I carefully disguised the braid from the cat by weaving it into my hair. It was a barely noticeable dark gray spot against the lighter gray.

Thinking of Martin made me all the more determined to find him. Unfortunately, thinking of him didn't make him appear, but it provided a distraction that might keep me from brooding about my own death. The how and why didn't matter anyway because there was nothing to be done about it. But the cat didn't seem to agree with that sentiment.

It was stupid to hope. I didn't even remember enough details to help. There had been an attack, and then a bright light that shattered me in every direction. I had refused to go towards a light because I knew what that meant, and when something tried to pull from me, I instinctively fought back.

Something or someone had demanded the light inside me, but I had refused to give it up. There wasn't much else to the memory other than a fear that left me mindlessly screaming until I ran, stuffing the light into a place that was opposite the direction of the pull.

And then in that instant, it was too late. I was here and not ready to be dead.

I turned and smacked right into Martin.

"Eeeeep!" Quiet as a ghost, he had snuck up on me. The shock of bouncing off him nearly sent me straight back into the weave.

I glared at him to no avail. He merely drifted to the right and began crooning over a pile of gray. Nothing unusual there; the man was always singing at something.

Rather than wait for him to cease his yodeling, I told him I'd seen Roberto and Lynx again. I left out the part about Lynx throwing me the braid. Even though Martin had said the bloodstone was for me back when Roberto had handed it to him, Martin had never passed the gift to me. Not that I had any idea what to do with it. Such a powerful object from the land of the living would only make me a target of every hungry beast In Between.

Martin sang around my words, but he was listening. When I stopped talking, he puffed himself up with air for no apparent reason.

"That cat is a good cat, curious and smart. Now that they found you, maybe he and the witch can call you back."

"You really think I'm still alive?"

Martin let all the air out of his essence, but released it carefully so he didn't swish away. "There are many stages to death, and you've always been different from the rest of us here. Your voice isn't hollow, and you trail phantom juice behind you that reaches for the other side when you aren't paying attention to it."

"I do?"

"You're more contained now that you have practice, but you have a ghost."

"I *am* a ghost!" I left off the 'you idiot,' but it was a near thing.

He nodded and hummed. "But you have this double impression. It took me a while to figure it out, but whenever you are near the edge, your mirror image hops right over like it belongs there."

This was news to me, although, admittedly, I was constantly having to collect myself. Bits and pieces were frequently sliced and diced off me or melting away on what seemed like an hourly basis.

"If I'm still alive, how do I find myself? And how the hell do I go where I want to be? If my body exists, I'd rather peer through at it instead of random hospital rooms!" One other question burned inside me, but the answer might be too frightening to face. *Who am I?*

"Stop fighting the weave. It is just a form of energy, doing what it is meant to do. Use your own energy to coax the weave along. Of course, if you aren't careful you'll break apart, but you can nudge the edge along in front of you if you are careful. It doesn't like us so it will skitter out of the way for us, but yet it must contain us. You can't fight it. Sing to it."

"Martin." I started to tell him that not everyone wanted to float around crooning like an insane madman, but he chuckled, turning it into an all-out cackle before he regained control of himself.

"Not lucky enough to have a beautiful voice like me? Heh-heh." He wafted away, beckoning. "It's not the voice that has to sing. It's the energy."

He was headed back to the edge. I hesitated, but Martin would merely wander away if I didn't follow. Nervously I puffed myself after him. "The last time I visited the edge with you...Is it required to be naked to coerce the weave into doing what you want?"

Martin laughed so hard he nearly blew himself halfway across In Between. His mirth started as a ghostly shout and dissolved into chuckles that pushed him around in a circle of fits and starts. "Heh-heh. Oh, heheheehee. No, but my nakedness irks the witch. Adriel is an amazing power, but she could stand to unbend some." Martin cackled some more.

"Good thing because I don't even know how to get naked," I muttered.

That set him off again.

When he could finally speak, he said, "I dress myself with bits of this and that, same as when I was topside. This place isn't earth, but it has a voice. If you listen, you can gentle it and bend it where you might want. Same as earth."

I wasn't certain of that. But at least any follow-up ordeal wouldn't require me to stand naked in front of the cat and his friends. And most of the time Martin didn't bother to fully form himself, which was fine. His granite face was more than enough.

As we sidled back to the edge, he asked me to list all the rooms and people I'd seen. Predictably, those memories brought us near the hospital. Reminiscent of walking through a graveyard, only the opposite, I could see blurred images of the living walking the corridors. There were at least two nurses, a doctor in a lab coat, and a gaggle of visitors whispering. The group nearly ran over the cleaning lady when she stepped around the linen cart to hand an orderly a set of clean sheets.

"Oh, hey Julia," the guy acknowledged her, glancing up from his phone. His name tag read "Paul" in big black letters. "Since you haven't filled the linen closet just yet, can you also drop a set of those in room 202 on your way by?" Without waiting for an answer, Paul smashed the clean sheets in the crook of his elbow and ducked into the doorway next to the one with the visitors.

The patient in that room was facing the wall, but turned with a groan when Paul walked in. Something about the man's bald head sparked a memory, but Martin distracted me when he sang, "Well, lookee there."

I drifted his way to find him in front of a chilled storage area containing rows of bagged blood. If blood spatters on a sheet could attract a demon, I certainly didn't intend to frequent a blood bank on a regular basis. There were bags of the stuff just waiting for a demon—or a vamp. My mouth dropped open.

A female vampire, dead as could be, picked up two of the bags, scanning one of them with a handheld device. She was dressed in a purple nurse's smock, but it fit her curves well, making her somehow very elegant, even in death. Her hair was smoothed into a French twist, and like Patrick, a bat-like visage hovered behind her.

Just how many vampires were walking around dirt-side, anyway?

I backed off until the fog rolled in and obscured every single bit of the other side.

"Odd, those vampires," Martin said. "Did you notice the aura of death?"

"Their lifelines are gone. Patrick was like that too. Dead, but the glow of life radiates through them from borrowed energy."

He tapped one finger on his nose. "It's not easy to meditate here with all these distractions. You can't learn if you are busy watching people and wishing you were there. Come along, and I'll teach you elsewhere."

We drifted peacefully for a while before Martin coaxed the weave to reveal an empty canyon. The location didn't surprise me. "Did you die here?"

He hummed. "I came here from there."

"That sounds like a yes." He might choose to Mickey Mouse around with the idea of death, but I wasn't inclined to float around fooling myself. Maybe there was a part of me left alive over there, but for now, I was as good as dead and just as hampered.

"It's easier for me in this spot," he agreed. "Feel the wind."

Martin drifted into meditation. His near constant singing became a buzzing.

I watched in silence. The edge didn't attack him, nor did it expand to allow him more freedom. Martin's life force didn't exactly drift over to the other side either, but he didn't appear to be trying very hard to go anywhere at all.

It's easy to be patient as a ghost. You really don't have a lot of appointments to keep. I didn't feel the wind at first, mainly because I wasn't paying attention and didn't have much use for air. But as I watched Martin and the canyon, the tiniest bit of a living breeze slipped through to our side. Martin sucked in the air and puffed it out carefully, in rings.

Now he was singing in smoke signals?

Since there was no sense in wasting the energy, I hungrily enveloped the bits of warmth and air that drifted my way.

"You blend with it," Martin intoned. "You sing to the earth, and she brings you treasure. You sing to the weave, and it accepts you."

"I'm not the weave."

"But it knows you."

"And it hates me," I muttered.

Martin was not deterred by my lack of enthusiasm. With nothing better to do, I tried shaping my form to match that of the weave. Maybe it liked thread. I could look like a bunch of strings. Of course, it wasn't all that easy, and with my eyeballs stretched into a thin line my vision was warped, but anything to tame the lion.

Then again, Martin still held his shape except he was thinner. He rarely bothered with legs or arms, even now. He was a very utilitarian ghost. He didn't waste energy, unless you counted his singing.

I was pretty sure the weave would not appreciate my singing. But what did it want from me? Nothing. I had nothing to offer.

Stretched out as I was, for the first time ever, straying fabric wasn't slashing at me. I still couldn't penetrate it, though.

I pulled my head together, but like Martin, I kept the rest of me bottled into a small space. Less of me to be available for the cutting block.

Martin breezed back and forth, dancing to his chant. After a bit, I noticed that he ebbed and flowed with the fabric of the weave. He drifted closer and then floated away. The weave often gave way before him, creating a space. Anytime it did so, the fabric was temporarily thinner as it stretched.

I stopped watching him and watched the steel bands. In the past, I had worried only about it coming after me or how close it was or wasn't. The weave was very elastic, but because it flowed, it also resembled running water. It billowed past at a steady rate, bobbing in and out, over and across, and up and down.

Whenever Martin drifted close, it flowed *around* him rather than attacking him, but like real water, since he floated slowly, the weave didn't splash against him. It just thinned, making room until the flow became more uniform.

The breeze from the canyon, with all its wonderful desert smells, came through every time the weave was sheer enough. The sounds of birds could be heard, a caw here, a twitter there.

No wonder Martin never had to spend his time hunting energy. He was perfectly capable of meditating his way around the edge, collecting whatever he needed. In this remote area, there was no one on the other side to see or disturb him.

The thought was a magnet for trouble, or perhaps my intuition worked better with my essence all tucked into my head. A sound, a different pressure, something was behind me.

I spun sideways, accidentally ricocheting off Martin. He nearly smashed into the weave. My bounce sent me flying over the hellhound, but barely.

The ugly devil hit the weave as it sprang at me.

I briefly considered leaping over the pack, but the hounds were skilled jumpers. With such a large pack, one of them was bound to score.

There were a lot of monsters In Between, but the primal scream that burst through the gray from the living side was so horrendous, shards of the weave froze in place. The howl commanded fear and enough threat to change the ever-present mist of In Between to icicles.

Freezing or not, it didn't stop me from launching myself over the hellhounds, all of which had turned to the threat, ready to rend whatever offered that challenge.

Luckily for the cat, he was dirt-side. Lynx's human head was ghosted around that of the cat this time instead of the other way around. The weave, despite freezing in that one spot, was thickening and undulating dangerously. The fabric didn't shut out the bobcat's next feral scream or the slice of his claws. The hound closest to the edge howled as some part of the magic did him injury. The claws may not have breached the weave, but the edge bent away from the feline form, slicing into the devil dog.

I puffed and twirled, bouncing off the back of another four-legged beast and landing on the other side of the pack. My essence burned where it had touched the monster.

One of my displaced and swiveling eyeballs searched out Martin.

I needn't have worried. He was already ahead of me, but instead of his usual genie head, he had grown legs, a streaker from the bleachers, jumping and dodging around the snarling hounds.

The weave was thin enough that the two lead dogs wasted time tearing at the fabric as if they might capture the howling cat. The challenging snarls provided us with precious time as Lynx paced the edge, slashing with lethal intent.

We ran. That cat had tremendous life energy to freeze the gray of the weave.

One of my eyes swiveled behind me, tracking the canine hunters while the other searched for a protective batch of rocks.

The beasts from hell bayed hungrily, eager to devour the energy we had just harvested from the other side. If only I could throw energy like the cat, maybe we could escape.

Then again, if Lynx could somehow throw it from across the barrier, why couldn't I? And what could I throw? I had nothing but bits of my own gray and the braid. I'd rather die than sacrifice the talisman the cat had given me. It was my hope.

Everything I owned was long dead. Supposedly so was I.

I screamed, pain burning across my foot. The fangs of the nearest hellhound snapped at what would have been an ankle had it not been formless essence that hadn't quite kept up with the rest of me.

Martin turned one wild eye back, but there was nothing he could do to save me.

I forced the part of my essence that was ankle to thin and flow through the grasping teeth, depriving the dog of his prize.

Once freed, I called the pieces of myself back to me while still flitting away in sheer terror.

If energy was a weapon, maybe a small piece would do. I twisted off a blob of gray cloth from the bottom of my shirt. Martin said he dressed with bits of this and that, but apparently he hadn't bothered to find any bits today.

I pulled the injured piece of me close and dabbed at the leak with the shirttail, still dodging and flying with ghost maneuvers born of desperation. A growing blotch of ectoplasm from my wound clung to the bit of shirt.

I took a huge breath, intending to snap the strip of cloth like a towel, but sulfuric hound breath convinced me to shove it down the throat of the nearest threat instead.

Hell's creature gagged on a shrill bark and flung his head left and right. The energy was stuck there like a bone lodged in his throat.

The beast's second head snapped down on the wisps of my fingers before I could snatch them far enough away.

"Aaaa!" I half swallowed a wail and let my fingers disintegrate away from the jaws before drawing them close again. Panicked now, I somersaulted low, using the time to squeeze off another piece of gray cloth with my uninjured hand. There were at least eight of the beasts still slobbering after us, and I was already leaking parts of me all over the terrain.

Martin was no dummy. As soon as he figured out what I was up to, he harvested some of the pieces he claimed dressed him. He might be dead, but his energy was no dead weight. He threw what looked like a handful of dehydrated juniper berries, possibly from Troy's tree. The dried gray balls hit a hellhound and exploded.

The dogs were eager to devour our energy, but they didn't appreciate it wielded as a weapon.

Martin tripped, or maybe teeth biting into him caused him to stumble. I threw my ball of cloth at the nearest dog, ripped off a jacket sleeve and swung it at the hellhound about to feast on Martin. I wished heartily for a stick to stab it in the eye, but at least had the space to snap the sleeve, letting the energy spark off the end. If the cat could use screaming as a weapon, anything was worth a try.

Martin jabbed the hound with the quill end of a ghost bird feather.

The beast leaped away in a panicked frenzy. Dangerous saliva spattered in every direction, causing two nearby dogs to yelp. It wasn't clear whether the hound was trying to eat the feather or dislodge it.

Neither of us waited to find out.

Martin grabbed at a wisp of me and yanked me towards a small clump of rocks. The two boulders weren't large enough to hide one person, never mind two, but it was either the rocks or keep attempting to flay full grown beasts from hell with my sleeve.

Martin made a ten-point dive with a burst of released air. Unless I was mistaken, the man had just farted his way underground.

Oddly enough, that was a technique that I'd never thought to try.

Instinct would have had me dodging the resulting breeze, but Martin didn't release my arm.

I let out my last breath, and we both sank into a very small air pocket beneath the rocks.

Chapter 10

Our hideout was larger than it appeared from the surface, but not by much. There was barely room to breathe; good thing we didn't need to. My essence was pushed up against rocks and dirt in all directions except the side where Martin rested. Both of us trailed pieces into crevices until we were more worm than human ghost.

"Did you know there was an air pocket under here?" I asked.

"The earth is different this side, but I have learned to read it. I can sense the pockets if I try hard enough."

"You were kind of busy."

"Heh. Desperate too."He leaked more essence deeper underground.

Eventually, I located a few more cracks and spaces. We'd have to wait out the dogs, but they'd wander elsewhere as soon as they realized the futility of trying to overturn the larger stone.

Martin was so thin, I could discern a few bits and pieces of his collection. The one that drew my immediate attention was the bloodstone. He apparently stored it inside his ear.

He noticed me staring at it. A ghostly set of fingers retrieved the bloodstone and pushed it my way. "I figured I'd gift this to you after I showed you how to manipulate the edge. I needed it for a time because I couldn't reach those on the other side easily anymore. I think my time here might be ending. The bloodstone helped."

My heart, wherever the wisps were floating, sank. I didn't have many friends and now one of them might be moving on. On top of that, Troy was in trouble of fading or worse. "You keep it, then. For as long as you need it."

Thinking of Troy had me blurting out the original reason I'd been hunting for Martin. "What besides a demon leaves a mark on a ghost? And what does it mean?"

Martin was little more than an ear, a mouth and two eyeballs. Both of his eyes blinked. "Demon mark?"

In a tangled rush of details, I told him about Cinderspark and what she had said about Troy. "And he's tired all the time, fading."

"Did you see any mark on Troy?" he finally asked.

I shook my head. "I looked very carefully. He seems fine, but admitted that he has to replenish all the time now."

"My energy's been drying up quicker'n a beer buzz, too," Martin mused. "That was why I couldn't visit dirt-side easily anymore and the reason I needed the bloodstone. It links quickly to earth. Now it's yours. I give it to you freely."

The bloodstone floated against me. I stared at it and then back at his guileless, almost childlike eyes. "Don't you still need it?"

"I'm stronger now. And maybe the problem isn't that my time is up. If Troy is marked by a demon or something powerful from that realm, that changes everything. That means a demon-like creature is stuck here, and it's throwing the balance off, including mine."

He was right about his balance being off, but I doubted a demon was wholly responsible. "You keep the bloodstone for now. I've got my own." It took some effort to shift the braid to where he could see it.

Martin chuckled gleefully. The bloodstone disappeared. "If you need it, it's yours."

"Let's hope I don't."

Martin hummed a bit. "The demon wants a way to the other side to feed on souls and wallow in the pain of others. The most likely cause of a demon being stuck here is that it escaped the control of whoever summoned it, but for some reason, it was unable to take over the summoner and stay dirt-side."

I told him about the young demon I had seen digging into the laundry room. "There was no one calling it. It was repelled and blasted back. I don't think it stayed here."

He nodded. "That's what normally happens. They steal enough energy from each other or the creatures like the hounds to make it to In Between. When they try to break all the way across, most fail. To reach and stay dirt-side they have to have a vessel to live in."

"Then why would a demon or something like one mark Troy?"

He swirled a finger. "A demon might use us as a temporary food source. With enough energy, it could stay here while it gathered power to cross. But raw power isn't enough. It would still need a body to inhabit dirt-side."

"Is that what the mark is for? To draw power?"

He nodded. "Mother Earth marked me long ago. Not the same as a demon mark, because it's a sharing with her. Something could have marked Troy and be harvesting his energy."

I could close my eyes, but not my ears. The good news was that his musing kept him from humming at least part of the time.

We waited until dusk before squeezing back out into the half light. My sleeve didn't reattach itself, but it was easy to just wear it along my arm. I'd use the silly thing again if necessary, assuming I had enough life force to wield it as a weapon.

I wasn't ready to handle demon marks, sleeve weapons and cats who could scream right through the weave. I didn't know how to help Troy, either. But in order to survive, I had to figure out what was happening or die trying.

Then again, I didn't even *have* a life, so what was I saving?

Chapter 11

Séances and mediums were of no interest to me before I died. Turns out, no ghost is obligated to attend a séance. Of course, most of the time being dead can be damned boring. When a live human has a talent to be heard in the gray area In Between, some spirits will rush to attend. They aren't necessarily relatives, friends, or even from the same century as those still alive. They're just groupies. They'll answer questions too if the medium is strong enough to hear, but most of the time the attending shades can't do more than rattle china cups or offer up a ghostly moan.

I drifted into a séance one time when an actual ghost of one of the attendees showed up. These situations are to be avoided. The ghost just hung there in misery, unable or unwilling to answer any questions or derive any kind of comfort from the contact. The older séance ghosts, the groupies, either left or tried in vain to console the ghost who was nothing more than a shell-shocked, numb presence.

Funny thing is, the mediums always seem to assume the ghosts are compelled to answer. Instead, we spirits come and go like open night at a bar, mingling with each other and watching the live humans. The only time there's any compulsion is when there's blood—and that's not a séance, that's a calling that threatens to drain any remaining life force. Enough blood and it will summon something else from one of the other realms. Nothing kills a party faster than bloodshed.

If I hadn't been practicing reaching the other side, I might have ignored the séance, but a séance meant someone was attempting to open a portal. That meant the two of us were after the same goal, and one of us had energy to spare on the task.

For the most part, the weave attempted to keep bits from crossing in either direction. When wisps of life entered, the weave often shattered them into tiny pieces. In the case of a séance, the medium sent across little bursts of life energy that were like beacons flashing bright before sparking out.

It didn't take me long to hone in on the sparks. The edge thinned near a hospital room where the aunt and the little girl, Espy, waited. They had been able to easily see and talk to me before, so it wasn't a total surprise to discover the aunt had the knowledge to pull off a séance. The room was stark compared to my first visit. The pink bedspread was still there, but there were no shelves with stuffed animals and the stillness of the little girl belied life.

Instead of pushing closer, I sat patiently as Martin had taught me. I called the drifting bits of energy to me. Slowly, the bursts formed an open tunnel now that the two of us were focusing.

I drifted closer.

The aunt was perceptive. "Espy?"

During a séance the medium always calls someone specific. Espy had been sitting up and talking during my previous visit, but now she was hooked up to a ventilator, IV bags and beeping monitors.

"Espy?" My voice hit the weave and splattered sideways. The sounds that leaked through were nothing more than distorted moans. Martin swore the barrier could be bent to my advantage, but one wrong twitch would have me sliced by shards of the weave.

"Is Esperanza there? Has she crossed?"

I pointed at the bed, and this time when I spoke, I leaned into a sheer spot in the fabric. "Essspy?"

"Her name is Esperanza, Espy for short. Is—what has happened to her?"

The aunt's concentration faltered with her grief, and the weave snapped my way. Instead of fighting it, I let it push me. The sharp energy crackled like lightning. It burned, but I kept ahead of it enough to avoid being sliced.

Aunt Brenda regained her composure, muttering a prayer.

I used the time to search for Espy's lifeline. She could easily have crossed when I wasn't paying attention. Despite being attuned to this area there was no way I heard every person who crossed. Many of them were nothing but arrows arcing through on their way elsewhere.

There was no sign of Espy's life force. Her energy may have already crossed, but it wasn't in the process now. Nothing else In Between was like a life coming over or through.

I puffed myself a tiny bit closer to the girl. The aunt seemed to understand right away and hurried to her side. She reached down to hold the girl's hand.

There. It was nothing more than a spark, just as her aunt touched her. I shook my head at the aunt. "I don't think she is here." My words didn't make it across intact. I looked for a way to show her. The problem was that there was no way to tell how much of Espy was still on the living side, though some certainly remained.

Little in the room was of use to me. As I explored, the door from the hallway swung open into the room. The aunt's concentration immediately dropped, snapping the weave right through me.

Rather than fight it, I allowed it to shred me and push me back. I helped myself by not struggling.

Even though the IV monitor was beeping, the nurse who entered was completely focused on the aunt, probably because, with a moan, Aunt Brenda collapsed on top of Espy. The séance had extracted too much from her.

I stitched myself back together, letting the weave slowly bind itself more tightly between worlds.

To my surprise, the nurse was attentive, but not very panicked over the aunt. She pressed the call button and hung a fresh IV on the hook next to the nearly empty one. The badge clipped to the bottom of her shirt read, "Sonya."

She checked the aunt's pulse, peeled back an eyelid, and then slid her carefully onto the armchair near the bed.

Aunt Brenda was already coming around. "Espy?" she asked weakly.

"No, it's Sonya, the nurse. Espy is right here. You sit still," she instructed. "You can't keep staying here all day and night. You fainted again."

The nurse swiveled back to Espy and the beeping IV monitor. She changed out the bag and reset the monitor. A trail of blood had spattered onto the sheets and bedspread around Espy's arm where the IV went in, but was already dried, a messy splotch of dark dribbles.

The guy I'd seen before when he requested sheets from the cleaning lady came through the door. Paul still wore his badge around his neck. His hair was spiked and bleached on the ends. He had clean linens in one hand and his phone in the other.

As soon as he saw Sonya, the phone disappeared into one of the loose pockets at the front of his uniform.

Sonya accepted the sheets and turned the call light off. "Thanks, Paul. Can you bring some ice water and have the kitchen send up some juice, please? I'll start on the bed."

"Sure." Paul spun on silent soles.

With practiced ease, Sonya pulled the soiled linens free and made the bed with the fresh ones. She bundled the sheets and dropped them on the floor at the bottom of the bed. "Have you eaten yet today?" she asked the aunt.

Brenda nodded. "I even brought in some crackers."

While Sonya opened the packet of crackers and fussed over the aunt, I watched Espy. The blood bag seemed to contain more life energy than the girl. The dark red liquid shown with a brightness along the edges. Surely the energy would help. Why hadn't someone given me something with so much energy that might have kept me alive?

It affected Espy almost instantly too, nearly reviving her from the coma. Her body stiffened, and around the fabric that was rapidly thickening between us, the ghost of an image formed across her face.

The ghost girl saw me and screamed. A spindle of life sparked in her heart and was drawn towards the blood slowly traveling into her veins.

I raised my hands, empty palms out, to show I was not a threat.

"Heeeeellp!" Her life force stalled in its journey along her veins to the fresh blood. She reached with her ghost hands towards me and the edge.

Alarmed, I shook my head. "You don't want to come here! Let the medicine—"

I scowled. During my own death there had been a violent pull on my life force. Had I been fighting something trying to save me? Had I gone the opposite direction due to stubbornness and ended up here? There hadn't been any ghosts willing to advise me, that was for sure. I stared at the blood traveling from the IV bag to her arm. It definitely pulled on the girl's life force. Was that a glow of life force in the blood or flames licking along the surface?

The nurse was assisting Espy's aunt with a drink of water, but she glanced over at Espy suddenly, staring at her for a moment. With a puzzled frown, she looked around the room before turning back to the aunt. "You really shouldn't stay here all day. This is the second time you've fainted."

The fabric was now knit too tightly for me to see anything clearly.

The girl hadn't made it across, not this time, but something was after her life force. I had felt it, and she had too.

Chapter 12

I floated aimlessly through the gray for longer than was wise, wondering about that glow in the blood. My cairn was a better bet for me than wandering because once again the weave had left me leaking. Instead of heading for shelter, I used my sleeve to soak up essence.

I stared at the cloth and the ghost essence. Both were gray blobs, one with shape, the other without. The blood that had attracted Espy's life force was dark red or black. It was darker than the blood already in her veins. There had been bright orange flashes of energy licking at the blood.

In Between, we were all hungry. But the only thing I'd ever seen flash that color was a demon. And something was eating at Troy. And Martin claimed his beer buzz wasn't buzzing.

What if something in the blood was killing Espy? What had threatened me when I was dying? Was that same thing threatening Espy?

If I found myself, would I still feel foreign fingers grasping at my essence, preventing me from fully claiming myself? Maybe I was here because it was safer than my own body.

The only way to find out was to find myself.

Martin was attracted to the canyon. That is where we'd met Roberto and the others. When Martin trained me, we went to his canyon. Where did I keep finding myself? The hospital. It couldn't be coincidence.

The only real question was whether or not I'd have to search room by room. Was my body in a morgue? A cold drawer somewhere?

Any action might be better than no action, especially with constant reminders that time was my enemy. If my body was still alive, it couldn't remain that way indefinitely, not with my essence here.

I closed my eyes, drew myself in and ghosted along the edge. I searched not only for a weakness in the weave, but for any life that called to my soul.

Martin had merely hummed. There was nothing beckoning me, but nothing in particular had enticed him either, not really. He just waited by the weave, and his last strong connection dirt-side had appeared.

I watched the weave and nudged it into thinning just the way Martin had taught me. Most of the hospital rooms were empty shells, floating past with no clues.

Disappointment filled me when my first glimpse of a person was that of a stranger. She was nothing but a gaunt, sallow face on the hospital bed. Straw-like hair made the whole picture into a morbid scarecrow. Just another needy, nearly dead person.

It wasn't until I noticed the cat that the realization hit me. My eyes went from Lynx to the mummified form on the bed. "Wow." My living body was in worse shape than my current ghost form. "Yikes."

The cat held his hand out as if maybe he had felt a cold breeze. It was possible he sensed my presence.

His blurry form leaned over mine and quick as a cat, he brushed his lips against my cold, dead ones.

I shrank back, horrified. How could he touch that thing? Did he think, like Sleeping Beauty, he could bring back that half mummy on the bed with his gallant gesture? And to be sure, it was gallant. The body was no more attractive than a day old corpse. Who would want to touch it?

The weird thing was that I felt it. Not the me lying in the bed, because there was no association there, or so I had thought. But a shot of warmth, of energy that was almost visible, radiated across the weave.

I reached up and touched my lips, my ghost fingertips tingling from the odd energy. As if he were here with me, raw emotion pulsed through me. The feeling was almost the same as a ghost touch, but Lynx was very much alive, giving off a heat and aura. I might be dead, but, oh, I wished I weren't.

The edge had thinned even further without me noticing. He must have sensed me because he whirled to find me hovering. I didn't think it was possible for a ghost to blush, but sudden shyness gripped me.

"Hey'ya Shadow."

I don't know what I expected, but it wasn't cat casualness. Did he see ghosts every day?

"If you don't belong there, how do we get you back here? I have the other half of the spell bundle I gave you." He held up another braid. I felt the resonance tingle through my hair as the bundle he had thrown me responded to the nearness of its mate.

"I don't know." I enunciated carefully, although he didn't seem to have much trouble hearing me.

"You're in a special ward," Lynx said. "There's two or three other people here too."

"Is there a girl named Espy there? Her life force tried to come across, but I told her to stay. Something was trying to capture her on your side. I think that may be what happened to me. Something was after me, and I ended up here!" It all came out in a rush, confused. I had put the thoughts together but not organized them enough to be coherent. But the cat, maybe the cat could help anyway.

"I haven't seen her, but I haven't checked around. Patrick recognized you as soon as he saw you. He's one of the special nurses assigned to this ward a few times a week."

"The vampire? Do you think he could be stealing our lives by imbibing our life force?"

Lynx shook his head, adamant. "'Trick is cool. He gets blood from the hospital bank. He doesn't need to run around draining patients."

"But what if he does? Or what if it's another vampire? I saw a female at the blood bank. What if they require more than just blood to stay alive? In Between the things that steal aren't after blood. We don't have any. They want the sparks of life. Maybe it works that way for vampires too!"

His ears twitched then, followed by his eyes slanting towards the door. Without even a whisper of sound, he casually tucked himself along the wall where he wouldn't be readily visible and if seen, he was nothing more than a tired visitor brooding over a dying patient.

I had a bad feeling. It was going to be the vampire, I just knew it. What if he was the thing I felt calling to my life force, the thing I'd run from before they could save me?

The door opened slowly. A single, bony hand held the edge of the door. A short person in a dark uniform backed partway into the room. The cleaning lady maneuvered a cart that was more than half full of dirty sheets. I recognized her gray head of hair and stooped shoulders as she scanned the room. The guy asking for sheets had called her Julia, but I couldn't see her badge from this vantage point.

She gave a short nod directed somewhere between the body on the bed and Lynx. She might have seen him or she might just be noting that there were no sheets to pick up. The body on the bed didn't look as though it had done anything as ambitious as sweat in a long time. They probably didn't have to change the sheets more than once a month.

The cleaning lady pushed the cart back out, leaving the door hanging partially ajar as she exited.

Lynx padded to the door, pushing it closed.

Maybe the vampire was after Espy, maybe not. But whatever had come after me was still in this hospital. Espy was proof enough for me. Her fear had been a choking tendril of desperation, an echo of the bone chilling panic I'd felt when dying. "The girl. Her name is Espy. She's probably in this ward now, in a coma like me. You need to get her out."

I stared at the near-corpse on the bed. It might be too late for me, but if we hurried, maybe we could prevent Espy from coming across.

Chapter 13

Seeing my body had not been the victory I'd expected. The husk that remained on the side of the living was well past its expiration date. The whole experience had exhausted me and yielded little by way of answers to my questions. It was a long shot, but the only person I could think of who might be able to tell me about the blood I'd seen was Cinderspark. Maybe she had changed her mind and decided to dally here one more time.

Once I determined my destination, it didn't take long to puff myself there.

Troy's juniper was the same looming gray as always. The color that had appeared when he was nearby wasn't evident now.

Before I could drift any closer, Spook materialized in front of me. I tamped down my hunger, even though Spook would have already sniffed out my longing for energy. The tree had been a temptation ever since I'd followed Troy through, and it was embarrassing to be caught blatantly coveting what was not mine.

Spook barked.

I was surprised because he usually ignored me. His tentative hello was filled with the same wariness he always exhibited.

"Is Troy around?" I asked.

He whined, worried.

"Yeah, me too." I sat on the nearest rock, wishing I could run up to the tree and jump inside and gather sparks and be full forever. But without Troy here, the tree was probably dormant.

I forgot myself for a moment and reached over to pet Spook. To my surprise, he scooted one hop closer and accepted my hand. "Cinderspark told me that Troy is marked by something. Maybe a demon, or something similar. Can you see the mark on Troy, Spook? Is there one on me? I was hoping Cinder had returned and would tell me more. Martin says a mark can't be good and that the balance In Between is all wrong right now."

Spook whined and barked again, a quiet sound of desperation mixed with urgency. He trotted in a circle, undecided, but then hopped quickly towards the tree. He barked encouragement, planting his feet as though inviting me to play, but his tone was not that of a game.

I hesitated, but Spook whined again. "Is Troy in there?"

Spook turned stubborn then, sitting and barking, demanding that I get up. He wasn't interested in sharing Troy's whereabouts, but he wanted me to follow him.

"Okay. You know this is dangerous, right?"

Spook barked a low growl, his version of a snort. He was right.

Everywhere In Between was dangerous.

The tree was silent. When Troy was around, the jagged side sometimes shifted as though swaying in the breeze, but today it was as still as a rock.

Spook sat next to the tree and waited for me to approach.

"Can't you enter without me?"

He didn't answer. I reached for the smooth surface, feeling it immediately, a warmth that wasn't felt In Between often. Troy had to be inside. I wasn't sure whether it would be good news or bad if I ran into him, but there was no point in standing here with my back exposed.

I slipped into the darkness, Spook at my heels. Just as before, there was a nighttime sky, but with less stars this time. Maybe it was cloudy. The ley line was barely visible in the distance to my right. I would have headed that way, but Spook took the lead, pressing me towards the starlight, precisely where I had no desire to go.

Without the constant hazy light of In Between, my eyesight was lacking. I reached for Spook and held on. The further we drifted, the more out of breath I felt, which was entirely strange because the dead don't need air. There was no edge to fray me, yet there seemed to be less of me.

The tunnel was narrow with rocks that contained varying hints of color; dull reds and yellowish browns as if they might be real, might be part of dirt-side.

As we floated upwards, larger tree roots began to appear, a darker color than gray, poking through the rocks. The further we ventured, the thicker the roots, until they were crossing the tunnel and running along the bottom. My ghostly feet brushed against them, and I wasn't too proud to slurp up the energy they contained.

Water trickled somewhere, feeding these roots. The happy sound scared me because water In Between was an open invitation to another realm.

Spook didn't care about my fear or the water. He whined and coaxed me along.

The tunnel narrowed further, forcing us to float single file.

A dip was followed by a Y-shaped choice. The surface, probably full dirt-side, was still impossibly far away, but Spook chose that tunnel. The ley line was the other direction, beaming light down the corridors in a flickering dance even as we traveled away from it.

Finally, Spook halted. He pushed his ghostly nose into an impression in the rocks. The dim glow from the ley line illuminated lighter brown roots. An odd shaped piece of metal, a ring, glinted up at us.

I knelt, wondering about the root that had grown through the ring. The gemstone was flat and winked with color, a deep red with flecks of gold from the band that housed it. The band was engraved, but was too far embedded in dirt for me to read.

Troy had played football. His jacket had a number on it that was clearly visible when he was near the tree. "Was this Troy's class ring? Or some kind of athletic ring?" Just how close were we to the surface anyway? Worried, I glanced up at the stars, but the tiny pricks of light held no answer.

When I might have touched the ring, Spook growled. He deliberately butted into me, knocking me back. "Okay, okay. I wasn't planning on stealing it." But I had wanted to touch it. It seemed so real, so full of color.

Spook whined then, and when I turned to find him, he was loping back down the tunnel. He hadn't warned of any impending danger, but he certainly wasn't lingering. He knew these tunnels far better than me.

I took a last longing look at the ring and followed Spook out. The tree roots had filled my hunger, but my questions remained without answers.

Chapter 14

Spook flopped down near the base of the tree as soon as we slipped out of the trunk. He remained on guard—or waiting for Troy. There was no sign of my wayward friend, though.

I wasn't certain what Spook had been trying to tell me. I could understand the dog's yips and barks almost as well as Troy, but Spook was still a dog. He didn't sit and chat, divulging deep secrets. He shared information his way, and something had been lost in the translation.

As I dithered on an errant breeze, Spook barked once, a reprimand. He was disappointed in me.

I was disappointed too. "He needs the ring, right?"

Spook barked agreement, nudging me.

Was Troy supposed to pry the ring out of the tree? But if he hadn't died with it, how would he keep something that solid here? Maybe it could cross like the braid Lynx had given me. Maybe he needed that ring or some part of it to survive.

Spook half-whined, half-growled. He wanted action. So did I.

"You want me to retrieve the ring?"

He yipped a response that wasn't a wholehearted agreement. The answer couldn't be so simple because Spook hadn't even let me touch the ring while inside the tree.

Before I could ask more questions, a tingling death crossing drifted through the ether, pinging my soul harder than usual.

Spook lifted his head and sniffed, but didn't stand.

I peered into the growing fog and frowned. This death had a different feel to it, a familiar pulse. I hoped that didn't mean it was someone I knew, someone I had met recently like a certain cat or...Espy.

With regret, I hurriedly patted Spook on the head. "I'll find a way to help, Spook, as soon as I figure out what to do. I'll be back. Soon, I hope."

The fog hampered my progress. It was tread carefully or be sliced and diced because it was hard to tell where the weave might begin and end in the dense clouds. I hurried along, but after what seemed only a short distance, the weave interfered. I'd step towards the crossing and then retreat, seeing nothing but the bands of fabric ebbing and flowing.

The weave finally compressed and undulated in the right direction, allowing me to see the spark of a soul making its way through.

Violet was wrinkled, pale and tired. As soon as her name came through, I realized I'd known her in life. Maybe she thought of me as she died.

The instant she fully crossed over, I remembered her putting something in my hands, hands that were still those of a child. She was training me to...the thought faded, filled with impressions of teacher or friend. Maybe even a relative. Where the information should have been, I flashed instead to fighting the man who had slashed at me with a deadly knife. I hadn't recalled the knife before. My arms had blocked it, both of them raised in defense. I had fought, angry I was without my weapons.

Had Violet trained me?

There was a lot of blood, and I couldn't retreat, not even when the man fell to his knees. He circled. I couldn't escape. His snarling face was embellished with a nose and tongue ring. His shouts and threats were long since lost. He had crawled away. No, he crawled, but he kept coming back at me like a nightmare, first in front, then to the side, then from behind.

My memories were interrupted by the rest of Violet's life line. She didn't require an escort. Her soul leaked slowly through In Between, a strong line floating to the other side. I used to think we were doing people a favor witnessing their last moments in silent respect, but these peaceful passings, they were the real gift.

The ribbon of life didn't stretch very far. What had been nothing but gray space pushed aside, and the link touched the other side. A small dot of light indicated when it hit. The backwash was calm, slow and peaceful. It ran the length of the thread all the way back to the living world.

Standing near, just as I suffered the backwash of drifting too close to the edge, I received the benefit of the white light. My own gray was suddenly lighter, refreshed, despite the strain I'd been under.

I raised a hand in salute as Violet sailed past. I would never touch her; it was too much of a violation, but she reached out to me on her final passage, filling me with a soft peace and strength, a gift I cherished greatly.

My focus had been so completely on Violet, I didn't see the others until Amy spoke. "Sweet. We could have helped had we arrived sooner." She was holding hands with Troy. The two of them stood next to Kyle, the musician I'd recently helped.

"That was beautiful; a perfect song." Kyle strummed his guitar. "She didn't need anyone to help her cross. Is that the way it's supposed to be?"

I nodded, but was too busy trying to glimpse Troy's hand to say more. It was impossible to tell if he had a ghost ring or not given that his fingers were wrapped up in Amy's. He wasn't drained today, but the wariness in his eyes remained.

Amy leaned into him. Her dangling earrings caught my attention. Good. If I could see those, it meant that I'd be able to tell if Troy had died with his ring or not. I wasn't sure whether that knowledge was truly helpful, though.

"Troy, I wondered if you've talked to Spook about...well, maybe Martin can help with our problem." I really *had* meant Spook, but felt stupid suggesting that the pup had any answers in front of Amy. I could explain to Troy in private that the dog had shared a possible clue, but I still needed Troy to fill in the rest of the pieces to the puzzle.

"I'm fine. Better I think." He half-waved, already drifting away. "I just need to stay close to home and replenish often. It's like having a cold, nothing really." He didn't sound convinced, and he paused for a moment as if he had more to say.

Surprised, Amy finally stopped and waited.

"Never mind," I said. Belatedly, I realized Spook wasn't with him. I'd assumed that Troy was somewhere around the tree because I'd seen Spook there, but obviously Spook hadn't left the tree after showing me the ring. I wondered why. "I'll stop by later, okay?"

But Troy was already gone, his head tilted towards Amy. I had to admit he seemed to light up when she was around. Maybe she could help him somehow.

"I didn't know there could be any kind of relationships after dying," Kyle said. "But maybe if you die young and didn't have anyone back home, you can find someone here?"

I had certainly become a shade far earlier than was right. The stray thought of my death caused a flash of *wrongness* with a sharp stab of resentment. The pain of it was so intense, it was likely to kill me completely someday, but I'm a fast learner. I immediately put the thought aside.

I gritted my teeth. "Yeah. He seems happy with her."

Kyle tilted his head. "I guess love exists even here."

"Did you happen to notice if Troy was wearing a ring?" I asked.

"A wedding ring?" He lifted his own ghostly finger. "Is that what has you all bothered? You think he's cheating on an earthly wife? Or did you think I was planning on cheating on my wife just because I mentioned that love was possible here?"

"No, no. I meant a class ring. Or a football ring. Never mind, I can ask him when I see him again."

"Oh, that ring. Yes, he did have one. He told me he gave it to Amy. That's what I meant about realizing ghosts have relationships. I thought love died. It feels dead to me. But the music still plays, and Troy found someone even though he's dead."

I stared at Kyle, my mouth agape. I stayed that way so long, the gray of my jaw unhinged and started drifting away. I finally pulled together and spun away.

"Hey, where are you going?"

But I was already puffing. I had to find Spook and ask him what this meant, but it seemed obvious. Troy had to get his ghost ring back. Why else would Spook have showed me the ring in the tree when I asked for help with all my problems?

Chapter 15

I ran. In Between wavered and undulated and generally threatened me with edges that had a strong desire to cut me to shreds. Usually when I was in this big of a hurry, it meant something hungry and ugly was after me. Today, I needed to locate Spook before Troy returned to the tree.

When I finally swooshed to a halt, most of me was temporarily deformed with bits trailing far behind. "Spook?" I reeled myself in, not worrying about where the pieces landed. If Spook wasn't with Troy, he had to be here.

The surface of the tree was smooth and cool to the touch. I didn't dare go inside. "Spook? I understand what you were telling me! Amy has the ring!"

Spook barked from behind me, causing me to jump forward far enough to land partially inside the tree. It was dark. The ley line to the right was nothing more than a pinprick. This portal to dirt-side was shrinking and shrinking fast. Without this source of energy, what would happen to Troy?

I scooted out quickly. "Spook! We have to force Amy to give the ring back, don't we?"

He barked a hearty agreement.

"Will Troy help, do you think?"

Spook ran in a circle, chasing his own tail. His whine was an unsure, "No."

"Can he help?"

Same circle, same whine. Spook didn't know either.

"Amy isn't going to want to give up the ring, is she?"

One succinct bark. "No." Now he was certain.

I caressed the tree trunk. "Somehow that ring is his tie here, as much as the tree itself."

When I looked back at Spook, he had multiplied. There were now two 'coons sitting near the dog, a squirrel and a possum. "You guys don't hang around with Amy either." Somehow that ring was the key to Troy obtaining energy. But if that was true, did it work for Amy too? Didn't she care that Troy was fading? Didn't she notice?

Before I could make any more observations, Troy drifted into sight. He was barely visible. His legs were missing completely and the rest of him was hunched into his jacket. He sported the look of someone who was allowing In Between to carry him wherever the mists blew.

"Troy!"

His face was blurry, and it took him more than a moment to recognize me. "You...I thought for a second you were roadkill."

Energy was never overabundant, but I wasn't starved. His hesitation was either an excuse or he couldn't focus. "Troy, do you still have the grass you showed me before?"

He shook his head. "Sorry. I'm tapped out." He drifted closer and would have reached for the tree, but with me standing right in front of it, he couldn't. He floated aimlessly as if he wasn't sure how to solve the problem.

"Can I see your hands?"

Too tired to care or resist, he pulled his hands from his pockets. Even this close to the tree, his fingers didn't properly form.

"You need your ring back, Troy."

His face blurred worse than before. "Have to go through."

"The tree is closing. You can't continue on this way."

Instead of denying or agreeing, he drifted sideways and then reached for the smooth surface. His arm leaked into the tree. I started to help him, but touch was bad enough during ordinary circumstances. What if whatever marked him was contagious?

I looked at Spook, but the dog just whined. "I'll go with him, Spook. Get the rest of the crew. Send a scout. See if you can find Amy. We're going to have to steal the ring back."

Spook yipped in agreement. The animals scattered. I slipped inside, next to Troy. The way In Between worked, a ghost could sit and partially regenerate, but it was akin to lying down and hoping you didn't die.

There was energy here, bits and pieces, but even that would take time to absorb. We floated to the left, where the tunnel was located. More tree roots had grown, filling the entire trail. We didn't make it far before Troy sat down. He pushed his arms forward into narrower parts of the tunnel. "Sometimes the ley line leaks. Can't touch it directly, but the little leaks are pure magic."

I had felt the heat from the ley line. A direct hit would be akin to a lightning strike. The magic might be feeding the tree and the roots here, but digging around hoping to find a trickle seemed like a quick way to burn your candle to the ground.

"Why does Amy wear your ring?"

"It doesn't hurt anything."

"It's linked to you!" I wasn't smart enough to figure out how all the pieces were related. "Did the ring keep this portal open?"

He shook his head. "No. After I made my peace dirt-side, the fairies spun magic so that the portal would close. It was leaking too much magic dirt-side."

"But why do you need more energy than you needed before?" Somehow that ring was crucial. Without it, he was missing an essential piece of himself. With the kind of energy available from the tree, he shouldn't require replenishing so quickly, not unless something or someone was draining him.

I thought of how snapping my sleeve at the hellhound had hurt it. That ring was tied to Troy and this tree. This tree was energy. The ring was part of his energy. "I think maybe Amy is using your ring to steal your energy. You come here and harvest more, but it is absorbed into that ring. Amy figured that out and uses it to draw energy from you."

"I am pretty sure I was tired before I gave it to her." He frowned in confusion. "My energy is just gone. She's not some kind of ghoul. She's human. You've seen her!"

I couldn't argue that. "Maybe being a human ghost doesn't stop her from drinking like a ghoul." She had always clung to Troy. Maybe it wasn't just because she liked him.

"Did she ask you for the ring?"

His face was formed enough now that I could read the expression in his eyes, and it was too much like feverish addiction. "Just a few sparks, and I'll be myself again!" He leaned towards me as if I were the energy line here.

Talk like that was worse than scary. "You don't feed off friends, Troy."

"I don't mean that! I wouldn't take—" He stopped then and rubbed a half hand where his hair would be. "The last roadkill. I could barely escort it through the tunnel. I think I killed it."

"Isn't roadkill already dead?"

He nodded. "But there's always residual energy. I brought it into the tunnel, but the fairies are closing the tunnel with a new tree. We were in the tunnel, and I guided it like I always do." His voice fell to a croaking whisper. "I was so hungry."

It would be too obvious if I scooted away from him. I raised my hands, wishing for a rock, a staff...I slid my jacket sleeve loose. It was already torn off anyway.

He stared at me, his eyes larger and brighter than they should have been, but holding no malice. The crazed look was replaced by wariness. "I offered you energy, and you never complained. Why is sharing with Amy any different?"

"You gave me bits of life force from dirt-side! I never took any of *your* essence." He knew the difference. He'd been one of the ones to explain it to me when I first arrived. "Did you give her the ring or did she take it?"

"That ring isn't me. It's not life force."

I nodded emphatically. "It's part of you. Let me see your hands."

He held them out again, not even having the energy to be impatient with me.

He had replenished enough that most of his fingers formed. Where his ring finger would have been, there was a darker stub than his other fingers, but nothing more, definitely no ring. I stared at that spot for a long time. "There's a mark where your ring belongs. Cinderspark said you had a mark, but not a demon mark. Amy took that ring and left her mark, tying your energy to her or the ring. By giving it to her, you entered some kind of agreement."

"But it's just a ring. It doesn't matter, and I can't remember. I gave it to her to help her. She calls it a promise ring."

I stared at my sleeve. It had come over with me. It was cotton. It retained enough energy to let me fight hellhounds, especially if I soaked it with leaking essence. "Your real ring, the one that belongs dirt-side is here."

His head swirled, he turned it so fast. "You saw it? I can't reach that spot anymore. The last trip to dirt-side I...tried digging. But the roots are everywhere now. I can't slide through them anymore."

"Troy, we have to retrieve your ring somehow."

He held up his hand. Two of his fingers formed completely right down to fingernails, but he was pale and shaky shimmers all over. The tree roots still fed him, but Cinderspark was right. Something about his essence was wrong, damaged. Where his ring should have been, there was only a dark band. "I don't think the ring will fix it," he said.

"It can't make it any worse. We have to try."

He shook his head in denial or despair.

I left him to soak up whatever energy the tree was willing to share.

Spook was waiting for me outside the tree, a ball of hyper puppy, spinning and jumping eagerly. His whole body shouted, "At last!"

The tree roots should have energized me, but I was coated with dread. Spook was a dog. He wouldn't be able to slide the ring off Amy's finger. I was the only one with opposable thumbs.

Spook woofed and growled. Two 'coons swirled into position. One took point with Spook, the other lined up next to me. I heard a piercing challenge from above and nearly lost my jacket sleeve before I realized it was a hawk. His gray down feathers stuck out at funny angles as though he hadn't yet fully recovered his ghost shape and was still partially smashed from being hit by a car.

Spook barked once, and we headed out. If only I had died with the knife that had been used in the attack against me, I'd happily cut her hand off and run away. I needed a weapon, maybe a ghost Uzi or at the very least a stout club. The thought made my hands clench, craving a baton that I could twirl as a weapon while keeping my distance. Maybe we should have bribed a ghoul or an imp. Would the mermaids help if I fed them fish?

This rescue attempt was a horrible idea. I was going to end up as fodder for some hideous not-demon. Well, I was already dead, right?

There were bad portals In Between, veils that led places no one wanted to go. I scanned for them and the creatures they housed as Spook loped around boulders, trotted across murky fog-filled patches and led us deeper into gloom. Maybe I stayed near the dirt-side edge more than I realized because the path Spook chose was fog with no boundaries. The gray was thick and full of obstacles; misshapen tree limbs coated with black moss and craggy outcrops that we either climbed or drifted around.

Ah. It wasn't that we were so deep inside In Between. The dense fog and rocks were because we were nearing the lake. Or maybe it was the River Styx like Martin speculated, but I'd always envisioned the river as narrower and flowing. There were waves lapping along most of the visible shoreline, but they were directed at the rocky beach, not flowing like a river.

Nearly obscured by the fog in the distance, a half mountain butted against the water. Larger waves broke heavily against the sheer rock face.

Spook stopped, turned his head my way, but made no sound. When he crept forward again, he did so cautiously, crouching low and putting one stealthy paw down at a time. It was actually harder to make noise In Between than be quiet. I barely had feet. When you're puffing yourself or drifting, feet don't matter much. But Spook was a dog. He wasn't changing his instincts just because he was dead. I followed his example, tucking myself small and advancing furtively.

When we rounded the side of the rock, Amy came into view. She knelt, staring into the water. Her hands splayed out in front of her body, forming a sort of circle as though she were holding something flat, but her hands were empty. The water swelled around the sides of her knees, while under her hands the water was strangely still.

Spook halted abruptly, his tail straight out, nose and eyes locked on the target. There was no sign of the other animals, but a flickering shadow near my feet might have been the hawk overhead. It might have been nothing more than floating gray mist, too.

I crept forward. Grabbing the ring with her bent forward like that was probably impossible, but if I pushed her in the water, maybe I could snatch it off her hand while she was floundering.

When I was nearly upon her, she spoke, "What do you mean she's gone? She didn't die. I'd know!"

The murmured reply was mostly lost in the lapping of the waves. "...another hospital...not my fault..."

"We can't keep starting over," Amy shouted. "I have to get out of here! We need that girl!"

"Who is that behind you?"

I didn't realize in time that Amy was talking through an open portal, and the person on the other side could see me.

Amy whirled.

I kicked out hoping to stun her, but a flash of released energy from the portal pushed her sideways as the portal snapped closed. My kick missed. I slapped my jacket sleeve across her face, blinding her with a small blast of energy.

Her legs swirled, pushing her upright. At least her hands were closer to me now; they were wrapped around my neck. The edge of my jacket collar buffered me from one of her hands, but her other hand might as well have been full of vampire fangs.

Dizziness and a sudden weakness overwhelmed me.

Her grip was incredibly strong. The emotion transferred with her touch seared with a hatred worse than the rancid breath of the hellhounds.

A raccoon darted forward and attached itself to her ankle. She released one hand from around my neck, but instead of backhanding the raccoon, she laughed. "The more the merrier, vermin."

She grabbed it by the neck and to my horror, she absorbed it. Just like that, all that was left was the barest of sucking sounds.

I dragged myself away from her, realizing her touch had weakened me considerably. My jacket collar had completely dissolved. She hadn't been attempting to choke me; she'd been absorbing me. My neck didn't hurt, but it felt as though a gaping hole existed where my neck had once been.

Spook barked in the background, smarter than the 'coon. He dove in and out, daring her to come and get him. With her back against the water, he couldn't maneuver around behind her. Neither could the fat squirrel that landed on her head. It bounced off immediately rather than risk being sucked into nothingness.

"Filth," she screamed, her swipe barely missing it.

I lunged for the ring again, but she was fast, smacking me with her fist. She knew the trick to throwing her energy around. Maybe if I'd been willing to absorb her energy like she was attempting to steal mine it would have been a fair fight, but I wanted nothing of her essence other than the ring.

Another squirrel leaped, but fell short. It scampered up her back, claws out, digging in. She was ready for it. There was a small pop, and the critter was gone, absorbed right through her back.

"Shit." If she touched me again, I was toast.

She advanced; I danced back. I slapped at her again with my jacket sleeve, fast. Even still, she nearly grabbed it away. The flash of energy when the sleeve snapped must have hurt her, but she forced her hand right around the spark. Her lips peeled back against the pain as she drank it in.

"Give me the ring." It was almost a whisper from behind me.

One eye roved to locate the source. "Troy!" Boy, was I glad to see him.

He stood not six feet away. "I come back for it every time I replenish my energy, don't I? And you manage to talk me out of it."

"Troy, darling, call off your beasts. We've been happy together!"

Her claim would have been more believable if her hand wasn't glowing with stolen power and her face contorted with the pain of absorbing it all at once.

"They aren't beasts," Troy said. "They are what they were born to be. My time was up here. I made my peace and was ready to move on until you talked me out of it." He sighed. "The ring calls me back to you every time. I didn't realize it until Shadow pointed it out. It keeps me here. I can't leave until I get it back. I can't rest."

"Okay. Sure. You can have it." She held out her hand. "We can share it."

"Uh, Troy..." If I tried for the ring, she'd pull her hand back. If Troy touched it or her, she'd start absorbing his energy. He'd either collapse entirely or end up so drained, we'd be lucky to make it back to the tree. The cycle would start all over.

Troy's eyes focused on the ring. His face went slack as he reached out. Thankfully, he was too far away. I scooted in front of the ring, blocking his view. He immediately shifted to keep the goal in sight. Mindless, he drifted forward. Spook shot right through him, whining, barking, begging.

Troy flinched when the dog touched him. He stopped, momentarily confused, but then refocused on his goal.

If I could somersault over her arm and grab the ring on the way...I'd land in the lake. The lake was dangerous, but it might be the only chance we had.

Because the fog muted most sounds, we were all equally unprepared when the strumming of the song, *Stairway To Heaven,* floated across the water.

I wasted a millisecond scanning the black surface, but there was nothing out there. When I finally whirled sideways, I saw Kyle, the musician I'd recently escorted, perched on the outcropping of rocks that bordered the lake. "Kyle!"

He strummed his guitar, the haunting tune floating across the gray. The blankness on Troy's face was replaced by realization for half an instant.

Amy's hand was still beckoning him, her fingers extended. It was now or never.

"Aaaaaaawk!" The scream jarred me almost as much as the music had, and Kyle hit a wrong note, but to a man, we looked up.

The hawk dove so fast, it took precious seconds for me to realize it had slammed into Amy's hand and either pried the ring loose or ripped her finger right off.

We all pounced towards the prize and ghost or no, I bet Troy and I earned perfect Olympic scores that rivaled the hawk's dive.

The ring was tuned to Troy, spiraling his way in the fog even as he reached for it. His hand wrapped around the ruby.

Amy may have been closest to it, but my foot snapped energy against her knees.

She tilted over, knocked flat. Stunned from the loss of the ring, she stayed that way.

As I rolled to my feet, her wide eyes stared up at me in horror. Her hair began to fade, losing the individual strands and waves, but despite only a blobbing mass atop her facial features, her beauty remained.

Her hand clenched and unclenched, missing a finger and more importantly, missing the ring. A strange darkness flickered around her edges like a black flame, reminding me of the blood in Espy's IV. Was Amy part demon? Was that how she marked Troy, leaving a demon mark, but not one that Cinderspark had recognized immediately because Amy was part human too?

Kyle continued to play, while off in the distance, something joined in. Discordant violin shrieks sliced across Kyle's music, nearly breaking his melody in half. He missed more than a note, but manfully he held the tune, and played even louder.

Amy screamed, writhing in agony.

I backed up more than one step. Kyle began sinking into the rocks.

Amy shouted, "Give it back! You wanted me to have it! It keeps me hidden from him! You saved me!"

She was suddenly crawling, stalking Troy. Flashes of dark flickered along the veins of her ghostly arms, neck, and even her face. Like the tarnished band on Troy's finger, the elongated patches were a dark glow that surged through her bloodstream. She had been marked by something, and it had expanded much further than the small mark Troy had on his hand.

Without the ring, her real essence was no longer hidden behind stolen energy.

Troy ignored her and touched my arm briefly. "Time for me to take the next train out. I should have left right after I made my peace dirt-side. Take care of my friends for me, please? I owe them, big time."

What was a ghost like me supposed to do with a ragged menagerie of animals? I barely understood only the most obvious chatter.

I nodded my agreement anyway. He had guided them here, and now they were repaying the favor. I was a poor substitute.

"And tell Cinderspark goodbye and thanks?"

I nodded again, but knew I wouldn't see her again. My throat hurt, my heart hurt and there was no way for a ghost to relieve it all with tears.

Troy held up his fist, clenching his ring.

Color! I stared at the deep ruby glow, barely hearing the fading sounds as Kyle finished *Stairway To Heaven*.

A tiny spark drifted down, and then Troy was gone.

Chapter 16

The howling threat of the hounds gave my feet wings. I dove for the rocks, hitting the spaces and oozing in like water down a drain. The tattered ghost animals must have disappeared with Troy because the only one that was close on my heels was Spook.

Amy knelt at the water, her hands spread in an awkward circle shape. She shouted, "There isn't time! I need to cross now! It will be temporary, I promise!"

Kyle was already tucked inside the cavity with me, his guitar returned to the case resting comfortably across his back.

There was another odd screech of distorted violin chords and then a cackling laugh from hell.

After that, there was blessed silence if you ignored the howling of the hounds.

"What was that?" Kyle demanded.

I started to explain about the ring and Troy, but midway through he interrupted, "No. I meant that violin. Can music die? Because it sounded like it was dying."

"Oh." I shuddered. The sound of bent strings had been like a giant spider in my ear, a gross mobbing of something I wanted to claw out. "I don't know. That noise was here at the lake before, remember? When you first came through."

"Not like that."

He was right. The instrument hadn't been that horrifying before. It had been a threat, but not a lethal promise. "How did you find us? How did you know what to do?"

He stared at me, a blank expression on his face as though he were elsewhere. After Spook nudged his hand and gave it a ghostly lick, he said, "I come here to play and watch the mermaids that look like my wife. I know they aren't really Paula, but I'm afraid I'll forget her."

"Why don't you watch your wife instead?"

He sighed. "It hurts too much. She needs to...she's still alive. She needs to find someone else."

I understood all too well. "Don't we all."

"How? How do we do it? Do I just wait like that Troy guy and disappear one day when the time is right?"

I shrugged. "I don't know. Some of us seem to have a purpose, like Troy. But he did what he needed to, and apparently he would have gone sooner except that Amy had his ring. He was stuck here feeding her." I shivered again, my form threatening to break apart from fear and disgust.

"Why is that Amy chick here? Why are you here?"

"I don't know." Spook put his head where my lap would have been had I bothered to form legs. I gave him a pat.

Kyle swung his guitar onto his lap, but left it in the case.

"Is there something you need to do? Here? There?" I asked.

"There were a lot of things I needed to do there," he said bitterly. "Like raise my little girl. Play my music."

"Martin would tell you to play, then."

"What good does it do here?"

"I don't know that, either. But he'd tell you that if you were supposed to play, to keep playing. That's what he does." Even as I said it, I realized the truth of it. "He was of the earth there, so now he's of the earth here. He just keeps right on being Martin."

"What about you?"

"Well, there's a real mystery." Since we had nothing but time to kill until the hellhounds found a more interesting scent to track, I told him what Martin had said about me not being dead. "But I don't know if it matters. I've been practicing nudging the edge, but so far as I can tell, there is no way back over even though my body is in a coma in the hospital." I frowned. "I don't know how I ended up here either. I was running from something, something like Amy, that was trying to harvest my life force. But now almost everything I meet makes a grab for whatever is left of me. I'm not sure it's an improvement."

"You might go back?" He stared at me hungrily.

"No one knows. Least of all me."

"But if you do, then you can deliver a message for me. Right?"

I'd been worried he somehow wanted to piggyback or take my place. Compared to those things his request was an easy one. "Well, sure. But, Kyle." I held up a hand. "No one knows how to return dirt-side."

He nodded, but instead of losing hope, he strummed his suddenly available guitar and sang, "You can't go back home."

Unfortunately, I couldn't even remember home, so he was more right than he knew.

Chapter 17

As soon as we were able to leave the cairn, I headed for Troy's tree. Long before it was visible, I knew it was too late.

My throat caught, and I halted as the fog rolled forward and back. The juniper hadn't exactly vanished, but it wasn't there anymore either. Oh, there was a ghost of a tree, but the smooth side had completely disappeared. The remaining lump was more driftwood, a pile of jagged branches and a large trunk split down the middle. There was no hint of color, no shimmer of a connection to fairies or dirt-side. When I breathed deep, there was only the dampness of In Between, no earthy scents at all.

I drifted closer and held my hand over the ghosted wood. For the barest moment it whispered against my skin. It was a peaceful passing, one that energized and left a blossom of contentment, but sadness still struck me. The tree was dead and gone. So was Troy.

Spook woofed from behind me. Without turning I asked, "Where did the other roadkill go?"

He woofed again, a sound lacking concern.

"Well, I hope they are happy. And I hope they know how to find me or take care of themselves. I have a feeling I'm not much help otherwise."

He yipped, and we turned for home. I should have been exhausted, but between Troy's peaceful passing to the next part of his journey, wherever that was, and the gift from the tree, I was more rested than before the whole ordeal began. It hadn't hurt that instead of wallowing in self-pity, I'd been kept busy answering Kyle's questions.

Thinking about Amy sent my essence crawling. Who had she been talking to? Where had she gone?

She lacked the shapeless hulking black shape of most ghouls I'd seen, but maybe she was how ghouls got their start. Suck one person dry at a time. One soul here, another essence there. Then one day you're nothing but a monster with no face of your own, nothing but an eating machine destroying and poisoning everything in your path.

The calls to the edge were frequent enough now that I almost expected them, but with everything that had just happened, I was tempted to ignore the tug that jerked at me as I passed closer to the weave.

My scalp tingled. It wasn't a death rattle. It took me a long moment to realize the vibration was coming from the bundle the cat had given me. The waves resonated through me like a very low bass or maybe a drum beat you feel but don't really hear.

Not sure whether to hunt down the source or not, I floated on the vibrations, letting it draw me closer. The edge responded to the beat too, because the next thing I heard was the feral snarl that only a cat could make —or a certain human with a ghost of a cat face hovering. Maybe because I had practice with Troy's animals, or maybe because he was human and cat, I distinctly understood the snarl to say, "Your entrails are nothing but smear."

To my intense dismay, the edge cleared on a room at the hospital again. Next time I died, I was going to breathe my last in a beautiful canyon like Martin.

My complaints fled in a near panic as I realized the cat was under attack. A large, bald man with tattoos smeared across one side of his neck lumbered towards Lynx with one club-like arm swinging blindly. The attacker was still dressed in a hospital gown, but it was torn and bloody. The bed had been slammed into the wall. Half of the leg supports, including the wheels, were smashed. One had been ripped completely off.

The cat dodged a blow, but the man never blinked. His mouth hung open as if it was too much trouble to close it. The hospital gown swung sideways with his missed blow. Where his stomach would have been, the flesh was peeled aside and hanging. Inside, there was nothing but a dried black cavity. The guy was little more than a mummy brought back into action. He certainly wasn't alive, not with that hole.

When the club arm descended again, the cat darted faster than a streak of light, his claws tearing at the man's neck. Blood welled, but it was dark black and already coagulated as if the blood in his veins had long ago stopped circulating.

Why didn't the cat run away? The door was closed. Was it locked? There was no window. But how had the cat gotten locked in the room with a zombie?

My questions would have to wait. Lynx might be mangling this piece of rotting flesh, but even minus parts, the thing wasn't slowing down. It stalked Lynx with a single-minded purpose.

From the intensity of the fight, it was clear that unless the cat could slice the zombie into tiny pieces, he'd eventually run out of energy and then his life force would be headed here.

That would be very bad. And unfair. This cat had been trying to help me. But I was stuck here where I couldn't help him. Swinging my jacket sleeve with its bits of remaining life force wasn't going to slow this zombie down. It might even feed him. What was needed was to toss this creature where he deserved to be—the land of the dead.

Could the answer be so simple?

"Lynx!" My shout was probably nothing more than a hollow moan on his side, but the cat heard.

His eyes flicked to me, full of fear. Blood and mess covered one side of his face. He'd been hit with some zombie part that had splattered or exploded.

He hissed. I understood it as, *"Run, Shadow!"* Yellow eyes were wide, evaluating every possible option.

"Bring him to me." My wailing desperation pushed against the weave. I was trying too hard. Martin had taught me to sneak through the weave, not batter it into forming a hard resistant shell. "Bring him here, near me," I whispered.

Lynx evaded the club arm again, stumbling and panting. The zombie launched his entire body at Lynx's new location, but the cat twisted, an impossible feat for a normal human, climbed part of the wall and flipped back and out of the way.

Eventually, just by accident, the zombie might come in contact with the edge. The question was, which would have more power over the zombie, the In Between edge or the living world edge?

Lynx snarled, an incoherent threat. He went full cat, but the change cost him precious seconds.

The zombie caught him under the belly, tossing him callously into the hospital bed. It careened one direction and the cat went the other. Even as he hit the wall, Lynx rolled and swiped in one motion. The bed fell over, revealing blood-spattered sheets.

The spatters formed a map of intricate designs, the dots forming a pattern. I had seen another sheet with a lot of blood. The one in the laundry room had been wadded up, though. If there had been a pattern, it had been meaningless. This time, the spatters clearly formed at least two star points. "A pentagram!" Someone had tried to summon something from this side and had ended up creating a zombie, or calling one.

Lynx loosed another feral scream, dodged and raked his claws down the arm that swatted at him.

If we didn't do something lethal and quickly, Lynx would be joining me.

"To me," I said softly, already working the fabric of the edge more fully into the room. Only the knowledge that I could be blown to bits kept me carefully massaging it inward rather than hitting out in frustration. The fabric wasn't interested in our lives or our deaths, other than to separate one from the other.

The cat must have misunderstood my request because instead of tricking the zombie into the edge, he backed himself in my direction.

"No, cat. This is not an escape for you!"

I unbraided the bundle and waved it at the zombie. I looped it tightly around my ghost finger and tied a quick knot. "Life energy. For free, monster." Holding it against the edge caused the bubble to undulate away from me. I advanced.

The zombie came for the cat. The cat sprang away, already having realized the zombie was not quick to change direction.

A lumbering step brought it right to the edge.

I steeled myself and slammed the hand holding the braid through the weave right at the monster's dead face. There was no hair left on his head to grab, so I wrapped my dead fingers around his ear.

The weave parted just enough. As soon as the fabric bands touched the zombie, the beast emitted a hollow, surprised groan. The moan of despair must have been worse dirt-side because the cat flinched.

Red-hot pain splintered up my arm, but I pulled that one zombie ear as if we could change places.

The dead welcomed one of its own. The edge immediately expanded, embracing the entire body.

I screamed. I had yanked too hard. The head tore off completely, dangling from my fingers. I gagged on another scream. The eyes of the foul, disembodied head blinked at me once as its body spun off in another direction, shards of the edge flaying it. The head morphed in my hand, losing the bloated tissue and fading to gray ghost. The neck dripped ghost essence.

I shrieked. The dull, cruel eyes of the man who had sent me here stared back at me sightlessly. If he had been after my life force when I ended up here, he had failed. And whatever that pentagram had tried to do for him, it had failed as well. Finally, he paid the ultimate price.

I flung the head away from me, a cold ghost moan trapped in my throat.

The bald orb slammed into the already battered weave. Rotted essence shattered, splattering.

It is possible that the phantom juice from the man who had killed me protected me ever so slightly when the fabric rebounded, cutting me into pieces and spraying the pieces every which way. I lost myself completely. The gray disappeared into an unrelenting black as my essence spun uselessly away.

Chapter 18

Kyle found me. Or at least he found my ghostly hand still wrapped around the braid.

It was the music that penetrated my awareness first. Kyle played his ghostly guitar, a cross between a funeral march and a war song. The sorrowful lyrics of *Done With Bonaparte* called me to my floating hand. Never mind that according to the song, the soldier lost an eye, not a hand. On short notice, details apparently weren't all that important.

"It sounds better when accompanied by an accordion," Kyle apologized as I returned to consciousness.

I stared at the ghost guitar, hanging onto the music and vibrating with the receding notes. "You sure can play." My voice was raw, almost a croak.

"I thought I'd have to leave music behind once I died. Then after we talked, I feared my music might go bad, and I'd start sounding like that thing by the lake. I followed you to ask you about it. You don't stay out of trouble long, do you?"

I shook my head, and it nearly rolled off. Collecting myself took another minute. "If you were musical before, no reason you wouldn't be now."

He strummed the strings. "If everything else had to be taken away, thank God there's still music."

I was in complete agreement, because something in the magic of the song had just returned me to me.

Kyle looked up from strumming, but glanced away as soon as he caught my eyes. "I've thought about it, and I want to give you the message for Paula. Just in case you find a way across." He took a deep, unnecessary breath. "I've been stashing money for our daughter. It was supposed to be a surprise for Paula after she had the baby. But she won't know where to find it. It's in a false bottom in one of my guitar cases. You've got to tell her. She might sell the thing and never find the money!"

"Kyle..." I hated to burst his bubble.

"I saw you grab that thing. There was a portal open!"

"Not really. The weave was just thin. When the zombie came in contact with the edge, it was sucked in here. I didn't go back there. I can teach you what Martin taught me, and you can try to talk to Paula. Do you know if the guitar you play here—does she have the real one?"

His hand stroked the guitar unconsciously. "I don't know. I haven't looked."

"It might help, because there's often a link between the ghost thing and the real thing."

"What about a real portal? Amy had a portal open," he said.

"At the lake? You saw it too?"

"I sit there a lot. I hide if the hounds come. Even among the rocks, if you sit in the right place, the view out across the lake is clear. I saw the whole fight. When the violin started wailing, she went berserk. You ran for cover, but she knelt and drew something in the air. Next thing I knew, she jumped in the lake and vanished. She didn't swim away or sink down, she just disappeared."

If I'd needed to breathe, I'd have choked. "I saw her kneeling and talking to someone. The portal was open then. Later, I was too focused on surviving to pay attention to her! You're sure she went through the portal? Things do sometimes slip through the weave from dirt-side, but I haven't seen anything return there yet." Given that my body was waiting for me over there, I wanted badly to believe it was possible.

"I wasn't sure that what I saw at the lake was a portal until I saw you yank that zombie through. That's when I realized she used a portal."

"The lake or river is reputed to be a portal. But how did she know how to use it? And if she has a way across, what is she doing here?"

"She was damned anxious to leave after that violin started plinking those death threats. But so was I. I'd hide from that crazy sound no matter what."

I nodded vehemently. "You're right. She was scared, and not just because she lost her energy source. I don't know exactly what she meant, but she said Troy's ring kept her hidden 'from him.' Maybe she meant the demon because as soon as she lost the ring, that violin noise headed our way."

"But if she had a portal, why hang out here? Why did she wait to escape whatever she was afraid of?"

"I don't know. Martin says to cross and stay, you have to have a body. She was arguing with someone when we first arrived at the lake. She was angry because they had to start over, and there wasn't enough time for that. The girl had disappeared." The only girl I could think of was Espy, but I had no proof Amy had anything to do with her. I didn't even have any real proof that Espy had been in danger in the first place.

"If Amy is part demon, maybe she's waiting for someone to draw the right pentagram to hold her intact," I said. "Or maybe she was satisfied with staying here as long as she had Troy's energy to hide behind. No, that doesn't make sense. No one would willingly stay here. I know I'd return in a heartbeat."

"So why aren't you gone? You said your body is waiting."

"I still don't know if or how I can cross. There's a guy dirt-side who is able to hold the weave open for a short time, but no one has ever had a body waiting so we don't know if his talent will allow me to cross."

"Maybe you can use Amy's portal."

It wasn't possible for me to sweat, but I definitely had the shakes. "Using anything of hers might not be a good idea. And we don't know for sure that it was a portal. Or if it still exists."

"We should check it out."

I could have used more downtime, but we were both curious, and my own silly words had left me optimistic that a portal, a real usable tunnel, existed at the lake.

We floated our way back to the water.

Waves, just like before, lapped gently at the gray shore. The fog was thick today, sometimes obscuring even the nearby rocks.

"If she held a portal open, it required energy." I kicked a useless ghost leg against a few pebbles. "There's no obvious opening here now." My hope died a bit. "And we still don't know where a portal might lead if there is one here."

"Where else would a portal lead other than home?" Kyle asked.

"Hell?" I guessed. "Martin thinks this might be the legendary River Styx, but if it is, he believes it should also contain portals to other places as well." I floated along the shoreline, hunting for a glimpse of color, sniffing deep in case there was any taint of demon. "Wasn't the River Styx bound by a marsh? This is too rocky to be considered a marsh. But whatever it is, I don't really believe Amy voluntarily jumped into a portal to hell."

We both agreed on the spot where she had been kneeling, but there was nothing visibly different about the area. The water retained its mirror surface, and the shoreline was an unbroken, relentless gray with pebbles, large boulders and the occasional patch of sand.

I was afraid to lean too close to the water lest something from the depths reach out and drag me under, but if she had drawn something, she had to be following a pattern. I listened for hounds, and checked the large rocks out on the lake. There was no music now and nothing but curtains of fog across the open water.

My knees left no impression on the ground, nor was there any obvious pattern to be found. If Amy had formed any kind of link, it had to be under the water. "She'd need energy to forge a final connection. We ghosts don't have anything else to offer." Gingerly, I dipped my hand into the water. The gray lake could have been a black hole for all the visibility it offered, but as soon as my hand broke through, the water rippled, just like any of the other gray. The bottom was only a few inches down. "A rock!" The stone glimmered back, a wet blackness amid the gray.

"There are rocks all over this place."

"It's black. Not gray. It has a black blotch on it, which is close enough to real color. It just happens to be black."

Kyle slung his guitar over his shoulder and knelt next to me. Braver than I, he put his face nearly on the water, flicking his finger to break the surface. "You're right. There are more, too." He spread his hands, causing the water to ripple and reveal. The motion was almost as if he were smoothing cloth into a circle. Amy had held her hands almost the same way.

I leaned closer. "They're black on the top. The base is either under the sand or fading to gray."

"There's seven of them." He pointed, leaving one hand skimming the surface to keep the water from settling.

"How did she link them? Obviously it took energy, but how did she do it?"

"We have to try it," he said, his voice bright with excitement.

I sat back. "If she's on the other side of this, we don't want to open up a chat line and have her hop back on top of us."

"Who cares? We have to try it!" Kyle forgot himself and grabbed my arm.

I gasped as his emotion flowed through me.

He released me immediately. "Sorry. I forgot. I forget all the time. But I have to talk to Paula. If there's a portal here, maybe I can reach her."

I shivered. "Let's find Martin. He knows a lot more about this place than I do. These rocks aren't going to up and walk away."

When my gaze swept out across the lake, I wished I hadn't spoken so soon. The mermaids had returned. Either our presence or Kyle's emotion had beckoned them. "Let's get out of here."

Before hunting down Martin, I needed energy. More than that, I wanted to check on the cat. Worry gnawed my guts, affecting my ability to manipulate the edge because it responded to my emotion.

I drifted near the weave, hoarding bits and pieces the way Martin had taught me. The edge showed the hospital just like it usually did, but even with my best efforts, Lynx was nowhere to be found.

Had he escaped from the zombie room?

I shuddered. Good thing Kyle had come along when he did. Good thing some other monster hadn't found me before I stitched myself back together. And if the murdering zombie ever gathered enough pieces to form a ghost, I'd find a way to feed him to the hellhounds.

Bastard. He didn't sport a nose ring anymore, but I'd recognized his cold dead eyes. They hadn't been any more alive when he was still breathing.

I fingered the braid from Lynx. Instead of seeing him, the hospital corridors remained in soft focus. I connected here easily. Martin connected to his canyon. Kyle could see his wife, but since he hadn't died near her, the link wasn't likely to be strong enough for them to communicate. Even if he had died in her arms, they might not be able to speak. Some people sensed us. Most didn't.

Would the portal allow Kyle to convey his message if we could somehow activate it? If Roberto were there, it would probably remain open long enough for them to communicate. For all I knew, we only needed Roberto. But I was short a phone and a number.

I puffed back and forth, contorting my body this way and that; a ghost version of stretching. It didn't limber my mind any. If Amy knew how to open a portal, why stay here? Why steal from Troy?

Troy's ring was still on the side of the living. Maybe the ghost ring was the catalyst for opening the portal for her. Maybe she didn't have enough energy on her own.

I fingered the braid. Even if we could open a portal, it didn't mean I could go through.

But we could try.

Chapter 19

It took most of a day to locate Martin. When we told him about the rocks and Amy, a low buzzing filled the air. At first I feared there were bees from hell on the way, but it was just Martin with a new song.

"If it's Amy's portal, you may only have one chance to use it before it runs out of gas. That's if the magic works when someone else activates it."

My heart sank. "You mean, we can either try to reach Kyle's wife or try to reach the living me?"

Martin buzzed some more. "I don't know that it will work at all. It's not your circle. If she has the magic to create it, you may not. Any spell is limited. Magic has to be recreated with original materials or boosted every so often."

My fingers clenched around the braid. "Not just any energy works to open them?"

"If it is a portal, then it must be the River Styx." He shook his head, muttered and wafted back and forth, leaving swirls of himself that he picked up on the way back. "You are in the hospital. But how can we link Amy's portal, if it is a portal, to the hospital?"

"Can Roberto help us? But if we wait for Roberto to call us, we could be waiting for all of eternity!"

Now Martin shook his head. "The witch is good. The cat, he's on a mission. He will bust you out. An actual portal is a better doorway than Roberto trying to force the weave to stay open long enough. With just Roberto you could end up stretched to nothing when you tried to squeeze through."

By now we had reached the lake. Martin didn't bother to peer around the rocks, he just blasted through them and headed for the shoreline. I floated along the bank until the area looked familiar, but when we broke the surface there were no black stones. Nothing but water and random gray rippled back at us.

Luckily Kyle had better spatial memory than I did. He found the black stones after only two attempts.

Martin took one look and resumed pacing. "Broken violin. Portal." He spun suddenly, hovering directly over my face like a mad scientist. "You heard this broken music before. Did you ever see it?"

"The music?" I asked stupidly.

"No. The entity playing it!" Martin rarely shouted, but he was agitated now, bobbing up and down.

When the violin screeched, I had been running for my, well, I was running, not taking notes. "There were flames. Sparks of light. The second time Kyle played, I was already inside the cairn, hiding."

"Flames." Martin drifted away again, no humming. He finally put his own hand on the water next to Kyle's and stared into the depths. "We don't want to use this more than once. We'll have to contact Roberto first and make sure everyone is in position."

"Once?" Kyle stared at me, sadness in his eyes. "If you can slide through, you can deliver the message for me. If you can't manage to get through, it's not likely that I can talk to her anyway. No point in trying that."

Martin huffed. "If the thing opens, the problem is that *any of us can get through.*"

Kyle blinked. "What?"

Martin bounced again, his head stretching like a giant genie squeezing out of a lamp. "The issue, of course, is that once there, the only way to survive is to inhabit another human body. Quite problematic if you don't have one waiting, which is likely Amy's problem. This portal doesn't belong here. The weave has always been one direction, but permeable. There are leaks that provide the energy we squirrel away." He pointed to the rocks now invisible beneath the water. "If this is a portal that leads dirt-side, unlike the weave, it is not one-way. The power required to create it is neither simple nor small. And whatever owned that power was not Amy with a ghost ring that belonged to a dead guy."

I listened to the gray carefully, but the only sound was waves lapping and the cottony silence of the fog. The smell of dampness held no hint of sulfur. "You think she stole power from someone other than Troy?"

Martin nodded. *"Something* stronger than Troy owned the power that opened this portal. Since it has not taken that power back, the entity either can't find it or it can't use the portal because it has no body to inhabit. But once we activate it, whatever powers this thing will know we're using it. It's going to want to jump over and inhabit a body."

That was bad news because if we were the ones opening the portal, the only available body on the other side waiting would be mine.

Chapter 20

My job was to stand guard over my body, which was more than a little boring and kind of spooky. Sure, I was linked to the hospital room, so it was easy enough to sit there at the weave, but a coma was very nearly like sitting on a death watch. Unlike a death, there wasn't even the beauty or comfort of a life line.

My body never stirred, not even when I nudged myself from this side. My skin was gray. You'd think I would be used to that color by now, but somehow the gray of this side was healthier than the one dirt-side.

Martin assigned himself the more desirable job. He roamed the edge near the canyon waiting for Roberto and Lynx so he could tell them to set up a meeting back at the hospital. Even if Lynx were to show up on my watch, there was no guarantee he could understand me perfectly through the weave, not unless Roberto was around. After the zombie attack, maybe Lynx wasn't ever planning on setting foot in the hospital again.

It wasn't on the agenda, but I wandered. I snuck around checking for the aunt and little Espy who could see ghosts. The girl could definitely understand me, but only if she had recovered from her coma. I peeked into every room that the edge allowed me to see, but she wasn't to be found. That was probably a good thing for her. Maybe.

Kyle's job wasn't any more exciting than mine and just as morose. He had to monitor Paula and learn to manage the edge the way Martin had taught me.

He could only take so much of watching his wife before the sorrow engulfed him. Most days, he'd stop by once or twice to see if anything had changed with me.

I was patrolling the edge to make sure no hellhounds were near when he drifted into my zone.

"The music made it through," he said without preamble.

"To your wife? I wondered if it might. You're pretty powerful when you play."

"I wasn't even trying to cross or communicate with her. I just played."

I nodded. "That's what Martin says. He says the edge responds best when it isn't being forced. He allows it to flow around him, and then he grabs whatever comes through the thin spots. Your music, it's more dirt-side than here. It's not dead like us so why wouldn't it drift through?"

"She looked up. She..." he choked.

"She heard it," I finished for him.

He nodded. "Have you experienced that sort of magic, too?" He waved at the lifeless figure in the hospital bed that was me.

I snorted. "My body is oblivious, trust me. There are those who are more sensitive to ghosts. Maybe your wife is one. Maybe she'll become more sensitive with you watching."

He frowned. "You said a link is stronger if there's something that exists on both sides. If she has my guitar, that will be one thing. But I also wanted to give you this." He handed me a ghostly guitar pick.

"I don't know if I can take it across."

He shrugged. "But if you can, then a piece of here is there. I have more picks anyway. I must have had five in my jeans when I died."

I accepted the disc. It possessed an odd energy, a kind of vibration as if it stored pieces of music inside. I wrapped a length of hair around it and stowed it behind my ear. It might not stay there, but most ghostly essences seemed to stay put until situations blew up in our face, literally floating bits all over In Between. "I'll do my best."

"I should just move on, shouldn't I? And let her move on?"

"Nobody knows the answer to that sort of question," I replied. "Let's go check on Martin. Maybe he's having better luck. You can ask him your questions. He'll chant earth magic stuff and pretend he knows the answer, but it might be total nonsense."

"Heh. I'll keep that in mind."

It was easier traveling the edge with someone to watch my back. Sticking to one area was more dangerous anyway. Anytime energy gathered in a particular spot, it attracted feeders.

I heard the snort through the fog before either of us saw anything. The thing must have been facing away from us because we didn't see the eyes until it heard us and turned our way. The orbs lit the gray with the same dangerous red glow as hellhound eyes, a warning to anyone with sense enough to run. The creature was huge; a dirty gray with a snout and tusks that belonged on a mammoth or a giant boar.

"Holy..."

I pushed Kyle closer to the weave before he could finish his sentence. "Shhh. Push the weave between us and tamp down!" The tusks on this pig were far enough apart that even if we split up, it might be able to spear both of us with a single charge. I edged close to the weave, herding a chunk to undulate between myself and Kyle.

Kyle caught on quickly, but he was newer at manipulating the edges. I smelled ghost burn when he brushed too close, but he never uttered a sound. I'd have screamed bloody murder.

The glowing dots of red left laser trails as the boar shifted its head, sniffing.

Were pigs nearsighted? We'd best hope so.

The edge wasn't particularly quick about accommodating us, but we pushed a fat lip between us. It was almost enough for me to tuck behind, but that left me boxed in. There weren't many alternatives. I'd been carefully noting any good hiding places as we drifted, and we were in no man's land at the moment.

The pig snorted and stepped one cloven hoof closer.

The strains of a broken violin shattered the misty shuttered silence that was In Between.

The giant boar's snout lifted and spun as though tugged by a rope. Its feet beat an odd, grating rhythm as it rumbled away.

Pressure from the weave behind me had me scooting out into the open as soon as the pig disappeared.

Kyle joined me.

"Is it headed the same direction as us?"

I shook my head. "It isn't following the weave edge. It went towards the violin, I think."

"To the lake, then?"

"Things In Between aren't all that stationary. We'd better find Martin. If he's collecting energy while he waits, he could attract that pig or whatever summoned it."

"That noise from the violin is like dying all over again."

"Yeah."

We hurried, but it was for naught. By the time we reached Martin, there was no point in warning him away from the edge. He was deep in conversation with his friends, and we desperately needed the exchange of information.

The best Kyle and I could do was play lookout and hope that if anything showed, it would follow us if we ran, leaving Martin time to save himself.

Martin formed ghost words and puffed them across at Roberto like smoke signals. I'd never collected my words that way. I just shouted them and hoped. Martin was smarter. He literally formed them as bursts of air and energy and blew them to the other side.

Adriel, the witch, squeezed in a word between puffs. "You don't ask for much, do you?"

Martin ignored her and kept talking. "This portal is likely linked to a demon or its power. Something is stuck here upsetting the balance. Whatever it is, it's not nearly as powerful as the thing that came through when I closed the gap and ended up here, but it is an evil entity, not interested in the greater balance."

Adriel's eyes widened.

He nodded. "Whatever is powering that portal has a stake in making it through itself. You better have your vamp friend sit in with you at the hospital when we make our move."

"Patrick knows how to stop demons?"

Martin snorted. "Nothing stops demons. But the vamp is already dead. The demon will be less interested in him and more interested in living souls. Might provide the vamp a fighting chance to do something to destroy the demon."

White Feather broke in. "You don't have any idea how to stop this thing?"

Martin had to step back from the weave as it whipsawed for no reason at all. I scanned the fog around us, but saw nothing especially threatening.

Martin resumed speaking in his disembodied voice. "If I knew how to stop a demon, it would already be stopped."

Roberto fell forward just then. The cat grabbed his collar and yanked him back. The weave snapped shut, just missing Martin.

The faint discordant notes we had heard earlier snaked through the fog.

I stepped up. "Time to roll, Martin."

He was tired, but never stupid. The three of us scattered.

Chapter 21

Waiting for the cast to assemble in my hospital room involved a lot of pacing, worrying and wasting time. An anxious ghost is not a pretty sight, and yoga exercises don't do a damn thing to calm a frantic ghost who might have the opportunity to live again.

In desperation, I practiced jumping over hellhounds that didn't exist. I even considered singing to the weave, but discarded the notion as one that would scare off Lynx and his friends.

Once Lynx and his friends showed, I was to gather Kyle and Martin to try the portal. Finding Kyle was easy. He had made the cairn near the lake his shelter. I'd not have chosen that spot if you paid me, but if he found comfort there, well, you embrace any kind of peace wherever you can find it.

Martin was another story. Nothing on earth or In Between could stop his wandering nature. Every day I'd check the hospital room and then flit to the canyon or the lake or even Troy's tree searching for him.

He wasn't spending much time at his canyon. When I asked about it, he said, "Too dangerous. I sip the energy quickly and leave. There's a demon on the hunt."

After that, I completed my rounds in fear, harvesting from the edge as far from the hospital room as possible. I caught a glimpse of the girl, Espy, and her Aunt Brenda once. One or the other was doing the medium trick again, but they were no longer at the hospital. By the time I was able to hop closer, the weave was thickening, and there was no time to ask if Espy was better.

I saw the nurse Sonya frequently, sometimes working with Paul, the technician, or one of the vampires. The female vampire wore a tag identifying her as Tina. There were two male doctors, one of whom was an impossibly older guy who included me on his rounds. He wasn't as decrepit as the near-corpse on the bed, but it was a close second. He must love his job to still be working at his age. His badge was so old, the letters were faded beyond recognition, except for a "C."

There were other patients and technicians, but none ever glanced my way. I grabbed bits of energy and stayed on the move.

It must have been the third or fourth day after Martin had talked to his friends when he found me on the way to my hospital room.

"Now. Hurry." Rather than waiting for me to follow, he just spurted ahead. For an old guy, he was fast.

I kept up, but barely. "How do you know it's time?" I demanded.

"I stopped by your hospital room this morning."

"You can thin the weave there?"

"It was easier once Lynx showed up there with bloodstone. Been monitoring the room a bit, and since he had the bloodstone, as soon as he showed, I knew they were ready."

By the time we reached the lake, the broken violin was an ugly foghorn, echoing intermittently.

Martin bobbed up and down anxiously. "That demon is on his way. He's been popping in here like a man addicted to a whorehouse. With Amy no longer hiding the portal and herself behind Troy's essence, he knows right where the window is located. He must not be able to open the portal himself, and unless he has a body waiting, it wouldn't do him any good. Success depends on whether we can push you through fast enough."

Kyle perched on top of the cairn. He had his guitar out, but wasn't playing. "Now?"

Martin knelt at the water, muttering incoherently, the bloodstone out. "This will work. You ready?"

Was I ready? No. How did one get ready? I wasn't sure I wanted to accept that nearly dead body in the hospital room, but the key point was that it was nearly dead. I was currently dead-dead. "Yeah." I glanced at Kyle. He watched the water hungrily. "I'll tell your wife. I have the address. Given the condition of my body, it might take me a while, but I'll do my best."

His eyes flicked to me, and he ran a shaking ghost hand through his dark hair before he remembered there were no longer any individual strands to soothe him. "Will you remember? Or will everything suddenly be forgotten when you pop through?"

He knew that I retained little of who I'd been while alive. He answered with me. "I don't know."

"Right. Got it," he said then, resigned.

Because I was facing away from the water, I saw the enemy first. It was the red-eyed boar, waiting in the fog. This time, it was not alone. Its rider nodded at me with a smile that should have frozen the water behind me —or burned it up, given the flames that licked along his dark body.

"Uh, Martin," I squeaked.

Martin's hands formed a circle. He dropped the bloodstone into the center.

"Martin!"

The demon cackled. In Between rattled from one end to the other. "Go ahead." He slashed his violin with a flame instead of a bow. "When you go, I go. Or you can stay here. Either way you are my new host, and those on the other side will be totally unaware. They'll call you, and one way or another I will own your body." He laughed, spitting fire. "There will be room for both of us," he crooned. "You'll learn to love me. I've been waiting for a host ever since I was freed."

His evil chuckle was in perfect discord with the chords he ruined on the violin.

My ghost form shook with fear, but I was riveted in place, held by his promise.

I would not play host to a demon. I'd rather be dead. My eyes flicked to the circle.

When my eyes shifted back again, the demon was next to me. His glowing eyes haunted me, but they were beautiful in their own way. Red orbs, full of promises. I shrank inside myself, but could not break free.

If I took a single breath, I would live. The demon would flow through me, repairing all that was ruined. Wait. That didn't make sense.

The demon soothed my worries, explaining it all. "I was so lonely until I gained enough power to let my friends through. Once you are with me, they are yours to command. You'll never be lonely again. You will wield power you never dreamed of."

I realized now that he was the first demon I had seen. There had been no boar, no violin. He hadn't played music; he was simply a lost demon trying to survive, just like me. If I hadn't run then, we could have been friends so much earlier.

Barking and an intense cold made me shiver. Wait a minute. The demon hadn't been friends with Spook. Spook had lost a leg to the demon we fought. I frowned. Something wasn't right. Where was Spook? I could hear him. Why couldn't I turn my head or move my eyes to find him? It had been this way right before I died. I had been trapped then and now.

I fought, screaming at the voice inside my head, shrinking inside myself like I had done the last time something had come after me, but this time, there was nowhere to run. There was nothing but brilliant eyes, shining, promising, enveloping me.

Music with an actual melody slammed into me like a physical blow, rocking me with vibrations. I blinked, shutting out the red demon eyes for a millisecond. The notes continued, breaking the shrill chords of chaos that the demon was using to hold and choke me. The song started as a strumming, a note that floated and held, sneaking between the crying violin strings.

"Kyle!" I choked out his name. One eye floated free, finding him.

He was back on the rocks. He might not be safe there, but it was better than standing by an open portal waiting to be eaten by a demon.

Kyle played. The notes of *Bad Moon Rising* faded in and out.

The demon guffawed and cut the song into bits with flames streaming across his burning instrument. But Kyle's music had broken the demon's thrall, one that had gripped me before I had time to realize it. Troy had been like that, helpless against Amy. The only difference was that the demon didn't want to destroy me. He wanted to possess me. He needed me alive as much as I wanted to live.

When Kyle changed the song to *Help Is On Its Way,* I sucked in air that I didn't yet need to live, and puffed myself closer to Martin and the portal.

Kyle's music was stronger now, without the hesitation. His notes didn't drown out those of the demon, but just as the demon violin tried to cut Kyle's notes to shreds, Kyle's song suffocated the noise from the demon.

Despite the screaming in my head from the raw blistering notes, I hummed along with Kyle's melody. I wasn't completely in tune, but then, it was hard to hold the line when flames licked at your eyeballs and a demon pushed at your sanity with broken despair.

I refused to meet the demon's mesmerizing gaze again. I focused on the song, holding it to me like a physical presence. It was not fog, it was not In Between.

I pushed a ghostly foot forward.

From the other side, the side I longed for, a wind began to moan, echoing Kyle's music. There was no instrument, but the wind played nonetheless. I focused on the portal. Martin spread his hands, and as I watched, he slid one of the rocks further out.

I took another step and hit water. I couldn't afford to stop, not even if a mermaid started chewing on my feet.

The warlock, White Feather, stood inside the hospital room. His magic drifted on the breeze, squeezing out a flow of music, the sound of wind whistling through a canyon. His life force danced through the air, a beautiful blue flame that had no trouble outshining the burning flames from the demon.

I grabbed that life force and held it between me and the demon. When Kyle played the first bars of *The Devil Went Down to Georgia,* I knew it was now or never.

The demon shrieked with glee. "That song is a stupid myth!! You can't beat me by outplaying me!" His rumble of rage bounced against the portal, causing it to vibrate under the strain. Martin grunted, and his ghostly hands shook with the effort to hold the opening.

Kyle missed a note. The music around me shuddered, threatening to fall apart. My own singing wasn't enough to keep the thread of song together. The demon flamed closer, muscling me aside to fill the tunnel that led to the other side.

White Feather's whistling wind encompassed the gap in the nick of time.

Kyle picked up the tune again, not caring if the story in the song was true. He played with conviction and *life* even if he was already dead. Music was a living thing, and he was holding onto it and playing for all he was worth. The demon might covet life, but he didn't have it, nor could he create it with his empty and broken screeching.

I swam within the odd current of music, one hand clutching the braid.

Time to return it to its owner. Ghosts couldn't cry without leaking, but a part of me was in tears because it wasn't fair that I had a body to return to and these guys didn't.

Kyle kept plucking and strumming notes.

Roberto yelled, "Okay, I've got this end. Now! Hurry!"

Lynx said nothing, but his hand held mine, and I could feel the sister to the braid in my ghost hand. For the death of me, I could not figure out why Lynx was helping me, but his fingers wrapped around mine was enough.

I dove across the water, careful to keep singing, careful to keep drawing music between me and everything else. The jump was similar to gathering pieces of myself to me when I leaked. Jump, but contain.

The flame from the demon seared one side of the music, tearing at me. I screamed. Martin shoved a piece of his collection at the demon, severing his hold on me.

The surface beneath me was crystal clear. I fell, swimming frantically.

Lynx had his hand out, reaching for me as though I had fallen in the water, as though he would pull me out. He said my name, only he called me Shadow because it was the only name he knew.

A doctor or a maybe a nurse with long black hair held a hand to my forehead. She wasn't wearing a smock, but I could feel the warmth of her life force. Unlike the command that had tried to own my soul, her presence was only a welcoming warmth.

The devil clawed in a panic at the music. The second he neglected to play, I felt the last of the licking flames drop.

I puffed out the last of my air, aiming for the braid in Lynx's hand, wondering if I'd make a splash.

The last thing I heard was Martin, humming the song. For once, he was in tune.

Chapter 22

Kyle's melody was a steady stream across the open portal as I slipped through. His song wrapped around me, a protective life magic. The demon beat against it and me, causing the portal to shudder. Roberto's magic resembled a fog with an opening. The smoke of his magic cracked from the strain, fine lines splintering the surface.

The portal bent, but the demon bounced against Kyle's music. He raised his violin then, his attack paused for less than a second. Perhaps he intended to kill the music with his own evil cacophony.

In the space of that tiny pause, Troy's dog slipped in beside me as I tumbled towards the body on the bed. Even without my physical eyes open, I sensed the three-legged ghost come through. He passed right through Lynx.

The cat's hand jerked on mine, but he held fast.

Roberto's fingers, already held high, darted forward and nabbed the bloodstone from Martin, yanking it free.

The portal snapped shut, silencing the shrieking ugliness that was the demon version of music without a soul.

"Got it," Roberto shouted.

"I can't believe you agreed to try that after what happened last time," Adriel grumbled. She stepped away from him, her arms relaxing at her sides. Her magic, a pretty silver, slid away from Roberto and back into her bracelets. Her magic was full of life, protecting Roberto from sliding across the portal.

"Tara, how is she?" White Feather asked.

The girl with the long hair stepped away from my body, but she didn't answer White Feather. She watched Lynx watch me. The only time he looked away from me was when his slitted eyes followed Spook's progress.

Roberto asked, "Is that dog safe?"

I wanted to speak, but my body was too weak, even though my spirit was now safely in the same room.

Spook sat his haunches down near my feet and put his ghostly head across my knees.

"The dog doesn't look like he's planning on hurting her," Roberto observed, answering his own question.

"She has a *dog*?" The girl White Feather called Tara peered anxiously around the room, but she was unable to see Spook.

"Lynx, how is it that you are able to see ghosts so clearly even though the curtain is closed?" Adriel was now tucked protectively under the warlock's arm.

The cat shrugged. "Roberto taught me."

The witch swiveled to face Roberto. "You can teach that sort of thing?"

Roberto grinned. His words were less clear to me now, but still understandable. His fingers flew through sign language as he talked. Lynx translated. "All he had to do was point out that cats have the ability to see spirits."

Adriel tilted her head for a second or two. "So you call your ca—" She broke off and shrugged. "Call enough of your magic without changing." She nodded. "Excellent. Is the dog likely to attack?"

Lynx shrugged. "He ain't attacking right now."

Tara said, "My work is done." Her eyes were downcast as she brushed by White Feather and Adriel.

Adriel stopped her with a touch to her shoulder. "Tara. Thank you."

Tara lifted her eyes to Adriel before glancing at White Feather. He nodded his head in agreement.

"It's who I am, but in this case, I didn't do much. She wasn't sick." She frowned. "She was just missing. It was weird. Like it would be if you were without your magic. Then she reappeared in a surge. All I did was make sure she connected." She spun on her heel and walked out.

Lynx did not watch her go. He was watching me again.

I forced my eyes open, but that was a mistake. Blinding light cut through my eyeballs straight into my brain. The second I commanded my body, my spirit returned fully to it. The pain felt much like the weave slicing me to pieces. I hoped that hell wasn't waiting at the other end of the dark tunnel that engulfed me.

Chapter 23

Bits and pieces of arguing drifted through now and then. The gist of it was that Lynx knew the hospital wasn't safe. There were others who disturbed my darkness, working on my battered body. A stomach plug for food was removed. Some cruel idiot tested my reflexes, including exposing my eyeballs to more light.

I struggled against the invasions until someone offered me food through a straw. Once I discovered it was a chocolate milkshake, I was just plain greedy.

Twice I pushed away from the pain in my body and floated. The first time I watched from within the room, I witnessed the elderly doctor refusing to grant permission to have me moved.

The second time, Lynx was there with Patrick, the male vampire. The vampire encased my feet in fluffy socks and draped the sheet up over my head.

As I watched, Lynx went still, but he stared down at me. "We're breakin' you out."

"Where's Spook?" I whispered, but my spirit voice was too weak to be heard.

When they started rolling the bed with my body, I grabbed hold of myself and lost my senses again.

In the new location, there were more chocolate milkshakes and way too much vampire. The place was dark, and for hours or days, Patrick or the female vampire, the one I had seen at the blood bank, exercised the body that was me. The female vampire told me her name was Tina, but I had already seen her badge. She told me the day and time and asked me questions that I did not answer.

In the dim room, I could open my eyes. The bed had buttons to adjust it up and down. I began to test my fingers and arms and adjust the bed myself.

Once, when the vampires weren't around, I sat up, but promptly fell back over. The weakness didn't stop me, however. Crackers and protein drinks waited on a bedside table. I ate every time I was awake. The crackers hurt my throat, but nothing slowed down my appetite. I began to take tentative steps around the room, most of the time without falling.

The witch showed up with more clothes. I had been watching things from above, roaming the room and flitting just outside of it into a corridor. Spook hadn't been around since the move. Maybe he went back over, but that didn't stop the gnawing worry that raged in my guts. What had happened to him? I was on my own here. No money, no friends, no job and no memory of any of those things either.

I followed the witch back into the room. There was no reason to avoid her.

"Time to depart," she told my listless form softly. "If you're hunted, this is too close to where you were before. It would be too easy to track you."

They smuggled me out under cover of darkness. I stayed barely sideways from my body, listening to Adriel rant that I'd be better off with her and White Feather. Lynx didn't say anything; he just drove the four-door Prius. Spook showed up in the backseat rather suddenly. He pushed his ghost head into the front of the car between Lynx and Adriel.

The cat flinched. The car swerved into the wrong lane, but only briefly.

Adriel paused in her lecturing. She might not see Spook, but from her sudden silence, she sensed him.

"It's just the dog that came through with her," Lynx reassured her. He pulled into a drive-through burrito place. After he ordered, he handed Adriel a burrito, and by my count, kept four in the bag.

"What about the dog?" Adriel asked. "Does he need to be fed?"

"He's a ghost. He never complains." Lynx pulled back onto the road. "I've seen him a couple of times, checking things out."

"Yeah, there's an odd flicker there. Not as formed as when he came through with Shadow, but I can see him."

We finally turned off onto a short dirt road that led to a dark, isolated stucco house.

"You can call me any time," Adriel said. "Our place is as protected as yours. She'd be safer with us. I can call Mom or Tara to check her out if needed."

Fear radiated through me. I was at the mercy of these people. I still had no idea who I was, how I got here or where to go next. My memories were flitting pieces at best, the most vivid that of the guy who killed me. But now I wasn't dead. I still forgot that, especially when I was floating near my body and not in it.

White Feather was there waiting. He did some weird thing with the wind, floating me into the house, down a hall and into a bed. Halfway there I dove into my body, wanting to know what it felt like to fly. It wasn't much different than drifting around as a spirit, only heavier.

Lynx left a burrito and a milkshake on a table that contained a lamp, a dream catcher and a pouch. The room smelled faintly of herbs.

"You need anything, you call," Adriel instructed him.

"Yeah, yeah, got it. I have your mom's number too."

"Tara will help," White Feather said.

"He won't call her, and you know it," Adriel muttered.

Their voices faded as they left the room for the living room or kitchen.

My eyes popped open, and I reached for the milkshake. Chocolate. My favorite, and a thousand times better than the protein drinks. I nibbled on the burrito, but my stomach threatened to rebel. Too much too fast, and it would be more trouble than it was worth.

Still, I finished half of it. I longed for a hot shower and more food. *Escape.* Only I had nowhere to run. I still didn't even know my own name.

***

I slept better than the dead. If anyone spied on me, it was a waste of time.

Spook was at the foot of the bed, wagging his tail when I next woke. I slid partway away from my body and let him feel the warmth of my hand. "Spook. How are you?" My voice rasped so badly, he probably only understood his name.

Spook enjoyed the petting, wagging his tail and rolling over for a belly rub. I chatted with him a while before exploring the house in spirit form. No one was about, but I saw a water and food bowl just off the porch outside.

I hurried back to my body, barely remembering anything other than the location of the bathroom and shower. There was a pile of clothes, probably from Adriel, on top of a table near the window.

My first surprise was the mirror. The gaunt face was expected, but my hair was the color of ashes, ranging from almost white to a dark gray. When I had stared down at my own body from In Between, my hair had been blonde with darker streaks. Somehow, the gray had managed to leave its mark on me.

"Too bad." There were more important things to focus on, like hot water and food. The shower was almost more of a relief than coming back from In Between. I hadn't needed them there.

After standing under the hot water until it ran cold, I dressed and explored in person. The kitchen was sunny and bright, but the cupboards were nearly bare other than a bag of cat food for the bowl outside, animal crackers, chips and a jar of unopened salsa. The fridge yielded two dozen eggs, some tortillas, an entire shelf of sodas and a single bottle of milk that had soured.

I felt guilty eating without permission, but they had brought me here, and probably not to die since they'd gone to a lot of trouble to keep me alive. I scrambled two eggs, polished them off and then cooked two more. Doing the dishes exhausted the last of my resources.

The next couple of days and nights were no different. Lynx left another burrito and milkshake. The milkshake was half melted by the time I woke up, and the burrito was cold, but I devoured them without hesitation.

The next time he showed up in the doorway with a burrito, I was awake. He stood in the doorway with the bag, barefoot. "Hungry?"

"Most of the time." My voice was better than my first attempt, but Spook wasn't much of a conversationalist, so practicing had been limited to a few whispered greetings.

Lynx brought the burrito and milkshake in and set them down. His eyes never left mine. He acted as though he expected me to sprint away.

My own reaction was worried wariness, although I tried harder to hide my discomfort than he did.

"You keep making yourself at home," he ordered. "Adriel's been by. You were sleeping. She brought her mom."

I didn't remember the visit. I slurped the milkshake. He backed out, leaving the door open.

The next morning, when I floated sideways out of my body to check things out, Lynx was in the kitchen. He must have a job to go to every day because he hadn't been home before.

He was flipping bacon in a pan. The enticing smell of it was probably what had woken me. My body was little more than bones. I was constantly hungry.

He turned fast, cat eyes flashing. The fork was up and ready to serve as a weapon when he spotted me. "Shit! You died? Crap!"

He sprinted so fast, he actually beat me back to the room where I'd left myself. It didn't take me long to flash back there and open my eyes.

"I'm fine."

He was halfway to the bed before I blinked. Without a sound, he stilled, staring at me. "You're alive?"

Puzzled, I nodded. "Well, sure."

"But I just saw your ghost."

Understanding dawned. "Oh, no. That's not...well, I guess it is, kind of. I can still slide sideways out of my body, pretty much like when I was In Between, only now I'm here, not there."

His eyes widened. "Wait. You can ghost whenever you want? And you ain't dead?"

The feat hadn't impressed me at all, not until that moment. I had existed so long outside my body that when I decided to move around, it had come naturally. "I guess so. And no, I'm not dead." I flicked my arm with the opposite hand. "No more so than I was before." I sniffed. "I think the bacon is burning."

His head started to tilt, and then he was gone that fast, gliding on feet so silent there was no sound when he left, just a swirl of air and absence.

Since I slept in sweatpants and a t-shirt, changing clothes wasn't necessary. I followed him to the kitchen.

He had saved the bacon by dumping it on a plate. Eggs replaced the bacon in the pan, sizzling fast. "Still hungry?"

"Yeah." The t-shirt hung on me like a sack. "I think maybe going ghost takes energy too."

"You just leave your body like that? Empty?"

"I didn't really think about it. It was a way to get around. Check things out."

He dumped the eggs on a plate. Then he slid half onto the other plate with the bacon. Finally he put some of the bacon on the first egg plate and handed it to me. "I bought more milk. Chocolate."

"Thanks. It seems to be my favorite." I helped myself. The only table was across a small bar off to the side of the kitchen. It was homey, but not fancy.

"You like coffee? Or tea? Adriel makes tea. I don't have any, but I can get some."

"This works. I can heat the chocolate milk. I can't remember what I used to like. The eggs are great. Everything you've brought has been great. I'd eat a whole cow if it showed up, I think."

He nodded as though he understood my hunger. Or maybe he thought I could eat a whole cow based on the way I'd been pigging out.

We dug in, eating hard.

"Can you still feel your body when you're away from it?" he asked abruptly.

I thought about it. "No, not really."

"Sounds dangerous."

"Being a ghost was dangerous when I was In Between. I couldn't affect anything happening to my body or my ghost. I don't think I can here either when I'm ghost. Sometimes Spook stays with my body, but usually he follows me around."

"Spook is your ghost dog?"

He was really Troy's dog, but Troy was gone. "I guess he's mine now."

Lynx chewed some more. "Ghosting could be a useful talent. But leaving your body unprotected isn't wise." He gulped some chocolate milk. "This stuff is good, isn't it? I usually drink soda."

"I suppose I shouldn't roam very far from myself."

"You think you could get lost?"

"I never have unless you count losing my body while I was In Between. I didn't know where my body was for the longest time after arriving there. Martin helped me figure it out." Shy, I dropped my eyes. "And you. You kept calling me back to it until eventually I found it."

Lynx stopped chewing. He stared without blinking for a few seconds. "I never knew if what I did was helping. I threw you the packet that was linked to mine. Talked to you. But you just laid there. Not dead. But not alive."

He grabbed his plate and rinsed it at the sink. "If you're gonna be traveling around like that all the time, you're gonna need some protection."

"I could stop doing it, I suppose, but it's easier to talk to Spook there. Plus things look different when I'm ghost so I learn things."

"Different? How?"

"The vampires. They aren't the same creatures when I'm ghost. Patrick is more like a giant beast with wings."

Lynx nodded. "He's part bat or something. I know he can fly. Sometimes he's not there and then he is. Adriel thinks he might be part gargoyle, but one time..." He hesitated.

"One time what?"

"I smelled him when he was in his other form. Reminded me of a bat."

"Oh. What does a gargoyle smell like?"

He blinked, a slow cat blink that managed to convey amusement. "Probably not like a bat."

I smiled and slid sideways, but only a little, like when petting Spook. "You always have the ghost of your other self, the cat, around your head."

He froze. His ears went back, and his eyes shifted. "You sound different."

I nodded and let go. "I can slide partway."

"So that's how you knew...what I am?"

It took a minute to remember seeing him the first time. "Well, that and Martin told me. You have a gold energy line. It's the same whether you're cat or not. When you fought that zombie, the energy was the same even after you went cat. After you guys took me out of the hospital, I noticed that when you walked across the ground, there is a white color near your feet. You soak up life or energy and convert it to gold because you're always that color."

"You see everyone like that?"

I shrugged. "If I'm sideways. Adriel has a lot of silver energy. White Feather, now that was weird. His energy is a blue fire with icy white bands."

Lynx nodded. "He's one cool dude."

"I don't think I knew any of this stuff before I died. I certainly never saw it."

"Probably because dying halfway changed some things. It changed 'Trick, that's for sure."

"Patrick, the vampire?"

He nodded.

"He's not dead. He's like one of the creatures In Between. Maybe."

I expected Lynx to ask me more about In Between, but he didn't. He exhausted all the energy I had left asking about what I could and couldn't do while sideways. We tried a few things, but I was too tired, too fast.

He went for burritos for lunch, and I went back to bed.

Chapter 24

The next morning, I accompanied Lynx on a breakfast burrito run. Stepping out into the sunlight was like being born again. It was bright. Alive. Full of noise and smells. Full of life force. Energy was *everywhere.*

He filled the empty bowl with cat food and added water to the other one.

"You have a cat?"

"Nah. One adopted me a while back. She helped us out of a tight spot. I just feed her."

Most people would consider that having a cat, but apparently Lynx didn't apply those rules to his situation.

I walked over to the first line of juniper trees and breathed in the medicinal pine scent. Crouching, I grabbed up fistfuls of juniper berries. There were hundreds just lying all over the ground where any ghost could come along and eat for weeks.

I slid sideways and absorbed the sparks of energy until the berries in my hand shriveled. Guilt assailed me. I offered some to Spook. He didn't seem to mind that I had pigged out first. He probably didn't need my help harvesting energy either. He wagged his tail, conveying his happiness.

I gave him a pat on the head and asked if he planned to join us today. He looked at the car and then barked an enthusiastic yes.

"Okay." I rejoined my body.

Lynx could easily discern my sideways maneuver if he watched, but if he wondered what I was doing, he didn't ask. He just waited patiently as if everyone he knew collected juniper berries and talked to their ghost dog.

I brushed the shriveled berries off my hand, but was unable to resist harvesting a few more for my pocket. Just in case. Because they were still a little bit alive, and I couldn't quite forget being more than a little bit dead.

As we climbed into his white Mustang, he asked, "You know how to drive stick?"

I glanced at the gears. "Yeah. Blue car." I thought hard, but couldn't remember when or where or if it was my last car or my first. "I wonder what happened to everything that was me."

Lynx shrugged. "Doesn't matter."

He seemed more concerned about my future than my past.

I stared out the window. If I had seen much of Santa Fe before I died, there were no recent memories in my head. The desert had a familiar feel, but I had changed so much from seeing the world through the eyes of the dead, it was hard to be certain what was new and what wasn't.

We stopped at Walmart, and Lynx shuffled me inside before

demanding that I purchase better fitting sneakers, food and "whatever else you want."

"I don't need anything. Adriel's clothes are fine, and there was a fresh toothbrush in the bathroom."

He lifted my hand and dropped a credit card onto it. "I hate shopping. I ain't gonna do it, and Adriel's shoes are too small for you. You walk funny in them. When you need to run, you need the right shoes."

I couldn't argue with that. Maybe if I'd been able to run...I frowned.

"Will you just buy shoes already?" he hissed.

Absently, I grabbed a pair of white and gray size nines. "I couldn't run."

"That's what I just said. You gotta be able to run."

"During the attack. I was trying to break away, but I couldn't run. I can't remember why."

"Maybe you had bad shoes."

I snickered. "Fine, fine. I'm letting you buy me shoes. But now I owe you." I sighed. "More than I already do."

"Get other stuff. As long as you're running a tab, make it worthwhile."

During checkout, I asked the lady if they were hiring.

"It's easiest if you fill out an application online," she replied, bagging the purchases. "Takes almost an hour to answer all the questions."

Lynx didn't say anything, but his ears went flat against his head and stayed that way even after we were back in the car.

"'Trick has been tracking every nurse and doctor who helped treat you or Espy. But you were there long enough that just about everyone had access."

"What about Sonya? She was the nurse who brought in the IV for Espy that might have been tainted."

"So far, everyone is coming up clean. And almost anyone who works at the hospital has access to the blood bank—either legitimately or not. The place isn't that well guarded. The bags can also be tampered with before or after they were picked up."

"What happened to Espy?"

"Tara and Adriel's mom helped her. She's doing a lot better."

That was good news. And maybe her condition was just a coincidence. Maybe nothing had been after her. "Are you sure the vampires are on the up and up? I mean, anything like that on the other side viewed us as dinner."

"He's cool. He and his girlfriend, Tina, work at the hospital. They siphon off their meals from the blood bank."

"How'd he lose his arm?"

"Fighting a ghoul."

"Here or In Between?"

"He said he's never been to In Between. That's why he went vamp.

He didn't want to cross over."

"Ghouls are worse than hellhounds. They're mindless. They do nothing but eat souls, entire body and all. Bad news."

"Damn straight."

We didn't say anything more until we pulled up at the hospital. Instead of parking in the front, he backed the car behind a dumpster in the rear of the building.

I was tiring fast, but didn't admit it out loud.

Spook followed us out of the car this time and bound ahead as soon as Lynx opened a large metal door leading into the back of the hospital. Both Lynx and Spook paused and sniffed.

Lynx had let me enter first at Walmart, but here, he led the way. He glided along the wall, moving fast. "Door isn't open. I told 'Trick we were coming."

I didn't spot any doors, but Spook prowled ahead down the hallway and then stopped suddenly.

My new shoes made it easier for me to shadow Lynx silently down the concrete steps. I kept far enough behind him that we wouldn't interfere with one another, but his eyes had me beat in the dark until I slid sideways. "Nothing in the hallway," I whispered.

He eased forward, his feet soundless. "Can't get in if the door isn't open. This doesn't look good." He stood back from the wall, staring at the same section of painted cinder blocks that Spook watched.

"Maybe if we knock?"

"He always knows when we come here. You better wait in the car."

"I can check behind that wall. Watch my...me."

Before he could argue, I went fully sideways and hunted for the cracks that had to be there. There wasn't even enough of a gap for air, but then, vampires didn't need to breathe. Neither did my floating form.

I slithered through and got more than my money's worth.

Tina was surrounded by dots of blood that formed a strange pattern. Instead of a regular pentagram, the blood was a trail map of arrows forming a general circle shape. The lines wound in and around and were connected by black flames.

Patrick was balanced on his toes, just outside the line of blood surrounding Tina. A snarl peeled his face back, revealing fangs. There was barely room for him between the circle of blood droplets and a half full bag of blood that had been dropped nearby. A ghostly face hovered over the bag.

I gasped. "Amy!"

She would have noticed me if she hadn't been busy talking. "Either you welcome me, or I take your girlfriend. I assure you, it will be temporary until I find the host we prepared."

I hightailed it back through the door, hitting Spook in my haste. He was crouched low, waiting for a signal from me.

I slid back into my body so fast, I nearly knocked myself over. "Tina." I stopped to heave in air. "She's trapped in a blood circle. Amy is there!"

"Amy? Who is Amy?"

"Amy was In Between causing all kinds of havoc. But she's in there trying to convince one of the vampires to take her in!"

Lynx shook my arm. "Can you open the door? Getting the key will take forever and picking a vampire lock is worse than stupid!"

"It's tight in there." I didn't tell him just how tight or what the squeeze meant. It had been possible to knock things over when I was ghosted, but it required an enormous effort. Maybe I could still do something similar now, but it had hurt then, and in a tight spot like a lock, any energy was sure to ricochet.

I reached in my pocket and clutched the juniper berries. If nothing else, maybe I could hit Amy with them.

"Is there a turn lock on the inside?"

Lynx shook his head. "It's keys only. That's how I ended up stuck in that room with the zombie. I was checking rooms, helping Patrick investigate. That one room was locked, marked as a lab, so I knew something was up. I picked the lock, ducked in and closed the door to have privacy. A few seconds later, the lock clicked, and I was stuck in there with Beef for Brains."

There wasn't time for further explanation. "Be ready to push on the door if I succeed."

The berry was nothing more in my hand than a smear of ghost energy. There was no such thing as fingers with my essence squeezed to fit into the space. What I really required was a bomb of some sort. I couldn't snap the berry like a towel.

I shoved the berry essence into the lock mechanism, but there wasn't enough room to leverage it. I tried pushing my own essence at it, but there simply wasn't any momentum. Popping the berry might help. I could absorb its energy and possibly donate energy, but how much energy would be required before it would affect the physical lock?

Frustrated, I flitted inside the room. Patrick needed to open the door for Lynx.

I spun a berry hard at the female vampire, hoping to break her free. The gray energy hit an invisible wall and exploded back. That was more like it!

Spook took my action as a signal to attack. Without so much as a warning growl, he sprang at the enemy.

Amy screamed and dove for the female vampire, but Spook knocked her sideways.

"Open the door," I yelled at Patrick. He was dead; he should be able to hear me. From the way his cold stare flicked to me and then avoided me, I knew he could see me.

His nearly liquid motion was even faster than Lynx, but he wasn't interested in running for freedom.

His foot kicked the bag of blood with a vengeance, almost separating Amy from it.

The bloody container slid a good three feet from Tina. The weave sliced deep, and Amy's face wavered, half melting into shreds.

Patrick was suddenly at the door, slamming the key home before my eyes could track him.

Instead of the click of a lock turning, the door gave a muffled boom.

The noise didn't deter Lynx. He slammed into the room, claws out and ready to pounce.

I returned to my body and staggered after him.

Patrick went for the bag of blood again, but the weave stopped him dead in his tracks. With Amy focused on him, he couldn't close in. If she didn't claim him, the weave would.

He growled, fangs out, but was forced to step back before In Between could bid him welcome.

Amy still hovered over the bloody plastic, her face a nasty contortion of frayed bits. She pleaded with him. "I'm no different than you. I just want to live!"

Patrick kicked the door closed. I glanced at Lynx for reassurance, not liking being shut in here.

The vampire cursed. "The lock is blown." His dark eyes focused on Lynx. "Did you cram explosives in there?"

Lynx raised empty palms, never batting an eye my way. "Didn't bring any."

That cat knew how to keep secrets, although not even I understood exactly what had happened. When Patrick stuck the key in, it must have pushed against the juniper essence enough to explode it. Ghosted energy was unpredictable. It took enormous amounts to create a breeze, but a sensitive person—or cat—could feel the presence of it without any expenditure whatsoever.

"It might be a good idea if a few more people had a key," Lynx advised.

"It's not as if the lock kept out the vermin," Patrick snarled.

"What is preventing her from taking over Tina?" I asked.

Amy smirked. "I'm halfway there. She drank the demon blood when she picked up her lunch. That ties her to me." Amy indicated the IV bag below her. "The binding diagram is complete. It's her or her boyfriend here, but one or the other of them is mine."

"It doesn't look that way to me," I said. "You can't reach her now that

Patrick kicked away the portal to In Between. And Patrick isn't about to invite you to possess him just because you ask."

She bared her teeth and reached my way, but the weave held her tight. "None of this would have been necessary had you given me your body, you bitch. The vamp is only temporary. I need a living body!"

The truth clicked. "You were the reason I died. But you aren't the one who trapped me!"

Her smile was a black slick of oil across her face. "Ted cornered you inside a circle of your own blood, but you were fast. You just about killed him even though the demon blood made him incredibly strong. After you cut him, he finished linking the drops with his own blood. I thought we had you, but when I tried to possess you, your life force vanished. I didn't realize then that demon blood in your system was the key to forcing your cooperation."

I peeked sideways. The blood in the IV had a black, glowing energy. So did the trail along the floor encasing Tina. I slid back. "Demon blood. How in all of In Between did you persuade a demon to offer you blood?"

"I was still alive for the summoning. You can't entice a demon without life. We placed a syringe in the circle before we summoned it. The demon agreed to provide blood in exchange for human blood from one of the patients in the hospital."

"You gave human blood to the demon?"

"Of course not. We called him, took his blood and then banished him. If I'd really handed over human blood, I'd have had to break the circle, and we knew better. As soon as he used the syringe to extract blood, we told him to get lost."

"We? Who could possibly have been idiot enough to help you?"

From this side, she was all ghostly gray except for the surge of black that occasionally pulsed through the veins of her face. Her eyes flashed with that same black flame in response to my question. "Ted would have done anything to save me. Just like Troy was helping me until you interfered!"

"Ted. The murdering bastard I tried to fight off."

Patrick grunted. "He was briefly a patient here until someone spirited him away and locked him in a room marked as a lab after he started craving human flesh. Turning zombie was a side effect of the demon blood, no doubt."

That explained the zombie that had attacked Lynx. "You and Ted both injected the demon blood. But you died anyway?"

"I would have died sooner without the demon blood. Because of you, I ran out of time and died!"

Her pinprick eyes glared at me. "Ted welcomed me, but even with demon blood he was rotting away. I had to cross back to In Between. But the demon was there, and he could smell me."

Patrick had regained some of his composure. "It wasn't the demon blood or lack of it that killed Ted. It was you sucking him dry. When Ted's soul was consumed, you had no choice but to return to In Between. The demon blood kept Ted's body animated, and that same demon blood would still have craved human flesh." The vampire's eyes were cold, but with anger, not hatred. He might lack a soul, but he wasn't a soul sucker. Just a blood sucker.

"Why try to possess the vampire?" I didn't dare look at either vampire. "They are already dead."

"I only need a body for a short time. This is a perfect solution, and it won't hurt anyone. Vampires have already solved the problem of not dying or rotting. I only need it until I find the body we prepared." She turned her face to Patrick. "The demon blood will leave you stronger and better. It's an even trade!"

Patrick must not have cared for her assessment, because he placed himself between Tina and Amy in less than a heartbeat.

I kept my eyes on Amy since tracking the vampire wasn't possible anyway. "This won't work."

"Yes, it will! As soon as Tina picked the bag with the demon blood, I followed her here. Demon blood to demon blood, I can inhabit her body. It was the mistake I made when I tried to possess you. You didn't have any demon blood in your system so I couldn't force possession of your soul. But I've learned." She flung a hand at Patrick. "It was perfect until he showed up!"

I stared at the circle, at the physical drops of blood. "You didn't draw that circle from In Between. Ted is dead and gone, so he didn't do it either. Someone else is helping you."

Lynx hissed.

"The door was locked." I glanced back at it. "But someone living drew that circle."

Amy smirked. "I'm more powerful than you know."

I shook my head. "If you could survive for even a few seconds, you'd have bridged the gap and possessed Tina. But you haven't, because you can't. Who is helping you?"

"Tina would have heard any living heartbeat that followed her." Patrick's teeth were bared, his lips pulled back in an inhuman snarl. Fresh anger interfered with his speech. "Free her!"

If I hadn't learned to understand animals on the other side, I'm not sure I'd have understood him now.

Lynx planted himself in front of me. "How we gonna do that?"

I knew the answer. "We break the circle of blood. Only the living can break through it. Patrick can walk through it all day long, but it would only trap him. The berries I threw were ghost energy, which was dead, but I have the live ones."

I tossed one, then another, rapid fire. The circle wobbled, but didn't shatter. I'd have to cross the damn line.

Lynx's reflexes were faster than mine. He pushed a packet across the line between two drops of demon blood using a single claw. When he swiped that same claw back, the concrete screamed.

A high-pitched grating noise vibrated across my bones and shot through the weave. The sound of hounds baying split the air. It was mixed with what might have been a broken bow across an untuned violin.

Amy's wail as she was sucked backwards cut off when the weave snapped closed.

Chapter 25

I could have told Lynx that snapping the line the way he did was not the best idea. It could have blown him backwards or worse, sucked him into the circle. Luckily, between the berries I threw and whatever was in his packet that crossed the line before he did, the rogue energy circle burst outward.

Tucked completely inside my living body, the blast was a snapping wind that stung like sand. The smell of blood and sulfur tainted the air. My ghost self shivered.

Patrick ducked behind his leathery wing and grunted, but other than experiencing some level of pain, he appeared unscathed. Spook jumped behind me and stayed there.

Lynx stepped in front of me too late to buffer me had it mattered.

"Amy is out of time," I said. "Troy and the scent of his energy is gone. The demon is able to track her again. Somehow she escaped through the portal after we snatched Troy's ring back. Whoever was hosting her must have helped her with this diagram."

"Where's the body if she used up another host?" Lynx sniffed the air suspiciously.

"Whoever it is must have bolted after drawing the circle to ready Tina. Is there another way in and out of here? Secret or not, Amy could have discovered it from In Between."

Patrick's head spun my way. I held my hands up in a "not-threatening you" way. "Amy can watch through the weave without making a sound. I know because I did it often enough. She could have bounced back and forth from here to In Between, planning, spying and using a host to prepare the blood and the circle."

He turned back to Tina, lifting her gently. "Your warning is appreciated, late though it has proven to be. There was no one here when I entered other than the hole to that other place. I was barely in time to stop her from jumping into the circle."

"Why not just permanently possess whoever was helping her?" Lynx wondered.

I shrugged. "Maybe whoever is helping her is too strong and knows a way to hold her off without escaping to In Between like I did."

"Or the host is running out of soul to feed her," Patrick said.

On that ominous note, Lynx ushered me out of the room, leaving Patrick to care for Tina.

By the time we climbed in the car, Spook had appeared in the backseat. "Good dog." I wished he were more substantial so I could wrap my arms around him in a giant hug.

Lynx drove without saying a word until I asked, "Will Tina be okay even though she drank demon blood?"

He slanted his eyes at me. "Do you really care?"

"Dead people aren't inherently bad. The whole drinking blood thing is disturbing, but it beats a lot of other things I've seen."

"'Trick will take care of her. If anyone can save her, he can."

"I hope the demon's blood doesn't allow Amy to come back and make herself at home. Even if Amy finds a host here, the only way she can stay is to keep absorbing life."

"'Trick should have smelled the scent if someone else was in that room." He shook his head. "But there was a lot of blood smell and a lot of magic. The blood stinks like it's been dead a long time, yet it's mixed in with fresh blood. Either way, I didn't smell any humans."

"If Amy possessed someone even temporarily, maybe that person smells like Amy now."

He frowned. "When Roberto opens a portal to In Between, there's a smell of damp and dead. Sometimes magic, sometimes a whiff of burning, but mostly there's dampness mixed with scents I can't identify. The wet is like this buffer that blocks me from smelling what might be there. 'Trick's room smelled like that today. If there is a human helping her, there isn't much of one left because it doesn't smell human anymore."

That I could believe.

Chapter 26

Even with a relapse that left me able to do little more than sleep and eat the next day, by the following morning, it was time to start paying my debts. There didn't seem to be a way to accomplish much of anything without involving Lynx, so I shared the story about Kyle and his wife. "I need to deliver the message to her."

Lynx rubbed his face, his eyes closed. "Okay. I'll find them. Maybe Roberto can help."

My hands clenched. "I don't know if Kyle's music stopped the demon. He and Martin may not have escaped." I looked up in time to catch a Cheshire grin.

"Don't worry about Martin. He knows to have an escape hatch. I'll check out the address Kyle gave you. Meanwhile, you gotta get some protection. I don't know the right spell, but Adriel, she's the best there is. If there's a spell that can watch over you when you're roaming outside yourself, she'll know one or she'll invent one. I can always duplicate it later once we figure it out."

Lynx drove me to Adriel's and walked me to her doorstep. Instead of knocking, he turned away from the door. "She's in the garden around back. You don't need me for this. It'll just make her suspicious if I hang out. I'll check on the other business."

He strode back to the car, leaving me in front of the neat stucco residence. The house could have been carved straight out of the rocks around it. When I slid sideways, colored lines were visible, winding through and around it. The odd mix of silver and icy blue energy wrapped all the way around the house, flickering as I scooted around back to find Adriel.

Sure enough, she was standing in the midst of an herb garden. She must have heard me coming because she was staring right at me as I rounded the corner.

I stopped on a nearby sandy patch to avoid stepping on any of the plants. "Lynx says you're the go-to person for spells. Martin talked about you, too."

Adriel raised an eyebrow. Talking to her face-to-face for the first time, I noticed her left eye had a green streak dancing through the brown like a lightning bolt. My Aunt Violet flashed in my memory with the words, *witch mark*. I sucked in a breath because I'd seen Violet cross In Between, but hadn't realized she was my aunt at the time.

"You don't sound convinced that I can help," Adriel said.

Maybe she was insulted by my lack of faith. I pulled my attention back to the present. "It's a tough problem. I need protection."

She crossed her arms and studied the dirt at our feet as if she were reading critical information from it. Maybe she was. Martin and Lynx said she was an earth witch.

I waited patiently. Martin had often spent time like this, thinking far away. At least she wasn't singing.

Taking a chance, I slid sideways just enough to watch the energy around her. The ground at her feet was white, just as it was under Lynx. There were masses of silver energy coiled around her bracelet and neck. Her wedding ring was a blinding white.

"Did you tell Lynx what kind of protection you needed?"

I snapped back to myself, a little shaky from the rough transition. It wasn't difficult to shift sideways, but I'd done too much of it the day before yesterday and hadn't fully recovered. I needed to learn better control and strengthen my reserves.

"Are you okay?"

I nodded, but that made the ground tilt. "I need to sit down." And I did so, right on the dirt. It was a welcome relief. If I could learn to draw energy from the ground the way Lynx did, or store it in a bracelet, my life would be a lot easier. "What did you ask me?"

"The part about you being okay or the part about whether Lynx knows what kind of protection you need?"

"Oh. He said he could cover basic protections, but I needed something stronger."

A smile bloomed across her face. "I *knew* it! He's been copying my spells. I told him I'd train him, but being a sneaky cat, he's been learning on his own. His education would be much broader if he was willing to accept some direction."

Feeling better, I eased back to standing. "He prefers back doors."

"Yes, he does. Okay, you require more than basic protection then. He must have been disappointed. That kid loves to have all the answers."

That was one way of putting it. Lynx had thought long and hard on the problem, asking me all kinds of questions before deciding he needed Adriel to help.

There wasn't an easy explanation for my problem, but I gave it my best shot. "Let's say I was in the hospital, in a coma. And I didn't want anyone touching me, but I couldn't protect myself. I can't move. I don't want anyone taking my blood—Lynx said to add that part—and I don't want anyone giving me anything either."

She stared at me and blinked. Even without being sideways, I noticed a flash of electricity spark around her bracelet.

"Moonlight madness! Do you think someone will knock you into a coma again? Because it's a lot easier to keep you out of that state in the first place than it is to protect you after the fact."

I shook my head to stop the flow of words. "That won't work. It's a state I can achieve on my own whenever I need to. But when I do, I'm vulnerable. Even if Lynx follows me around and guards me, which he seems to do whether I'm in a coma or not, I have no way of protecting myself."

Adriel was quiet for so long, I thought she'd already given up on the problem until she asked, "You can visit that place—In Between, you called it. Whenever you want?"

"No."

She stared at me. "Okay. That's not where you go." Her fingers rubbed her turquoise bracelet. The electrical charge traveled up her arm. "I don't ask questions. I just help clients."

"He said he'd pay you, but I'd rather work off my own debts. I'm not entirely certain what I'm good at yet, but—"

She waved a hand. "We'll work something out. And even if we didn't, I have a running tab with Lynx. At any given time I probably owe him three hundred dollars."

"It's better if I pay my own way."

"But Lynx will do what he wants either way. He always does. If he says you need protection, then you need it, one way or the other. Can I assume he's given you something to hide your appearance?"

I nodded and pulled a packet from under my shirt. "It's good for blending and works especially well at night. But I'm not invisible, and there's no actual protection. He said to use it if I found myself in a tight spot, but it won't physically stop someone from harming me."

She shook her head. "The kid has a nose on him like—"

"A cat," I finished for her. "He said to tell you it took him a couple of tries."

Adriel rolled her eyes. "Yeah, because he probably added an improvement or two." She tilted her head. "Let's go to my lab."

Her lab was a combination kitchen and work area with tables, benches, and jars filled with an inventory of herbs, stones, and unidentifiable goo. There was a flat piece of wood with a circle in the center off to one side, piles of other wood, cabinets and books that looked too ancient to be real.

"First spell, first," she said, rummaging amongst the jars. "Cuttlefish! It's a huge improvement for the blending spell. Those creatures can change pigments at will, blending even as their environment changes. I'll add it to his spell. That way, even if you're in motion, be it light or dark or changing back and forth, you'll still be nearly invisible. I used smoke screens with the old spell, and that is great in half light or fog, but New Mexico isn't known for foggy days."

After she fixed the spell to her satisfaction, she started with a set of new ingredients. I told her what had happened the day before with the vampires and Amy even though she indicated that Lynx had called with details yesterday. "Do you think Tina will survive drinking the demon blood?"

Adriel shivered. "I don't know. I don't see why demon blood would harm her in particular because she already gave up her soul. I guess it could have poisoned her because drinking that stuff can't be healthy."

The soulless part had occurred to me.

She sighed. "I suppose I'll have to call Patrick and offer...I am not spelling anything that might help bring a vampire back from the dead. Whatever the hell that means. And demon blood?" She looked at me. "Moonlight madness."

It was definitely madness. "Can you store energy in a packet that you can give me? Like you store energy in your bracelet?"

She didn't set down the silver spikes she held in one hand. "My bracelet?"

"Or any of the spell packets you have here." I waved at the table. "Although your jewelry contains the most energy."

She lifted her arm, her eyes narrowing at me over the turquoise. "It's my conduit. You can see that?"

"It swirls with energy."

"Can you use the energy?"

"Probably. I haven't tried to take any of it, and I'm not sure what would happen if I did."

She held her arm out. "We won't know unless you try."

I could harvest the energy if I went sideways. Trying to utilize it without doing so probably wouldn't work. I slipped partway until the energy was clearly visible and placed one ghost finger on the bracelet. It was warm, then cold.

Adriel's eyes widened. She might not see it the way I did, but she felt the energy transfer.

The flow tingled, like a shock when you rub your feet on carpet. "That's more than enough." My voice was hoarse and then squeaked on the end. "It's not the same as other energy."

"Well. That makes things easier. I can store Mother Earth in silver or turquoise easily." She turned back to the table. "There's energy in every spell. We just need it contained in something you can use." She fiddled with things on the table for a while. "I'm not sure how this helps you with a weapon though. Can you push this energy at someone?"

"The hellhounds didn't like being slapped with it. That was In Between, though. It might not work as a weapon here."

"It's worth a try." She handed me a turquoise bead.

The energy was not nearly as plentiful as her bracelet, but a sideways glance showed it coiled neatly within the ball. "I can try, but I don't think I'd better hit you with it. If it works, that could be a big mistake."

"Good point." She waved a hand at the target on the other side of the lab. "Aim there."

Without going sideways, there was no hint of the energy. I could throw the bead. It would probably hit the target. But how to activate the energy within? "I don't think that will work."

"Why not?"

"The energy works against other energy. It's like...electricity."

"If you hit that board with an electric pulse, the board will be destroyed."

I drifted sideways again. The energy radiated from the little ball of earth. "I'm not sure what to do with it."

She sighed. "I don't blame you. These arts take training. You're like Lynx—a complete mystery to me. I'm not sure what you can or can't do."

"That makes two of us. I've only ever tried to use the energy as a weapon against something that had energy. If I throw the bead at the board, it isn't attached to me anymore, and I can't see how to release the force of it once I'm not attached to it. If I'm sideways, I might be able to use the energy in the ball as a weapon if I can figure out how to fling it."

"Sideways?"

I nodded. "Sideways is, well, it's ghosting without being trapped In Between. When I'm sideways, I can't protect my body because I'm not in it."

"That's going to make protecting you a real risky proposition."

"I know." I fingered the turquoise. "Maybe if I practice with this I'll come up with something."

"Be my guest."

Chapter 27

Lynx brought food when he returned to pick me up. There was plenty to share with Adriel and White Feather, but since White Feather wasn't there, Lynx ate his share too.

After we finished eating, Lynx drove me to the grocery store to stock up.

"I gotta run another errand. Just get everything. I'll be back in forty."

Forty days and forty nights? Okay, he probably meant minutes. He hadn't told me if he had found Paula. He was probably still working on it.

As I roamed the grocery aisles, I felt vulnerable using the credit card Lynx had insisted on providing me. Even though the food would be shared with him, guilt prickled me all through the store. Since meat was expensive, I'd have made lasagna without it, but Lynx hadn't eaten a meal that didn't include copious amounts of meat.

My personal memories might be mostly gone, but apparently cooking skills hadn't left me. I bet I could concoct the burritos with beans, meat, potatoes and chile that Lynx so loved. The Spanish rice did not ring a bell. He liked eggs. How about egg drop soup? Piece of cake. Hmm. Chocolate cake.

I bought more than was strictly necessary, but hunger, or the fear of it, gnawed at me.

Lynx was waiting outside when I rolled the cart out. He dropped me and the groceries off at his house and disappeared again, but he didn't take the Mustang.

He still hadn't reported any progress.

On the bright side, with all the shopping done, at least I had a worthwhile task ahead. Since Lynx's idea of cooking involved racing the Mustang to the nearest burrito stand, perhaps I could now contribute some other food.

After I started pasta boiling, I went outside and showed Spook my newly acquired turquoise bead. "I have to learn how to use this as a weapon the way we used our energy In Between. But I can't figure out how to force an explosion without just mashing it up against someone."

Spook nipped the ball gently between his teeth, but in his case that meant he grabbed the energy, not the physical bead. He trotted off a ways and then brought it back.

"Seriously? You want to play fetch with a packet of energy? What if you squash it?"

Spook snorted with disdain and wagged his tail.

I tossed the ghost ball of energy. Oddly enough, the physical bead stayed attached to me with an elastic link between it and the ghost ball.

Spook took off after the ghost image, his missing back leg not hindering his progress at all. Maybe the ghost ball had to stay within a certain distance of the real bead, but I couldn't tell if my throwing arm was weak or if the ball of energy couldn't sail very far past the tree line because of some ghostly restriction.

"Okay. You can deliver the packet of energy." If I exploded the physical bead, would the other one explode? I tossed the ghost energy into the trees while I pondered the situation.

Finding the ball of energy, even in the trees, wasn't a problem for Spook. He brought it back, gently depositing it in my hand where the physical bead waited.

"I can't do it, Spook. I can't do a thing with it once the energy or the physical bead leaves my hand." I placed the bead against the front door. The energy was warm. Tingly. I clutched the entire ball, including the ghost energy, and slapped it against the door. "Nothing. I can still see it and push it." I went sideways again. The pulsing force was visible and warmer now. I slapped the bead into the door again, flinging the ball of energy like a weapon, envisioning the contents arcing out with the swing.

It worked! The stored energy left the bead and splashed out, still attached to me and the bead, forming a long beam.

The blue light hit the door before the physical bead. Instead of pushing the door open, the energy splattered sideways. Beams of the power bounced right back at me, hitting me solidly in the arm and chest.

I flew backwards and smacked into a hard body, ricocheting sideways into the porch railing. My stomach took the brunt of the blow, leaving me without much air. "Ooof."

"What the hell was that?" Lynx sputtered from the ground where I'd knocked him two feet off the porch. He rolled into a crouch. One hand was down for balance, and the other up and ready to do battle. His claws were visible, and he was barefoot again.

I hung there for another second or two with no air to answer him. Finally, I half rolled, half fell onto the second step. "Uff." I rubbed my stomach. "Was trying...new weapon."

Lynx spent another minute scanning the surroundings, his ears swiveling faster than his eyes. He eventually stood all the way up. "You know you're supposed to use a weapon on someone *other* than yourself, right?"

I glared at him. "I was attacking the door."

He didn't even glance at it. "You missed."

"Did not." I used the rail to haul myself up. "It fought back. Bounced the energy right at me."

Now he focused on the door. "It's warded. It was warded first with

Adriel's stuff, and then I added my own protections. Guess the spells performed well." His lips tilted in his version of a happy smile, and I swear he purred.

"I didn't think I could attack an inanimate object with the energy at all. I expected a loud noise at best and nothing at worst." I had seen the protective lines on the door, just as I'd seen brighter ones at Adriel's, but hadn't taken them into consideration when trying to throw energy.

Lynx held out his hand. I dropped the bead into it. "Adriel gave this to you?"

"It doesn't work that well though. I have to be touching it and very nearly touching whatever I want to hit. And I have to be sideways to release the energy." I plucked the small remaining energy off his hand and tossed it into the trees. Spook promptly fetched the bit of ghost energy, but there was only a lingering faded blue light remaining. "From here, I can't do anything but see the pulse. So I tried to fling it against the door."

"Yeah." Lynx held his hand out for the invisible energy, but Spook ignored him and deposited it in my hand.

I absorbed it. "Now the energy is gone. It doesn't work as a weapon." I sighed.

"If you want to fling or throw it, you need something longer. Get the weapon away from you. How far can you direct it?"

"I don't know. I explained the problem to Adriel, but didn't start experimenting until I got back here."

I climbed the steps tentatively. He followed, dusting off his backside.

"Oh, shoot! The pasta!"

Luckily, dinner wasn't ruined, and it didn't take me long to finish layering the lasagna and put it in the oven.

"A sword would be a better weapon," Lynx said, beaming at the prospect. "If it was in your hand when you were visiting sideways, you could shoot energy down it. Probably."

"I wasn't dead that long, Lynx. I am pretty sure it is still illegal to carry a sword around."

"Not to mention you might spear yourself until you learn to keep from bouncing it off a door."

I ignored his mirth. "An umbrella would work. I could even perch it over the top of me while sideways."

He frowned. "Maybe you don't need this sideways thing."

"I should just carry around a big stick. Trees have energy. Even the leaves." I wrapped bread in foil and placed it in the oven. "Do you own a crockpot?"

"A what?"

"I'm guessing that's a no."

"You think you can use a crockpot for energy?"

"No. It's for cooking." I rolled my eyes, and then noticed he was silently laughing.

"I knew that," he said. "Smells good. Hope you didn't overdo the tomato stuff in that."

"Lots of cheese. And hamburger and sausage."

"Good."

Lynx either liked the lasagna or hadn't eaten in three full days. Since we'd been together for most meals, I knew he had eaten.

When we finished dinner, Lynx eyed the plates and the full sink. "I'll take care of the dishes, but I have business first. I'll help when I get back."

"Go on, then."

Not that he waited for me to finish the sentence. The door snicked closed before the last word was out of my mouth.

Chapter 28

By the time Lynx returned it was late. I'd cleaned the kitchen, taken a shower and fallen asleep. The clock on the bedside table told me it was eleven. I got up anyway.

Lynx was in the living room with a guitar and several tree limbs.

"Adriel says it's always best to harvest right from the trees. Then there's no chance of any rogue magic interfering. We could buy hardwood from her too, and it would probably contain some of her magic. But the tree has its own." Lynx held out three different lengths of wood, each carved differently.

"You made these?" I plucked the medium staff and twirled it. It flowed through my fingers. Surprised, I stopped twirling it.

"You—" he started to speak, and then just settled for watching me.

I twirled the bar across the fingers of my other hand. Memory twinged just outside my consciousness. I closed my eyes and danced with the staff, switching between hands and rotating it behind my back and across to the other hand. Lynx had carved the wood smooth, leaving no splinters. "Walnut." I opened my eyes. "Right?"

He nodded. "Where'd you learn that?"

I frowned. "Batons. Thicker than this and not tapered."

Lynx raised one of the other staffs and feinted a swipe at my neck. I parried. He lunged. I danced back, swiping low, smacking his stick. He had no trouble dodging my efforts.

He tossed me the extra. I caught it, spun it and attacked again. He was cat fast, but I was trained. He spun his body inside my swipe, hitting me in the chest, just enough to throw my balance off, but not enough to keep my other arm from automatically reaching across his throat in a choke hold. With an agility I couldn't match, he snuck under my arm.

The spinning staff caught his shoulder, but neither of us was playing for keeps. He was outside my range before the movement really registered with me.

"Someone taught you to do more than bang into doors." He wasn't out of breath.

I was breathing hard, but I'd been lying in a coma not too long ago. My fingers never stopped rotating the mesquite. "I wonder where I learned this."

"I wonder why you learned it. Adriel's about the only girl I know who can fight, and she doesn't have your balance. Shit. She hasn't got *any* balance because she tries to fight, run and throw spells all at the same time. If it weren't for her link to Mother Earth she'd be dead about ten times over.

As soon as I came at you, you set your feet right. And that spinning thing." He nodded. "I gotta learn that."

I stopped twirling the staff and grasped it with both hands. The hellhound had left scars across three of my fingers, but the marks didn't interfere with the automatic way I handled the weapon. "The question remains though. Can I push energy through it? And even if I can, it won't help me much unless we figure out how to make it trigger when my body is unaware." I started to slip sideways, but I had gone there a few too many times today. The light beams from the three staffs barely twinkled at me.

Lynx caught me as I swayed. "Enough, Shadow."

We didn't make it to the couch before I sat down again. It would have been a much harder landing had he not been there to ease me down. Swirls of color with a lot of black danced in front of my eyes. Somewhere in there I remembered. "Someone said to sit my ass down when I needed to!"

"Who?" Lynx tightened his fingers on my shoulder, still holding me even though we were sitting.

"I was trying to make it to a bench that was against the wall, but I fell and hit my head. It was after that she said to sit down when I needed to."

Lynx relaxed his hand and draped his arm across my shoulder. I rested my head in the crook of his arm. I was completely exhausted again.

"You don't remember who it was?"

Feeling as though sleep was but an instant away, I searched for the memory. On a soft sigh, I said, "My mom? No, my aunt. Maybe my Aunt Violet. But she's dead now. I saw her cross over." I frowned. "The memory is from a long time ago. I was small. We weren't fighting for real. I wanted to be a ballerina, and so we practiced in a dance, but always with the baton. I was safe though, like I am now." I lifted the staff Lynx had given me. "This is carved. The one I had then was rounded, smooth, white."

"Are you sure you're safe?"

I tilted my head back, smiling. The laugh died in my throat. Human eyes, eyes that caught my breath as surely as if I were hunted, held me instantly still. His arm tightened again, drawing my head closer to his.

I didn't start breathing again until he kissed me. I reached up to hold him to me, and promptly smacked him in the ear with the staff still clutched in my hand.

"Ow!"

"Sorry!" My elbow saved me from landing flat on the carpet when he released me. "Accident!" I fingered the wood still in my hand. "I forgot I was holding it. I think I must have carried one a lot."

He rubbed his ear. "Or something."

I sat up fast, nearly clocking him again. "When I was In Between I never lost your braid even when I held it in my hand." I switched the staff to my other hand and clenched my fist. "I never let it go. Holding this staff feels like that, like it belongs with me, and I'm used to carrying it."

"Good. You need a weapon. Not right this *second*," he clarified. "Unless you hit me again. Then you're gonna need it."

I grinned. "What's with the guitar? Do you play?"

He shook his head. "Nah. But after I found the address where Kyle's wife lives, Roberto said to make sure the wife had the guitar that Kyle crossed with. He said it was easier if something on this side was on that side."

"You stole the guitar from her?" I was confused.

He snorted. "No. After Kyle hit his head, he apparently decided to stay overnight in Albuquerque instead of driving home to Santa Fe. When he died at the hotel, the police and ambulance came, but somehow the hotel in Albuquerque ended up with the guitar, and they hocked it."

My eyes widened. "Oh no!"

Lynx shrugged. "Finding things is a specialty of mine. People, magic, information. Wasn't too hard to track this down. There was no money inside, but it does have a false bottom. He must have had a thing about hiding stuff in his cases."

Alarmed, I asked, "Do you think someone already took the money?"

"Did he say it was in the case he was carrying?"

I shook my head. "No. I don't think he would have carried the money to the concert that night. The way he worded it made it sound like it was in one of the cases at home with her."

"I didn't want to set anything up with his wife until you had some protection and we had the guitar. Roberto's good, but he can't hold that window open for very long on his own steam. He just about got himself yanked over there the first time when he gave the bloodstone to Martin. We're more careful now."

That reminded me of another problem. "Martin used the bloodstone to open the portal to send me back. He doesn't have it anymore."

Lynx nodded. "I know. In the canyon when we talked about what was needed to get you back, he told Roberto to hold onto the bloodstone and yank it the second you were through. We knew it might be difficult so Adriel had a hold of him to make sure everything pulled this way and not Martin's way."

"Can we throw more bloodstone to Martin?"

His ears swiveled forward. "Does he need it?"

I nodded. "It's..." Trying to describe how important it was made me relive In Between. Old desperation clawed through me, and I started to sweat. "It's like your braid. Like a lifeline. Even though we are dead and things from this side can't save us, it helps."

His eyebrow flicked the tiniest bit with surprise. "Can he come back here?"

I shook my head. "He wouldn't anyway. He's happy there. But the bloodstone is energy. It's..." I waved my hand, the one not holding the staff.

Lynx sat back, determining the answer before I did. "It's earth. For Martin that's about as close to life as it gets. He's an earth witch, like Adriel, but don't tell her I said that. She'll start yammering about how they are nothing alike."

"She doesn't like him?"

"He was a drunk when he was alive and liked to roam the desert naked."

My eyes widened. "He still does that!"

Lynx gave his silent cat chuckle. "Figures."

"So when can we visit Paula?"

"I can get more bloodstone from Adriel. She keeps the pure stuff. Roberto's recovered, but he's worried about Kyle's wife. She's pregnant and due soon."

I had conveniently forgotten that part. "Oh. We don't want to trigger any unexpected events."

"And even without that, it's dangerous. So you gotta make sure you have this protection stuff down before we take too many risks. We don't know what's on the other side."

Well, that wasn't entirely true. The problem was that I knew all too well about the hungry things waiting on the other side.

Chapter 29

I slept dead to the world again, but this time when morning rolled around, I had a plan. Lynx had an entire room that was nearly empty. It was perfect for practicing. I was out of shape. I'd already died once; no need for a premature repeat.

The add-on room had a concrete floor that was cold on my bare feet. Despite the chill, it felt natural to flow through the forms with no shoes. After the first practice, I put shoes on. It changed my balance, but practicing both ways was important because unlike Lynx, I didn't often run around without shoes.

The third practice was all the forms with me sideways. That took the most out of me, and my concentration wavered all over the place. By the time I finished, I was shaking and starved.

Lynx reappeared from whatever haunts he visited in the morning.

We crammed ourselves full of leftovers, and then he joined me for the afternoon practice.

He was a quick study, mirroring the forms without a staff. He was faster than me, and it wasn't because I was still regaining my strength. The cat was just amazingly agile. I'd never match his speed, not on my best day.

Once he had the basic pattern down, he flew through the forms, adding a wall climbing run that left me gasping. "I need to learn that!"

He shook his head. "Your center of gravity isn't right for it. I adjust mine as I go. You'll just land on your head."

But he was wrong. I used the staff as leverage, climbed and somersaulted backwards. I landed off-balance and had to roll. My staff stayed with me though.

"Not the same thing!" He then mimicked my straight up the wall without the benefit of a staff. He held it for an extra second before flipping all the way over and landing on his feet.

I shook my head. "You're amazing. Absolutely amazing."

His eyes flashed a smile. "You're not so bad yourself. Teach me that thing you do with the staff."

"Which thing?"

"All of 'em."

I laughed. "Okay."

Lynx was faster than a human and smart too. I only had to show him a technique once. The hand twirls gave him the most trouble, but it wouldn't be long before he'd outdo me there too. "It's not just the speed," I told him. "It's positioning it, being ready to fling it, switch it, bat with it, stab with it."

We sparred, using four different exercises, a light back and forth with the staffs. "These can be done with a knife too if you're careful enough." That thought stopped me cold. Pictures flashed through my mind; a dagger with a long wooden handle hitting the staff.

Lynx pulled the practice swing that he had aimed at my head, but left it a bit too late. The memories distracting me had kept me from deflecting the smack.

"Ow." I spun inside automatically, despite the sting.

He was good for the maneuver, grabbing for me as I spun. His arm snaked around my ribs, locking me in tight, but he had to drop his staff to hold me there. The move left him without a defense against my staff.

I slid my hand along the bar and then jabbed it backwards into his ribs. "Ha! You're fast, but with the stab, my point!"

He kicked my legs out from under me in retaliation. His hold loosened enough that I tumbled towards the concrete.

I grabbed his arm and forced him down using my weight.

Well, maybe that would have worked had I been twenty pounds heavier, in good shape and not running on empty.

He followed me down easily enough, but rolled me under him.

"Okay, we're even. Your point," I panted.

"I didn't use my claws. I'd have earned the first point too if I clawed you instead of grabbed you."

"There is that." I inhaled another deep breath, which wasn't all that easy with him pressed across me. "I used to teach this stuff."

"You remembered. That's good. But in a real fight, can you not stop to think about it so much?"

"Absolutely. No distractions allowed."

Despite my agreement, the worry in his eyes didn't disappear. He reached up and brushed away a gray lock that had fallen across my eyes. He felt along the side of my head searching for a bump, his fingers tangling in my hair. "We'll practice more." After failing to find any sign of an injury, very carefully, he extracted his fingers. He placed his palms against the concrete and lifted himself off me using just his arms, like a push-up. "Did I hurt you?"

I smiled. "No. Besides, it was my own fault." I reached over and traced his ribs in one gentle swipe, but I was certain I hadn't hurt him. He sucked in a breath, startled.

"Hey, your ribs aren't hurt! Pulling punches is part of training. We all learn that."

His eyes locked on mine. "I've never pulled a punch in my entire life. And I've almost never fought without my claws."

"Oh." That meant he'd never been in anything other than a real fight. And he had never shared his techniques with anyone other than me.

"You didn't hurt me," I said. "I forgot we were training because you're fast, and then the memories got in the way. Sorry."

He blinked. "Sorry? You're apologizing to me? I almost took your head off!"

I shrugged. "But it was my fault. Part of teaching is to know when the student is dangerous. Do you think maybe I made a living teaching?"

He rolled his eyes. "Will you quit worrying about money?"

"I don't like...being..."

He spun into a sitting position. "I know. I can't stand owing anyone anything either. But we'll settle. And I don't care about it, anyway." He stood and hauled me to my feet. I could tell he still didn't trust my assessment of not being hurt because he kept his hand under my elbow and the other ready to catch me.

I deliberately swayed towards his shoulder, forcing him to reach out and tuck me under his arm. Like any good warrior he was watching my eyes so he wasn't fooled. I giggled. "See. Told you I am fine."

"Shadow..." Conflict flashed across his eyes. He let go, dropping his arm without any warning.

Despite the surprise, my feet snapped to support me with only the slightest skip. I balanced on the balls of my feet, ready for whatever might come next.

He gave a clipped nod of approval. "You can't ever stop looking out for yourself even if you're with someone you can trust." He turned on his heel and walked back into the main part of the house.

I frowned, wondering if he was telling me he couldn't be trusted. But no, what he said was more complicated than that. More like he needed me to be able to take care of myself.

That idea didn't bother me in the least.

Chapter 30

Adriel and White Feather stopped by the next morning with breakfast, medicinal tea from her mother and some new weapons for me.

While we ate, she explained how she had fine-tuned the beads. "Since throwing them didn't work well, I spelled them to explode if anyone touches you after you activate them. Lynx will need to know how to disable them. White Feather and I already know, but we can't tell everyone how to rescue your body if you're not in it. The beads will explode away from you. You probably won't be hurt, but there is that possibility if the explosion hits something and bounces."

"Can you design something like that for the tip of her staff?" Lynx stood at the kitchen bar eating, but he paused long enough to toss me the mesquite weapon resting near him.

I caught it, spinning it along my body automatically before handing it to Adriel.

"You're teaching her to fight?" Adriel's eyes went wide.

"She knew how already." He gave her a blank cat stare. "You don't wanna mess with her either. She nearly kicked my ass."

I rolled my eyes. The ear shot didn't count, and he'd been my equal or bested me in practice every time. "I'm not sure I can fling energy from the end of a staff any better than I was able to when throwing energy from the turquoise bead."

Adriel stared at Lynx for another few seconds, but eventually she turned her attention to my new collection of staffs. She watched as I demonstrated with one. "Wood doesn't transfer magic very well. A staff with a silver liner might be useful. Or maybe we could line it with a silver rod."

"Wood doesn't transfer magic well? That's odd," I said.

She tapped her foot. "I thought you didn't know anything about magic?"

"I don't. But In Between, I could draw energy from anything living or that had any living residue. Pine needles, a branch—it didn't even have to be connected to its original source."

She paced, staring at the staff resting along my thigh. "I should have said wood doesn't work well for *me* in most spells. I do use wood to track items and find water." She shrugged. "Try throwing the energy from one place to another off the end of the staff."

I picked up the staff and attempted to toss energy while sideways, not sideways, pushing and pulling. My energy flowed readily along the wood and boy, it could pack an extra punch when I did that. But it didn't flow outside of the staff very far, not until I snapped it like a towel, a kind of punching, halted fling. I also missed the stone fireplace where I was aiming because I didn't expect anything to happen. The shot went wide. The television hanging off to the side of the mantel crackled with an odd popping noise when the force hit. A funny gray line sparked across the center, like an inert streak of lightning. "Uh-oh."

"I don't watch it anyways," Lynx said calmly. "It was payment from a buddy who didn't have any cash."

Adriel paced away from me, probably hoping for more distance between us in case I started throwing off invisible sparks.

"Interesting," she said. "We can tip the end with silver. That might very well cause the energy to arc away a bit, but it might not travel any further than it does now. It also doesn't solve the problem of protecting you when you're outside your body if you drift too far away." She handed me the silver balls and then looked at Lynx. "Is this too much silver for you if she carries them? Or will your bracelet protect you enough?"

Lynx didn't look at her, me or his bracelet. I hadn't noticed the skin colored sandy band at first. Then later I'd thought maybe it was just a streak of dirt, but eventually I realized it was a bracelet made from some kind of Zuni-like sand that expanded and contracted. He never took it off.

"I'm good," Lynx said.

She turned back to me. "Carry the silver with you. Remember to activate the spell if you leave yourself. Release the spell when you return. Try it once so I can make sure you have the hang of it."

I was exhausted already, but sliding sideways was nothing compared to flinging energy down the end of the stick. That had taken a big chunk out of me.

I set the spell as instructed, went sideways and saw the balls as little silver orbs of energy. Without thinking, I touched one, drawing the energy to me. It was like eating a full meal. I instantly felt better.

"Aztec—" Adriel closed her eyes. "You just drained that spell completely, didn't you?"

I shifted fully back. "Sorry. I was In Between a long time and there it sat, a happy little feast."

"Now I'll have to recharge it. Well, you have three others. Try not to drain them every time you see them. Save them for weapons!"

Feeling better, but still tired, I sat on the couch. Lynx handed me a glass of chocolate milk and perched on the arm. It felt nice to have him nearby. With the energy from Adriel's spell I wasn't in danger of falling over, but knowing he had my back warmed me from the inside out.

White Feather had remained at the kitchen table watching us the entire time. He finally asked, "Any luck tracking down the story on Amy?"

Lynx nodded. "She died about four months ago when she was twenty-one. She had been diagnosed with ovarian cancer about eight months earlier, but was still working as a tech at the blood bank next to the hospital. Ted ended up as a patient at the hospital when he started having convulsions and chewing on people. 'Trick says it's obvious Amy has another accomplice at the hospital, and whoever it is could have easily listed her death as the ovarian cancer rather than 'dumb ass who called a demon and tried to turn herself into a zombie.'"

"I'm not sure a forensic scientist would recognize death by demon blood," White Feather replied.

Adriel tilted her head. "The demon blood didn't kill her. It just failed to heal her body like she thought it would. But technically, the demon magic should have allowed her to possess another body."

I tucked my legs under me. "I wasn't a willing donor. She made it sound like she died because she didn't find a donor fast enough."

Adriel nodded. "After failing to possess you, she was probably drained with no backup plan. It's also probable that when she left her body to possess you, her body died and she had nothing to re-inhabit."

"Does anyone know how I ended up in the hospital?" I asked.

Lynx didn't look at me when he answered. "You were attacked in the park across from the Santa Fe Indian Hospital. If you'd been any further from assistance, you wouldn't have made it, but from what 'Trick gathered, someone saw the fight and called it in. The paramedics didn't have to do more than run across the street. You had no ID. You landed in his hospital, Specialty Center, because no one knew who you were. 'Trick said you had to be resuscitated twice."

That was a lot of information to digest, but it was also no information at all. "Do you know where Amy lived? I saw the blood from at least one pentagram at the hospital. The splatters attracted a minor demon. There were remnants of another drawing around Ted even though he was a zombie. Whoever helped Amy probably drew the pentagrams to allow her to jump back and forth from In Between, but whoever it is had to store supplies, or books, or something."

Lynx fidgeted but didn't say anything until Adriel crossed her arms and tapped her foot. "I know you must have found the place, Lynx."

He didn't blink, but he answered. "Ted still had an apartment, but it isn't paid up. Looked like Amy musta lived there before she died, but there was nothing significant there. Didn't even smell of magic or blood."

Adriel stopped tapping, but left her arms crossed.

"There wasn't any sign of the occult?" I found that hard to believe.

He flashed me a smug cat look. "The carpet was pretty new. Something burned there, but it was quite a while ago. It was in a small enough area that it could have been a pentagram."

"Maybe it was left over from when they called the demon to obtain the demon blood the first time?" Adriel threw up her hands. "We'll probably never know!"

"I could look," I suggested. "There might be something useful at the apartment that I can spot."

"Lynx can smell magic," Adriel said. "He wouldn't miss that."

I shrugged. "And he can see ghosts too, but maybe there's something there that I can see, some link to In Between."

Lynx's eyes flashed. "Not a good idea to go roaming around the place. You tell me what to look for and I'll find it. You get in too much trouble."

"I know what that's like," White Feather muttered, glancing in Adriel's direction.

He earned a glare from Adriel. "I can take care of myself," she huffed.

"Not really the point," was White Feather's reply.

"Shadow gets in way more trouble than Adriel," Lynx said.

White Feather slapped him across the shoulders. "That's simply not possible."

Lynx snorted. "Yeah? She got herself killed, and we had to drag her back. Adriel hasn't tried dying yet."

Adriel shook her head at me. "Men."

They were both right, but so was Adriel. There were things that needed to be done. I might as well go for broke. "I need to talk to Paula and give her Kyle's message too before it's too late. Time is different In Between. I know Paula's pregnant, but I'd rather contact Kyle sooner rather than later. In Between was bad enough before Amy set the demon loose there."

Adriel nodded. "I talked to Mom. She set the stage." Before I could ask how, Adriel explained. "My mom knows everyone or someone who knows everyone else. Paula's mom knows a friend of my mom. She has a friend who called Paula to break the news that you have a message from Kyle. If you walked in cold, she'd be certain you're a con artist."

"Roberto's ready," Lynx said, "but Shadow and I can visit first to tell her to search for the money. Then we can bring Roberto in to see if we can reach Kyle."

"I'm ready," I said, in case anyone had any doubts.

After White Feather and Adriel left, I gathered juniper berries and wrapped them in two cotton hankies. They stored energy better than the pine needles, but one or two of those wouldn't hurt either. I put extra bits in my own pocket, insurance that wasn't logical, but I didn't care.

I shaved two bits of wood from the staffs I'd been using and added that to the bundles before tying them tightly.

Lynx waited without asking questions. He held a quiet position better than a cat.

I finally grabbed two of my staffs. "Okay, let's go."

He led the way to the car.

Paula's apartment complex was a typical brown adobe structure. Musicians apparently weren't paid well even in Santa Fe, where art was considered a major part of the economy. The building was riddled with cracked stucco, uneven pavement and a general air of neglect.

We knocked and waited for less than a minute before Paula opened the door. She was quite short so her pregnant belly was not only prominent, it affected her balance. Her dark hair was pulled back into a long ponytail. She was barefoot.

I wished Roberto had come along. He could prove we weren't liars, but more than that, I wanted to make sure Martin and Kyle were okay. Without Roberto, we were just empty-handed messengers.

Well, except for the guitar. Lynx set the case upright while Paula stared at us from the doorway.

The apartment behind her was very small. From the boxes piled in the living room behind her, it appeared she was getting ready to move out. It was imperative she keep Kyle's guitar or he'd have a very hard time finding her from In Between.

I introduced myself and stuttered condolences, telling her we were there to return the guitar and had a message from Kyle.

She blocked the doorway with her person and her glare. "Kyle's grandmother is crazy. She said you'd stop by, but I don't believe a word you have to say."

Adriel had said she set the stage, but it hadn't helped. Paula wasn't a believer.

"We brought Kyle's guitar. It's the one that was in the hotel room with him."

"And I suppose your message is that he wants me to have it? *Very* original."

"No. The message is that he left some money in one of the guitar cases. He was saving it for a surprise when your daughter was born."

"Ha! That proves you are lying. We don't know the sex of the child."

Kyle had told me it was a daughter. I shrugged. "He said she was a girl."

"Right. And I would imagine you are here to help me find this fortune? And then what? You demand some of it, or you come back later with more messages telling me where to send it and any other money I have?"

I shook my head. "No. Kyle asked me to deliver the message and to hurry because he was afraid you'd sell the guitars. He wanted to make sure you found the money first. There was a false bottom in this case, but no money." She sucked in a deep breath, ready to lambast us, but I kept talking. "But it wouldn't be in this one anyway because he told me...well, he implied the money wasn't hidden in the one he had with him that night."

Her furious brown eyes were fast turning red with held back tears. "He had more than one guitar with him. He always does."

Lynx finally spoke. "There was only the one at the hotel. If he had others, he left them somewhere else."

"And this is your proof? I'm supposed to believe you because you show up pretending to be some mystic with gray hair and my husband's guitar?"

I blinked. The gray hair made me look silly, it was true, but there wasn't much I could do about it. "It really doesn't matter if you believe us or not. Check the cases. We can show you in this one how the inside has an extra piece of padding fit to the bottom. The others are probably constructed the same way. Kyle also wants you to have this guitar back because he had it with him when he died. He'd like you to keep it even if you can't keep the others."

My ear started to tingle. I glanced at the guitar case, but it hadn't changed. I clicked my fingernails, the signal Lynx and I had agreed upon if I intended to slide sideways. With the pressure building near my ear, I didn't wait to make sure he heard.

A soon as I drifted sideways, there was music, and I remembered the guitar pick. I'd searched for it once after my return, but not while sideways. I reached for it, and Kyle was suddenly standing next to Lynx, almost superimposed on him.

"Tell her it's in the acoustic guitar case, the Overton," Kyle said.

"Kyle!" He looked the same as when I'd last seen him, right down to strumming his guitar. "I'm really glad you're okay." It was a stupid thing to say to someone who was dead, but my relief pushed aside logic. "I brought you something. One for you and one for Martin." I threw the bags right at the side of Lynx's head because Kyle's face was at the top of the guitar case.

Lynx flinched. The bags disappeared through the weave.

"Kyle?" Paula gasped.

Lynx set the guitar on its end and edged away from it, settling closer to me.

Martin was suddenly there, puffing words at us. "Need. Demon. Name. Didn't get banished."

He was wispier than he should have been, maybe because he'd given up the bloodstone. Instead of a chiseled appearance of ghostly stone, his face was a blotch. "Did the demon find Amy?"

Martin shook his head, leaving ghost trails. "Chasing. Us. Daily."

"Kyle, is that really you?" Paula asked.

Kyle nodded at his wife, knowing better than to try words. Martin was better at delivering entire sentences, and even he sounded like a record on the wrong speed, warped and cutting to an odd stop before the words were finished.

"Is it really a girl?" Paula stepped next to me.

Kyle nodded again. The music to "My Girl" floated through the weave.

Paula was suddenly sobbing too hard to say more, but Lynx took over the conversation. "Can you force the demon name from Amy?"

Martin shook his head. "Aaaa...crossed back...over."

"She found a host? The demon will try to follow her," I shouted. Cold chills ran down my spine.

"Need. Demon...Name."

Paula put her hand out, reaching for Kyle. The weave snapped shut, a force that shook me right back into my own body. The slam threw me sideways into Lynx. The weave was capricious under the best of circumstances. I should have known better, but had never seen it in action from this side. Lynx held me up until I recovered my balance.

Paula still had her hand out. "Bring him back!"

"Not right now," I panted out. I grabbed the guitar and set it inside the doorway. "He has this guitar with him. You need to keep it."

She nodded around her tears.

"And search for the money," I instructed.

"Can I move out? How will he find me?"

I pointed. "The guitar. He gave me a guitar pick, but," I reached up behind my ear. There was nothing there but a slight tingle. I had no way to give it to her.

She yanked tissues from a box on the coffee table. After blowing her nose and wiping her eyes, she hurried back over to hug the guitar case.

We turned to leave, but she called after us. "Wait! Can you...can you tell him I love him?"

"He can hear you. At least most of the time. Do you hear music a lot?"

She hesitated. "Sometimes. When I tried moving the guitars around. I thought the strings were just vibrating."

"If you hear music, he can probably hear everything you say. You can tell him then."

"Really?"

"For now. He's in a place called In Between. I don't know how long he'll be there. Neither does he. But while he's there, you can talk to him. He can't answer, not most of the time, but he can hear you."

She sniffled again. "He'll be able to see the baby?"

I nodded. "Especially then."

"*My Girl* was the first song he ever played for me."

I was too tired and scared for Kyle and Martin to smile. "I guess it's now the first one he played for your little girl too."

She had a hand on her big, round tummy. "Yeah. Yeah."

Back in the Mustang, I got the shakes. I gripped the staff resting between us in the front seat. "I'm not leaving this in the car again." My voice cracked. I'd been afraid if Paula saw it, she'd become alarmed. But I hadn't had a weapon with me when I died. It had proven to be a costly mistake. "Can you make a staff that resembles a cane, thick on one end and thinner on the top? I don't need the handle part, but it would probably look more legit with a curved handle or one of those straight out handles that old guys lean on."

Lynx nodded. "Sure. It would be a good disguise. I can hollow it out too if you want to stash a little extra something in it."

I started to refuse and then thought better of it. "A small cavity." Berries would fit in there. Or other bits of life.

As he pulled out into traffic he said, "I didn't know you could do that Roberto thing, or I'd have brought the bloodstone."

"I didn't do it. The guitar was enough, plus Kyle has been waiting for this opportunity. Martin knows how to thin the weave, and with that guitar being a link to Kyle they managed it."

He drove for a while before asking, "This Amy chick. Can she find you?"

"She doesn't even know my name. Hell, I don't even know my name!"

"When we were at 'Trick's she said you were supposed to be her host, but you refused. But if she had picked you out, maybe she knew who you were. Maybe the two of you knew each other when you were alive."

I shook my head. "I recognized people I knew even stuck In Between. There just weren't many to recognize. And if she did know me, it doesn't matter. I'm not the same person. I don't know where the other me lived, or who she was. If Amy knows and looks there, she won't find me."

He nodded. "That's a good thing."

"I wonder who she found to inhabit? She can't just cross over at will. And the demon was hot on her trail, too. He isn't going to stop until he finds a way across."

Lynx had his own questions. "If this demon catches up with Kyle or Martin what does it mean?"

I sliced an imaginary cut across my throat. "Total destruction. Those creatures take everything and anything that is left of a person."

"This Amy chick. She has a soul?"

The idea caught me off guard. "Maybe not anymore. Could be that she traded part of it to the demon just by calling it. He knew her smell, but that was probably because she drank or injected his blood. If she had been stuck In Between without anyone to hide behind, she'd be toast already. But if she came back here like Martin said, she has to have found someone to accept her."

"Maybe the same person who has been helping her all along?"

I nodded. "That could be it, but we know that she can't or won't stay in that person forever or she wouldn't have been prepping Tina. Maybe whoever has been helping her is almost used up like Patrick said, or maybe Amy keeps that person in reserve for when she uses up other hosts."

He thought for a long time. "She told 'Trick that Tina was temporary too."

I pieced together the little bits we knew. "Tina *had* to be temporary because Tina has no soul. If her accomplice was temporary and Tina was temporary, they were after someone else." There was only one other person I knew of who might be a candidate. "Right before we grabbed Troy's ring back, Amy was yelling at someone through the portal saying they couldn't keep starting over. It was right after I told you to take Espy out of the hospital because I suspected Espy had been given demon's blood in her IV." We'd pulled up at the house, but I didn't leave the car.

"The kid is in a safe place." His eyes were cat flat, an expression I was beginning to recognize as worry.

"What if Amy found her?"

He shook his head. "The aunt would know, and they're both in a safe place."

"Maybe Amy started over again, but what if she didn't? If Espy ended up with demon blood from that IV, maybe Amy can smell her like the demon smelled Amy! Lynx, we need to check on them and make sure they stay hidden in case Amy is hunting! We can't just let them sit there with demon blood. Even if Amy hasn't found her yet, the demon might!"

"Okay, okay. I'll have Adriel get her mom to start the wheels turning." I shook my head frantically, but he kept talking. "You can't go springing this stuff on the normals. They don't take it so well. Paula wouldn't have believed a word we said if Kyle hadn't shown up."

"We don't need to wait. The aunt and Espy know me already. They'll believe me."

Lynx cut his eyes to me. "They know you from before you died?"

"No, they're like Roberto. They talked to me when I was In Between."

"You sure met a lot of people over there. Place sounds like a McDonald's with everyone stopping in to eat or use the bathroom on the way through."

That wasn't an entirely inaccurate description.

Lynx called Adriel and updated her with the basic details.

After he hung up, he said, "Okay it's set up. They'll meet us in a few hours. Adriel needs to create a protection spell first. She's gonna have to figure something out because she's short on demon protection spells." He shook his head. "She's good, but I don't think she can come up with enough fire to kill a demon."

"If she can't kill the demon, maybe she can hide Espy like Amy was using Troy's essence to hide from the demon. Can I borrow your cell to call

Adriel?"

He handed it to me and said, "Espy is already hiding."

I hit redial. When White Feather answered, I could hear Adriel muttering in the background. "How do you tear a demon into pieces? Have to keep it from capturing a human, but it would be easier to kill if it was human."

"Hang on," White Feather said before handing her the phone.

I started talking without preamble. "When I was In Between, Amy hid from the demon by hiding behind Troy's essence. His essence is sort of like his soul, but not his whole soul. She borrowed his essence by stealing his ring and his energy."

Nothing but silence.

"Adriel?" I looked at Lynx desperately, but he just shrugged. "I think we got cut off."

"No, no, I'm here." The phone crackled as she breathed out a big sigh. "You're telling me that all I need to do is hide her behind someone else's soul?"

"Exactly!"

"Great."

"So you can do that?"

Her voice sounded strangled when she answered. "I am guessing it's a blood spell. I don't do blood spells."

"Amy used Troy's ring, not his blood."

She was silent for a few moments and then said, "But the way you described it, anything you used In Between was life energy. So that's similar to blood. Or maybe a soul." The sound of objects clattering forced me to jerk the phone away from my ear. "Maybe we can hide her behind her aunt. Unless a blood relative is too close a match for a sniffing demon. How would I know? No one tells me these things!"

"I, uhm, guess we'll see you later?"

"Yeah, yeah," she grumbled back.

I hung up. "She doesn't know if she can hide Espy."

Lynx finally opened the car door. "We need to enhance your weapons."

We worked on the staffs until dark. Lynx had some basic tools, including a drill. He was skilled at carving, and the wood responded to him. He worked quickly, producing two canes to supplement my arsenal of straight weapons. "Remember to limp when you use these, but don't pretend to be an easy mark or you'll end up having to knock people left and right. Just don't look as bad-ass as you usually do or no one is going to believe you need a cane."

I snorted. "Bad-ass? My hair is prematurely gray, and I'm so thin I still resemble a corpse. That's bad-ass?"

He gave a last polish to the wood and then let his eyes travel all over me. "You look great. From the very first time I saw your ghost..." He sat perfectly still, as if the vivid memory captivated him. His eyes flashed, him seeing me through cat eyes. "You look great."

His sincere approval left me speechless, and my heart missed a beat.

He slipped a piece of wood over the point he had been crafting. "If you need a sharp object, just pull this chunk of wood off. It's tight, but it needs to be that way to stay on."

Even if I had never slipped sideways and seen the golden energy that glowed around him, I'd have sensed the magic that was Lynx. He had confidence and skill and a cunning that was not just because he was a cat. He was human with a soul that had somehow touched mine. He hadn't given up on me when I was dead. He didn't look ready to now, either. "Thanks."

He shrugged. "We can make better weapons, but I'll need more supplies."

I scooted my fingers along the staff until they touched his. "No, I mean thanks for...for rescuing me from In Between. For helping Espy. For—"

"You saved me from that zombie. We're even." He stood up abruptly. "It's dark enough now to check out Amy's place. We won't have much time before we have to meet Adriel and White Feather at the safe house. And we better hope Adriel comes up with a spell because there ain't a safer place than where we stashed the kid and her aunt."

He handed me the cane. As he stepped past, he brushed up against me, a tingling kind of hug that made me want to throw my arms around him and never let go.

Chapter 31

Lynx loaded one short and one long staff in the trunk. There was already a pack filled with supplies and a large jug of water in there, but there was plenty of room for my two weapons. I added a short baton to be on the extra safe side.

Spook hopped in the backseat, so Lynx placed my remaining cane on the floor in the back. I stopped at the juniper tree and collected more berries. Once in the car, I retrieved the cane and poured some of the berries down the hidden hollow.

Lynx took a roundabout route to our destination. Maybe he thought someone would tail us, or maybe he wanted the Mustang noticed in other areas of town. When we parked, it was behind older, yet modern buildings, none of which looked residential. Some had lights indicating occupants and others were dark.

We walked. There were streetlights showing everyone our route, but Lynx didn't seem too concerned.

We slinked through at least nine different alleyways, two behind restaurants. When we finally arrived at an apartment complex, we faced the back fence.

"Stay here until I give the all clear." That fast he was gone, at least half cat, springing over the privacy fence.

I scooted along the boards, letting Spook track Lynx. I remembered to use the cane and limp slightly.

Lynx was back in short order. "There's a dumpster a few yards ahead. If you climb the fence, you can use the dumpster to help you down this side."

I didn't need a dumpster. He'd shown me his cat trick for scaling a wall. I just had to use the staff as a pole to vault me to the top of the fence.

I backed up, checked to make sure there was nothing but desert and scrub visible and made the leap. Balancing on the top would not only be precarious, it would leave me silhouetted against the night, so I flipped over with just a light tap to support the proper arc.

The asphalt was harder than the dirt road behind the place, but I didn't dare roll.

There was enough ambient light from the buildings to spot Lynx standing up against the fence, a darker shadow against the wooden planks.

He beckoned me. "Come on."

Spook drifted through the fence without a problem and then trotted alongside us like a dog fully alive.

Amy and Ted's apartment was on the ground floor in the back. Lynx must have opened the door earlier because we slipped right inside.

He flipped on a light. "I closed the curtains last time, although I searched the place without lights. Eventually the police will hunt for Ted and ask the neighbors the last time anyone saw any activity here, so don't waste time."

I had expected a dump, but Amy and Ted hadn't spent a whole lot of time here lately. There was a couch, a fifty-inch flat panel on one wall and a coffee table. The lamp Lynx had turned on using the main switch was on a side table. A glass with old soda or maybe the dredges of an alcoholic drink was the only real sign of the former occupants in the living room.

"I'm sliding sideways."

He nodded, inching closer to me. There was no need really. My body didn't fall over. It just stood there, completely still. Once shifted, I stared back at us, realizing my body was barely breathing. No wonder it unnerved Lynx.

The light wasn't necessary anymore. Everything took on a gray cast as I floated into the kitchen and dining area. There were rinsed dishes on the sideboard and a few dirty ones in the sink; a bowl and coffee cup. The coffee maker still contained a low ring of coffee, and something in the pantry was attracting flies.

I drifted to the bedroom.

There were no mysterious colors or sparks of light.

Spook growled once, sniffing heavily before retreating to the doorway.

The bedroom was large and messier than the front room. There were clothes across an unmade bed. The closet door was open, revealing both men's and women's clothing.

On the dresser, there was a picture of Amy and from the resemblance, her mother. They were both dressed to the nines, probably for Amy's high school graduation. Amy looked several years younger in that picture compared to a more recent one where she posed with Ted.

I had never seen her alive, but even in a photograph, Amy beamed with color and life. Her rich auburn hair glinted in the sunlight and her smile was full of laughter. Her mom reminded me of someone, but I was positive I hadn't known either of them. Maybe she just reminded me of Amy because although her hair was a very dark brown compared to Amy's, she had the same eyes and full smile.

There were two other shots with Amy and her boyfriend, Ted.

I turned and fled. I didn't need air, not in this form, but I halted in the hallway, inspecting the bathroom while regaining my composure. Lynx was right. There was nothing here. There wasn't even a bookshelf in the living room or first bedroom. If they had done any occult studying, it hadn't happened recently.

The second bedroom was a hodgepodge, half lived-in, half storage. The closet had obviously been in use, mostly with Amy's clothes. There was no bed in this room, but there was another dresser with junk, including jewelry, a notebook, and some textbooks strewn across the top. Resting on a biology book was an award certificate from a hospital Christmas party. Signatures ran along the bottom of the photo of people from the hospital. There was an open gift certificate envelope with, "Thank you for your hard work," printed on it.

I recognized Nurse Sonya in the photo. It was impossible to tell who was a technician versus a nurse from the smocks, but the doctors wore lab jackets. The old guy who had been in charge of treating me was in the picture. I didn't even know his name. He had probably done his best to save me.

I had turned away when Spook floated over to one corner of the room and sniffed along the carpet. It must be the place on the carpet where Lynx had smelled old burn.

Maybe Amy had called the demon from here, maybe she hadn't. I looked back at the photos. Amy was quite striking in her party dress. I spotted Paul, the technician. He was in the back of the lineup with his head down, probably looking at his phone. The vamps were nowhere to be seen in the daylight photo.

The light in the living room went out, snapping me out of my thoughts.

I returned to my body with a whoosh. Lynx had a tight hold on one arm. "People passed by. You got anything? Do you need more time?"

I shook my head. "Let's roll."

"Hold tight. We'll leave a different way than we came in."

We exited the kitchen sliding door, and then Lynx trotted down a path that led to the front of the complex. From there, we hiked back to the car by strolling along the front of the buildings.

When we were nestled safely inside, I said, "There was a picture of Amy and her mother in there. Did you see it?"

His ear twitched. "I noticed the frames and her with her boyfriend. White Feather has an ear with the cops. His brother Gordon is on the force. Amy's next of kin listed was the boyfriend. But if the mom is still alive, we better check her out."

When we pulled up to a place called The Owl, I guessed Lynx had decided to eat before meeting the others. I wanted to argue in favor of getting to Espy without wasting any more time, but I had to admit that after my sideways exercise, I was hungry again.

Spook didn't follow us this time.

Lynx knew the secret to opening a side door that was boarded closed. Once inside, he led the way through a dim hallway to another locked door.

Strangely, behind that door was a regular seating area with a bar along one side. There were no other customers in the place, but I remembered to use the cane as though for balance.

"Burger okay?" he asked me, sliding into a booth.

"Sure. I'm easy."

He grinned at me. The candles flickered oddly, merging his cat shadow with his human face. It made me a little queasy when I glared at him for taking my statement suggestively. His foot touched mine under the table, and the wobbling images firmed into a steadier, normal looking Lynx.

"Illusion candles," he explained. He moved his foot away, and the uneven image returned. I played footsie with him, locking my ankles around his, grateful when the blurred images stilled.

"You're easy too," I said with a straight face.

A very plump lady came through a swinging door behind the bar. "The usual?" she called out. Her hair was not prematurely gray like mine; it was albino white. That couldn't be the reason for its lack of color though because her skin was a rich Hispanic hue. Maybe her appearance was just another lie caused by the illusion candles.

"Two," Lynx said. "We're in a hurry, and we'll eat at The Monastery later."

"We're eating twice?"

He waited until she disappeared behind the door before replying. "Nah, that's code to let Angel know that we're planning to take the back way to Tino's other restaurant. The Monastery is fancier. Costs more even though the food here is just as good. This place is better for most meets or talking business with Tino. Adriel and White Feather will meet us at The Monastery, but it's better if we don't all come in together. They'll arrive separately."

Before I could ask who Tino might be, a guy emerged from the door behind the bar. He was well over six feet, bald as a day-old baby and chewing on a wooden skewer. A shiny silver quetzal earring glinted long from one earlobe. He leaned on the bar, chewing away. "Business good?" His deep voice rumbled across the tile floor and skittered up the legs of the table.

I shivered, wondering how he managed such a timbre that had a life of its own.

"Might need to move things around," Lynx answered casually.

"Someone hiking on the trails?"

"Good tracker hunting out of season."

I decoded the conversation to mean that we might have to move Espy because someone was hunting her, but maybe Lynx was a big-game hunter and just talking shop.

Angel reappeared from the door carrying a platter with two of the largest burgers I'd ever seen. They dripped green chile and cheese from the sides. She set them down alongside two sodas and a basket of fries that even

Lynx probably couldn't finish on his own.

I started eating.

After a few short minutes, Angel brought us a takeout bag instead of a check. "Tino says to deliver. She likes his burgers."

"Smart." Lynx nodded around a mouthful of fries.

Now I was positive they were talking about Espy because I wasn't planning on eating another burger this size anytime soon, and Adriel wouldn't need it if she was at the other restaurant.

When we finished licking the last of the burgers from our fingers, Lynx stood and wrapped his fingers around mine. I froze in momentary shock, not sure what to make of his open display of affection. His hand was warm and steady, a force of emotion that hit me as strong as any touch had In Between.

The lights flicked off. The place went pitch black. My grip tightened around my staff, ready to swing. Lynx, expecting my reaction, held tight and brushed against me lightly, a quick reassuring touch of his body.

He then glided away, tugging me after him.

My sense of direction was pretty good. We walked to the edge of the bar or perhaps just behind it. When Lynx stepped down, he stayed close and squeezed my fingers so I wouldn't miss the step. As soon as the door snicked shut behind me, lights snapped on.

We were in a stone stairwell with a ceiling that was lower starting at the third step. I followed his crouched form down the steps.

He handed me a flashlight. "I don't like relying on Tino's lights, so I stashed a couple of lights down here just in case. Don't worry though; we can make it in the dark if we have to."

"And you know this because?"

"Lights failed when I was down here working once."

And he had found his way out anyway because he was Lynx. "What is this place?" I kept my voice low because he did, plus the situation seemed to call for it with the way the stone and dirt tunnel echoed back on us. The smell of dirt wasn't unpleasant. A stream of air swept past with enough of a breeze to keep it from becoming completely claustrophobic.

"It's part of an old Spanish monastery. Tino's other restaurant is the main building, but the place was a huge complex, its own little sheltered city a long time ago. Tino made it his business to buy up any buildings still standing that were a part of the complex. I worked for him for a few years mapping it out. Some of the old buildings are directly connected by these tunnels, but others were built side-by-side and are only up top. Parts of them, probably used for livestock, were torn down a long time ago, but he's bought and reconnected a lot of it."

"Why?"

"He bought the old monastery for the restaurant it is now. While cleaning it up, he musta found the records for the place because there ain't no way he could have figured out some of the stuff he did all on his own. He bought up the old dormitories, the chapels, a library, a school room, and some other stuff. If you plot out his restaurants, The Monastery is the center with the various buildings like arms."

"Wow."

"Not all of them were connected by tunnels, and he didn't reconnect all of the existing tunnels anyway. A couple of his places attract groupies and gangs. I've never found a tunnel at those places, but they were a part of the old complex."

The tunnel opened up into a wider area with multiple offshoots. Would that the space be only an old chapel or library rather than catacombs. Several wall spaces contained small offerings and statues. The plastered over rectangles and a lone gate leading to more of the same made it clear the place was a house for the dead.

The underground graveyard was rather creepy, probably more so for me because wisps of ghosts drifted past us. I couldn't make out any features, but given that New Mexico was dry as a desert skull, the gray mist couldn't be true fog. Lynx shied away from the forms, too.

"Because you helped map it, you get to use it?" I guessed.

He flashed me his self-satisfied cat-has-the-cream expression. "I'd use it anyway, but Tino's good people. He knows about us shifters and the rest of the magicals. He's got something himself, but I haven't figured out just what yet. This place has more than one safe house. Only rule is that the vamps can't use it. He doesn't have anything against them except they are dangerous, and he doesn't want to fight them over the territory."

"I can see where a vampire might consider this a nice homey atmosphere." It was underground, dark and protected. I shivered.

When we climbed up, this time using a set of packed dirt stairs, we entered a long hallway with broken and missing tiles. It quickly led us to a very old chapel. There was a place for an altar, but nothing remained except a rounded out area and a piece of a crumbling ledge. What might have once been stained glass windows were filled in with adobe bricks. "The ceiling isn't a dome on the outside like it is in here," Lynx said. "On the outside it's a square building with just the front accessible so no one has a clue this is here. No doors or windows in this section." He hurried through as if the lack of exits bothered him.

Blue and white paint had once been an angel on the ceiling, but it was now a half-halo, an arm and part of a dress.

We traveled underground again, changing directions twice. At the top of the next set of stone stairs, there was a large room with three additional arched exits crumbling under dust and age.

"There's another restaurant several buildings over." He waved at the exit on our left.

This particular room looked newer and was swept cleaner than the previous ones, but it was crowded with what might have been the remains of the other buildings. There were at least three statues of praying saints and a large table that was probably an old altar. Only two carved legs remained, so someone had taken the time to prop the side with no legs against a set of adobe bricks that formed a shelf along one partially tiled wall. No plaster remained on the bricks; they just hung on the wall, pieces of straw and dirt.

Gilded paint on several items was now little more than tarnished brown specks. An old chandelier, the type that required real candles, rested on the floor. Deep niches three-quarters of the way up the walls still held candelabra and half-melted candles.

As we exited beneath an arched doorway, I swear the gargoyle perched on the edge blinked at me. Must have been the dusty light. The half-bat, half-dog stone statue was an odd, mismatched piece for a monastery, but Lynx did say that Tino had reclaimed several old buildings. Some of them had to have been used as something other than a monastery at some point.

We were almost through the next corridor when Spook showed up, nearly giving me a heart attack. He nipped at my jeans, chiding me for leaving him behind. "I didn't know we were going this way," I told him.

Lynx looked back and shook his head. "That dog is spooky."

Spook wagged his tail in happy acknowledgment.

The next doorway was obviously the back of a building in use. The wooden staircase with thick, scuffed planks led to a second floor. The space housed two simple bedrooms with a modern bath. Muted kitchen noise floated up from the floor below. "This is the back of The Monastery restaurant, second floor. The other half of the second floor is behind this wall. It's a balcony where the musicians play on weekends. There's an emergency exit that way, but we don't use it because of the crowds.

"The first floor is the dining area. There aren't any meeting rooms like at The Owl, but it's easy to come and go here without being noticed because it looks like you're just coming for a meal and then leaving a couple of hours later."

The second bedroom had a hidden doorway. The stairway past the door was tight.

The bell tower contained an old bronze bell that was anchored into place and sealed around the edges. There was space for a single bed, an antique oak desk and a matching set of drawers. The wood floor was warped in places and hadn't been polished in a long time. One frayed Navajo rug bordered the side of the bed.

Adriel and White Feather were crammed inside next to Aunt Brenda and Espy. The aunt had lost weight and worry was adding wrinkles to her face.

The aunt recognized me immediately, the girl shortly thereafter.

She jumped in front of Espy. "You!"

Her vehement reaction wasn't a huge surprise. It wasn't every day a ghost showed up in the flesh.

Lynx stepped closer to me. "She's the one who made sure you got out of the hospital."

Espy peeked around her Aunt Brenda. "Shadow." She stared at me with big brown eyes. Her cute braids were starting to grow out, frizzing near her head. She was far more serious than any nine-year- old deserved to be. Fear radiated from her so loudly, it was sound and touch.

"You know my name?" The weave wasn't such a one-way ticket after all, not for the right people.

"Did you follow us here?" she asked instead.

I shook my head. "I didn't know where you were, only that staying in the hospital was a bad idea."

Her Aunt Brenda closed her eyes briefly, her shoulders relaxing. "We sneak out to the park in the mornings, and this afternoon we took a second jaunt because Espy was so restless. I thought you had seen us and followed us back."

"Leaving here isn't very safe," Adriel scolded. "Even with the new protection spell, it's not a good idea. I'm not certain anything but another soul can disguise her from a demon."

Aunt Brenda tightened her arm around Espy. "It may not be safe, but she needs exercise. We can't stay cooped up here forever." She hesitated. "I've watched carefully. It's hard to tell if anyone follows us. So many people come to eat here."

That was the point of the place. My mouth was dry when I tried to swallow. I wondered what else Espy had picked up from In Between besides my name. Names were important. They were always attached to the life lines that leaked through. Everyone knew their name, except me. I had forgotten mine, left it behind or it had been ripped from me. But the new name had stuck, and she had felt it from across the weave. Maybe she had picked up other things as well. "Do you know the name of the creature stalking you?"

Espy's eyes widened. "The stuff in my blood? It does have a name. But it's all jumbled. There's more than one name like it's tacked on every person that it's touched."

"Is your name there?" Fear nearly choked my voice.

Every eye was on her. Lynx was barely breathing.

She sniffled and stared at Spook. He had floated to the top of the bell and sat there watching us. "I don't like to get close to it. I can't get rid of the blood. The other witches came, the healers. But they said they can't separate it out."

Adriel's head jerked. "Mom and Tara came earlier today. Tara tried the trick she used on the tat ink last year, but it didn't work."

I didn't know what trick had been tried, but the girl was marked just as surely as Troy had been marked. "It's demon blood. It's after your soul."

Aunt Brenda's face tightened.

"There's not a lot of it," Espy reassured her aunt. "And besides, I told you, I keep it away."

"We have to bleed it out!" her aunt hissed.

I shook my head. "It's not really blood like our blood. It's something else. But I don't think she was infected with much of it. The problem is that if the demon comes through, it can track its own blood. I am not sure it's possible to hide from it."

"Even though we're in a monastery? Doesn't that protect us?" her aunt asked.

Adriel answered for me. "There are old lines of magic here. Some are protective. I've added new ones too, here and where you sleep. There's holy water in the spells. That will help, but I'm not sure it can dilute the smell of the blood." She turned to me. "Does the demon have any of her blood?"

"I don't know. It depends on whether anyone extracted blood from Espy and somehow gave it to the demon." I hesitated. "I saw the demon blood mix with Espy's, but Espy was hiding from it."

"We moved her out as soon as you told me to," Lynx said.

I nodded. "But time is warped by the weave. Just because I didn't see anyone extract blood doesn't mean it didn't happen."

Espy made a fist. "It does not have any of me or my soul. Aunt Brenda taught me a long time ago how to shut the ghosts out. I can't banish them the way she does, but I can shut them out. So when it came for me, I shut it out. But I can't make it leave." Tears welled in her eyes. "Can you get it out?"

I clicked my fingernails to signal Lynx and slipped sideways. The tip of Espy's finger was a boiling black. The energy churned against itself, unable to leave or merge with her energy.

"What about an exorcism?" her Aunt Brenda asked.

I slipped back inside my body. Everyone was looking at me with high expectations. I hated to let them down. "She's right. She has it contained. By itself it doesn't have much power. If we banish the demon back to where it belongs, the demon blood may go with it. Or lose any potency. Right now what she carries is more like a mark that the demon can smell."

"How do we send it back?" Aunt Brenda demanded.

Lynx and Adriel answered at the same time, "We need the demon's name."

Espy held up her finger. "There are sounds there, sort of like when I hear the name of a ghost. But I never saw the demon, not the whole thing. Just this thing in my blood."

"She's only nine," her aunt cried. "You can't expect her to hunt down and exorcise a demon!"

"Maybe one of the names is enough," I hoped aloud.

Espy sighed. "It's not exactly a name." She waved the infected hand. "It's a sound. More like...like a song, but it's ugly."

I shuddered, thinking of the hellish music the demon had played. "Well, that fits. Can you duplicate the sound?"

She shook her head vehemently. "No way. It's just an ugly scream. There are names, but it's an awful noise like the time my brother ran over my bike in the driveway. Only it's longer than that."

I nodded. "Like a violin played with a rusty metal bow, breaking the strings right in the middle of the notes. But maybe if you can't play back the names there is someone who can. We just have to figure out how to let him hear what you hear."

"Can't I just give him the demon blood? Won't he hear the sound too?"

All eyes were on me again. "Well. The problem is, he's dead." The room sucked in a disappointed breath.

Before dismay could take further hold, Espy giggled. "That's not really a problem, not for me. I just need to meet this friend of yours."

"We are *not* going demon hunting," her aunt protested again.

"No, no," I agreed. I turned to Lynx.

He answered before I asked. "Roberto. Maybe we should have kept that guitar a little longer. He might need it to reach Kyle."

I smiled and clicked my fingernails. Slipping just a little bit sideways, I felt behind my ear before sliding back. "I still have Kyle's guitar pick. All we need is Roberto to tell the guys where to be. Then maybe Espy can help Kyle hear the name that's contained in the blood."

Chapter 32

We retreated single-file down the stairs, but instead of accessing the tunnels, we turned right and used an unmarked door that led to a closet. White Feather did an air check to make sure the hallway was empty before we stepped out. The flooring here was a beautiful new hardwood that matched the woodwork that swallowed the door as it shut silently behind us.

Across the hall from where we emerged there was a door labeled, "Employees Only." From the sounds behind it, it must lead to the kitchens. Another door along the hallway led to the employee bathrooms.

White Feather and Adriel left via the door at the opposite end of the hallway that led to the restaurant.

"They'll meet us out front and drive us back to The Owl," Lynx explained.

We waited a few seconds before strolling up to the same door they had used. Noise from the front leaked back here, and the only lighting was a small scone.

Lynx fidgeted, his head cocked back towards the hidden exit. He could probably hear whether anyone was close by outside the door, but I couldn't. If I really needed to know I could have floated sideways or sent Spook, although the dog seemed able to hear too because he stepped forward right as Lynx reached back and grabbed my hand again.

I tensed, waiting for the lights to go out.

His smirk told me I'd been had.

As we slipped forward again, the door marked "Employees only" opened and a lady with a mop stepped through.

I recognized her from the hospital and finally placed the picture in Amy's apartment. The cleaning lady was dressed nearly the same as when I'd seen her through the weave doing laundry. She did not wear her name tag with "Julia" this time, but no one paid attention to cleaning staff anyway. If she had smelled Espy and found her outside earlier, all she had to do was grab a mop and show up to clean. No one would stop her and no one but me could see Amy's face hovering over hers.

Amy's mother was stooped over and far more aged than the face that had been next to Amy in the photo. Her smile from the picture was nothing but bitter wrinkles now. Dead shark eyes sunken into her face matched the lifeless set of Amy's ghost eyes floating in the head above hers.

"Lynx!"

Spook yelped a warning and spun around in a dead run back the way we had come, zipping faster than most four-legged dogs. I didn't blame him. Even without sliding sideways, the ghosted image around Amy's mother's head was clearly visible.

Amy's youth and beauty had been stripped away. A few remaining strands of hair stuck out from her head, like straw pieces clinging to an adobe brick. Her ghost face was a demented screaming thing with elongated teeth and a jaw that was completely unhinged.

Lynx ruined every diner's meal in the restaurant with a high-pitched cat scream.

I don't know what he saw. Maybe to him it was just a cleaning lady, but the body that housed Amy spurted forward faster than any normal human was capable of moving.

Lynx grabbed my shirt and twisted it, crushing the pack underneath. I had forgotten about the illusion spell he and Adriel had given me. There wasn't time for it anyway. Lynx had badly misjudged Amy's speed and abilities.

My staff was up and behind him as he faced me. I hugged him between the staff and my hands, stopping Amy's claws from connecting with his back. I knew what her touch could do. She wasn't stealing any part of Lynx, not his flesh and not his energy. With my arms around him, he was momentarily trapped, but he heard the scrape of danger as my staff connected with her raw power.

The illusion spell snapped into place. Other than an odd wavering fog, it made no difference to me.

Lynx twisted under my arms as I spun sideways and around him, jabbing to keep Amy back.

Lynx yelled, "Run!"

The kitchens and back door were behind us. So were the tunnels, but those led to Espy, and she was Amy's real target. With matching blood, Amy would have a younger body, a fresh soul and more power.

"Not in this lifetime," I ground out. Lynx couldn't fight the thing that was Amy on his own.

Then again, the swipe he took at her arm not only left a bloody gash, it almost tore it off.

White Feather and Adriel burst through the door leading to the restaurant. A stiff wind slammed into Julia's body, but Amy wasn't deterred in the least, and she was by far the larger danger.

I snapped the staff at her ghostly figure, dead center with splash of energy meant to kill. No point in wasting my efforts.

The pulse slammed into her, forcing her face down directly on top of Julia's head. With Amy slightly dazed, the physical shell nearly collapsed. There was nothing of Julia left. Amy must have finally consumed her soul. She may not have wanted to use her mother up, but it was beyond too late now.

Adriel threw something and yelled, but I didn't see it hit because the lights went out.

Lynx grabbed my staff and yanked me back towards the door we had just exited. As we dove through it, there was a flash behind us. I chanced a backwards glance as I pushed the door closed.

"Oh—No!" My shout was lost behind the door. Adriel had thrown explosive power. Instead of blasting Julia, Amy had sucked it up. The situation had gone from bad to worse.

I stopped. "They need our help!" Adriel and White Feather didn't know how to fight the gray sucking energy. If she hit Amy again it would only empower her further.

Lynx already had the door to the tunnels open.

Before we could dive one direction or the other, the panel leading up to the bell tower opened. Spook barked. He dashed out, herding Aunt Brenda and Espy.

"Aw, shit," Lynx said. "Let's move."

We were just inside the tunnels when the hidden door to the hallway crashed open behind us.

Chapter 33

Lynx slammed the tunnel door shut.

We had to get Espy clear of Amy. "Run! Don't stop!" I yelled at them.

"The tunnel door should hold—" It blasted open before Lynx could finish. "Damn! That wood had more spells on it than Adriel's place!"

We dashed for the storage room, pushing Espy and her aunt ahead of us. There were multiple exits from the storage room; maybe we could confuse Amy.

"Uh-oh." The weave was thinning, I could feel it. "Lynx, get them out of here." I turned back and set my feet. Amy came through the archway, standing just under the gargoyle as she assessed the situation.

Running was for naught. She was battling the weave, but Julia's body was no match for the demon forcing his way through.

"Tell me the demon's name!" I screamed at Julia's body.

She bared her teeth and reached for me. I was afraid to hit her with energy because the demon might grab it or learn the scent of me if he didn't already know it. I had gotten lucky with my first strike because she hadn't expected it.

Music.

The sound of a far off melody drifted through the thinning weave before being abruptly cut off by the screeching chords from hell. Black claws with red-hot tips ripped into the weave.

Amy dragged Julia's body several steps away. "You'll not have me," she snarled. "I have a host, and you can't have it!"

Tell that to the boar that leaped at the break in the weave. The weave fought against the giant pig, trapping its squealing girth for precious seconds, tearing away at its essence. That only made it easier for the beast. It went from mammoth size to that of a large horse and squeezed through.

The smell of burning offal filled the room.

"Holy—" Lynx snarled and went cat. He could escape faster and better than any of us, but he planted himself next to me.

I smacked the boar across the head before jabbing my staff into its eye. The top of the staff blackened, but I didn't fear the heat.

The boar bellowed in outrage, swinging its pitted and twisted tusks. Fire leaked from its injured eye, but that didn't slow it down.

I spun under the lethal horns.

"What the hell is that?" Lynx darted in and out, swiping his claws along one flank, drawing more fire.

"Don't touch it too long," I shouted.

Adriel rolled into the room just under the flapping weave where the boar had come through. White Feather sailed in after her, somersaulting through the air and landing on his feet. They were both ready to do damage.

"Don't touch," I shouted again.

The weave was doing its level best to repair itself, but discordant notes cracked through, followed at times by a more melodic strumming of a guitar. Kyle was fighting for us, and Martin couldn't be too far away either.

"Name the demon," I demanded again, smacking Julia's body with my staff. Forcing Amy out of Julia's body now didn't matter. The weave had already partially opened. Kyle's music couldn't fill the void forever, and the notes certainly weren't going to wrap protectively around Amy to keep the demon out. She'd kill any music with her demon touch.

Amy dragged Julia's ruined body closer to the back end of the pig. The feral monster ignored her.

White Feather smacked the creature with a windstorm hard enough to blow over any normal animal. Lynx swiped at it with another bloody hit.

Amy wasn't headed for the weave even if it wanted her back. That meant she had decided to retreat through the arched doorway we had just entered.

Panicked, and more than a little angry, I flipped the staff to throw it. I hadn't practiced this, at least not in this lifetime. I loathed the idea of losing my staff even for a second, but there was little choice.

Adriel was suddenly beside me, her arm also back to throw, completing the arc before I could stop her.

"No! Power just feeds her!"

"Yeah, I picked up on that from my first try," she panted. Her magic left a trail of energy, escaping as a beautiful blue silver light even before it hit the gargoyle. The timing was perfect. The stone cracked. The falling gargoyle might not hurt Amy, but it would finish Julia's body.

Only the gargoyle didn't fall. The explosion that should have rocked it was sucked away, blowing the gargoyle's wings straight back. The gargoyle blinked.

Adriel's mouth gaped open, matching mine.

The beast tucked in and dove, its feet ripping Julia's head off on the way past as it sailed off the ledge.

Amy's ghost head now sat atop a body gushing blood.

Lynx screamed then, that same cat bellow that had saved me once In Between. Knowing it as a warning, I slammed the staff hard at the pig while Adriel ducked.

Fighting was natural to me, an exercise that allowed me to beat my fears against something else instead of my own head. I pivoted and hit the pig again, snapping the energy off the end of the staff.

It backed up with a grunt, distracted enough that Lynx leaped on its back, raking his claws and tearing before he was suddenly by my side again.

He snarled something unintelligible, but my training from Troy helped.

"No idea if the gargoyle is friend or foe!" I answered.

The gargoyle supplied his own answer by charging into the pig, nearly ripping one tusk completely free.

Music swelled from behind us. The wall inside one of the candle niches flickered, wavered and then a ghostly face appeared.

"Kyle!"

He didn't respond. He was too busy playing.

Martin yelled, "The name! We must have the name!"

Adriel lobbed a dark rock in his direction, probably bloodstone.

From the deadly screech emanating from the original breach in the weave, it was too late anyway. The curtain shred again and, music or no, this time the demon stepped through. His talons wrapped around Amy, cutting off her scream.

I thought her ghost face was melted before, but that was nothing compared to the elongated mess it became. The demon fed off pain and misery. From the way she was clawing at him, there was some anger transferring too.

"Let me tell the guitar guy the name."

It was a whisper under the screams. It was a tiny voice that caused me to pull my punch or I might have knocked Espy all the way to the catacombs.

She stood behind me, her fingers tangled in Spook's ghostly fur.

I stared at her, my mouth trying to form words and failing.

"I have to give him the name." She held up her finger, the one with the demon mark. "Hurry."

Hurry? White Feather was pulsing the feral pig away from us, but the damn thing breathed fire. It singed the very oxygen around us.

The demon was not in a hurry. It clearly was enjoying a leisurely lunch in front of our eyes, polishing off both Amy and Julia. No doubt it would come after one of us very soon.

I looked up. Kyle and Martin had thinned the weave, but the opening was near the ceiling. Well, any port in a storm.

I grabbed Espy's hand and we nearly flew over to the altar. As soon as Lynx figured out my plan, he leaped up, reached a hand down and hauled her on top of the table. It wobbled. The ceiling was arched and still too far away.

He lifted her.

I climbed up on the table with them.

The demon laughed, an odd cross between his broken music and a human gag.

"Lift me and then I'll lift her!" I shouted. The two of us stacked might still not be high enough. And Lynx might not be able to hold both of us at once, skinny though I might be.

Adriel yelled, "White Feather, lift!"

White Feather's face was black from the flames that had scorched him. He blasted another sheer wind across the pig. Adriel pitched silver balls similar to the ones she had given me. The energy crackled against the floor, forming a wall between us and the pig.

Before White Feather could respond to Adriel's plea, the gargoyle swooped down, lifted Espy high and hovered over the niche. She set one foot down, scooped up the candelabra, and then sat, teetering.

Lynx grabbed me in time to break my fall as the altar slid from its perch atop the adobe bricks.

Espy jabbed her finger against the brass edge of the candle holder. Without hesitating, she reached into the weave, dripping black flames across the strings of Kyle's guitar.

Kyle, bless his heart, played, even when four strings snapped. The sound of music dying echoed from here to hell. It was the demon's name.

Chapter 34

The walls shook.

Kyle lifted his face from his music. It was full of tears.

The first time I'd seen him, those tears had been real. They were still energy now, but the broken strings had taken their toll. He was splintering.

Martin was visible behind him, chanting and waving juniper berries, the smear of berry bits and juice forming a small, foggy pentagram.

The demon surged towards us, but his name demanded his presence. The weave snapped into him, trapping him, shredding him, and finally forcing him back over. The curtain undulated, sucking the oxygen from the room as it repaired itself.

The feral pig charged.

I slapped out with my staff, only to have it snap in two. I rolled, the heat from hooves blasting past me.

The wall didn't just shake when the pig hit, it crumpled, tearing out huge chunks of plaster and knocking a hole right through the adobe.

"Shouldn't that thing be disintegrating?" Adriel shouted. "Isn't its power source from the demon?" She ran behind it, cutting the flank with the smallest dagger I'd ever seen, but that dagger sparked with magic, cutting a chunk of pig fat free.

The boar ignored any pain and turned to charge again, squealing a challenge.

Our weapons were the wrong kind of energy. They were too alive. Lynx couldn't possibly hear me click my fingernails with the pig's hooves churning and roaring as it attacked.

"I'm going sideways," I yelled.

"Don't!" But he stood guard near my body anyway.

I slid into gray, reaching up to pluck the guitar pick from behind my ear. Spook rushed the boar from behind. He'd fought this kind before. He knew to bite and not touch anything for long.

There wasn't a lot of energy in the guitar pick, but it was the right kind. It was In Between. The pig was nearly blind and bleeding fire from several cuts.

I floated high and dove down, my hand with the pick aimed for the remaining good eye. Spook attacked a leg, providing a distraction.

It was now or never.

I plowed my fist into its remaining red orb and flicked the guitar pick with my fingers, shoving it deep, but yanking my hand free before my presence could register with the boar.

It whipped its head sideways. The momentum flipped me away, fire chasing me.

"Aaaaii!" The pain was like slamming into the weave, but the burn across my chest and arm didn't shatter, it ate at me. My living body gasped.

I yanked at the gray essence of my shirt, ripping it and the pig snot away from me.

I slammed back into my body and reached for the juniper berries. "Stand clear!"

Lynx didn't listen. He grabbed me as if he intended to haul me away. Adriel yelled, "I've got the left," flanking him on one side and White Feather the other.

These people did not follow directions.

Berries in hand, I slid sideways again and pelted the boar, little stabs that exploded into it, driving it back, slicing deep. The fire that licked the edges banked, drawing in.

The demonic creature gave a mighty snort and bore down on us anyway.

I threw the last berry and shouted, "Scatter!" There was nothing more I could do and even my last gasp wasn't enough to save anyone. Either they didn't hear me because I was sideways or they ignored me again.

Just as I hit my body, the gargoyle dove at the beast and grabbed the remaining boar tusk. The boar spun halfway around as the gargoyle wrestled with it.

"Duck," I yelled.

The tusk ripped free, belching stored fire, but the gargoyle turned to stone, dropping through the flame to the floor with an earth-shattering crash.

The flame fed on itself, exploding the pig outward in a huge fireball.

I flew backwards so hard, I took Lynx down. He landed on top of Adriel. White Feather must have reached for her or tried to yank her away because he ended up on the bottom. For a moment, it was difficult to tell whether I was in my body or still sideways.

Stumbling badly, I rolled to my feet, hunting for threats in the bits and pieces that burned along the floor.

Lynx rolled the opposite direction, and came up facing the wrong way.

Adriel groaned and slid onto a piece of clay tile without making it to her feet. The tile under her cracked like a bullet, splintering into pieces. White Feather sucked in air loud enough to be heard in the sudden silence.

A tiny voice from the candle alcove said, "Are y'all okay?"

Espy was barely stable on the ledge. Kyle and Martin were gone. So was the pig. There was a distinct smell of sulfur and burned meat. I gagged. No fresh bacon here.

I sat down, hard. My shirt had nearly disintegrated; barely holding on by a few threads. Whatever life was contained in the cotton fibers had been removed when I ripped the essence of it away from me while sideways.

Spook scooted next to me, panting. I'd have reached to pet him, but lifting my arm was too much effort.

The gargoyle retrieved and then landed with Espy, settling gently near our pile of bodies.

"I must say, well met," it said.

I stared at it, speechless.

Chapter 35

Oddly enough, the first thought to wander through my tired brain was to wonder whether the gargoyle smelled like a bat or not. He stood upright in a hunched gargoyle kind of way; from that position, he met me eye to eye even though I was sitting. His ears were almost as long as his entire head. Now that I had time to notice, his skin was several shades of gray and black. Leathery wings folded neatly behind him, almost invisible, making his arms resemble those of a human.

Spook didn't seem alarmed or surprised by the nearness of the bat-beast.

"Thank you, witch," the gargoyle rumbled at Adriel. "Your magic set me free."

"Uhm, yeah." Adriel muttered something about the moonlight, but it was little more than a puff of air followed by, "I didn't know that spell could be absorbed through stone."

"My name is Horacio." He spoke with a clipped Spanish accent and a hurried cadence to his words. "I was trapped as stone for a very long time."

"Who trapped you?" Lynx wanted to know.

"The prior was an old fashioned fellow who brought me over from Spain. Following in a long line of tiresome customs, he was granted my companionship for protection as a favor."

"What happened to him?" I asked.

"The idiot died before passing on the proper release spells or granting me my freedom. It is in our nature to turn to stone and back, but as part of my promise, much to my regret, he held the key to that power for the time of my indenture. His death was rather sudden. There were things here he did not understand, and he did not learn readily despite my passing along wisdom."

"No one else could release you?" Adriel asked.

The bat-head nodded. "Just so."

I did some quick calculations of my own. "Your term is surely over, so you're now free to go about your business?"

"Just so." His smile was a bit toothy and rather fearsome. He was going to create some interesting dynamics in the world. Of course, if shifters, witches and vampires were all over the place, what was one small gargoyle?

"Thanks for the help." I swept my arm to include the spattered mess around us. "We were having a time of it, and I'm not sure we'd have gotten Espy up there fast enough. Speaking of Espy," I gave her a quizzical look. "Where is your aunt?"

"Somewhere that way. We were running, but I stopped." She leaned tiredly against Horacio. "I knew the demon was coming through. I felt the tear in the fabric of the world. It was hunting me anyway. So I figured I may as well come back and see if I could tell you his name so you could pass it on to the guy you talked about."

"That was very brave," White Feather said softly.

"Damn straight," Lynx added.

I slipped sideways just enough to see her finger. The black mark was gone. I would have told her so, but once back in my own body, her eyes met mine. She already knew. "Your aunt will be thrilled that the demon mark is gone," I said instead.

She nodded. "Me too."

White Feather and Adriel helped each other stand. Adriel surveyed the area in disgust. "We'll need to come back and help Tino clean up this mess."

"And find out where she lived." White Feather pointed to Julia's mangled body.

"At least we know Amy's mother was the accomplice," I said. "She worked at the hospital and had complete access to everyone involved."

Lynx agreed. "It would be great if she left behind answers to some of our other questions."

No argument there.

Chapter 36

After Adriel and White Feather dropped us off at The Owl, we picked up burgers for the way home. Tino appeared long enough to make sure we were okay and to complain about the mess at The Monastery. Apparently a very damaging wind storm had destroyed windows, dishes and tablecloths when White Feather attempted to stop Julia from following us.

I was pretty sure that the burn marks Tino described on his hardwood floors had nothing to do with Adriel or White Feather. Amy had more than enough demon in her to have left scorched footprints with ease.

The smell of sulfur clung to every pore, and I was almost too tired to eat. "We need to send Kyle a new set of guitar strings," I said as Lynx parked the car in front of his house.

"Tonight?" His face fell as though I had stolen his burger.

I opened the car door and groaned my way out. Every part of me was stiff and sore. "No, but soon. And I am not sure I can talk to Kyle without Roberto's help anymore so can we invite him too?" I explained how I had used the guitar pick. "It's gone now. It was my only link to Kyle." Sadness gripped my heart.

"Good thing he was already married," Lynx grumbled.

He surprised a laugh out of me. "You have nothing to worry about."

"Yeah?"

"Yeah." I reached out and linked his fingers with mine. He rarely smiled, but his eyes lit up and not with the glow of cat yellow.

***

I remembered showering, but not falling asleep.

Next thing I knew, Lynx was shaking me awake. "It's gone, Shadow. The javelina from hell is gone. Wake up."

I stared up at him, breathing hard. My fists were clenched as though holding a staff between them. Lynx was right where the bar would be, holding my hands apart with his shoulders.

"You sure it's gone?"

"Well, it's not here right now."

He was such an optimist. "I was back In Between." My voice cracked. "In the dream I couldn't leave without knowing my name. I don't want to go back there."

"You might have to someday, but we can plan it better."

"I wonder what happened to my name."

"It doesn't matter. I don't know my name either," he admitted.

The window let in light from the coming dawn, but he was still only half visible, his face cloaked in shadows. "What do you mean, you don't know your name?"

"Names are important. The ones you're given, the ones you come to own. There's power in a name, that's why it banished the demon. Once they had his name and blood, Martin knew the right rituals. He's one cool witch dude."

I sat up. "When people crossed into In Between, I could sense their names. We all could, but no one knew my name."

"So you either lost yours or you left it behind." He shrugged. "When a thing like that Amy chick is chasing you, it might be good to lose your name."

"What happened to your name?"

He shrugged, his eyes dropping, but only for a moment. "My mom never gave me one."

There was probably a lot more to that story, but it didn't matter right now. "So your name is Lynx."

He nodded. "And your name is Shadow." He said it with such finality, it was like a promise.

I threw my arms around him and kissed him with every bit of need inside me, enough to kill him had we been In Between. But I wasn't dead, and he was alive with his own passion that may have come close to matching mine.

He leaned in, giving as good as he got, pressing me back against the pillows.

I wrapped my legs around him, not caring if he felt trapped. He moved against me, closer, his hands gripping my arms so hard he might well leave bruises. I didn't care. Our bodies tangled, tasting, nipping, *feeling*. I'd have begged for his touch, but was too busy ripping at his stubborn shirt, trying to convey everything all at once.

He pulled back, breathing hard, his eyes glinting in the dark with his own need. "Shadow...are you sure?"

"Lynx, don't make me beat you up again."

He smiled. A real, honest-to-goodness smile.

The warmth of it stayed with me, even as he ducked his head under his shirt and threw it across the room.

It was wonderful to be alive.

Chapter 37

From the outside, Julia Inkstar's home was a quiet little place, especially in the dark. There was no grass in the front yard, but hardy roses, yarrow and lilacs lined the porch. Lynx had picked the time of one hour after midnight.

Adriel carried a flashlight, but she left it off.

White Feather blew a questing breeze through the place. Then Adriel did some sort of earth check. "It's contaminated. I don't even want to try to find silver or gold." She sounded like her teeth were grinding.

Since everyone was being cautious, I was prepared to investigate next, but Spook beat me to it.

He trotted back out, and I clicked my fingers before drifting sideways. "Well, Spook?"

"Woof." He coughed, hung his head and gagged.

"But is it safe?"

He sat and looked at me.

"Well, okay not safe and great, but we won't die, right?"

He barked a pitiful "woooof" that was half wail as though he accepted we had to enter the place, but he didn't like it.

I shifted back. "He says it smells bad, and he's completely against us being here, but he won't stop us."

"He said all that?" White Feather asked.

I shrugged. "More or less."

"I can attest to the smell," White Feather agreed. "Amy must not have taken care of much after she inhabited her mother."

Worse than a lack of care was the flickering portal visible as soon as we squeezed through the front door. White Feather turned on the lights.

I might not have recognized the gateway to In Between had Amy not used water before, but a claw foot tub in the living room would have gotten our attention regardless.

"Don't stand too close to it," I warned. "I don't think it's an open portal right now, but it might suck you right into In Between. Martin said some portals are doors that will let anything through."

"How do we close it?" Adriel demanded.

"Martin used a bloodstone to activate the other portal. Amy used Troy's life energy to activate it. I never saw how Martin destroyed the portal. It closed when Roberto yanked the bloodstone, but Martin would have had to destroy the circle of stones Amy had set there."

Spook barked and circled the tub. I knew what he wanted, but it made me sigh. "Sideways again."

"Don't get too close," Lynx muttered.

I circled first. The portal didn't appear to be open, not exactly. Like the water In Between, there was an odd sheen to it. Nothing other than the tub bottom should have been visible, but there was a gray swirl underneath the surface. I had a bad feeling that if any of us touched it, it would use us to open the portal. I sank back into myself.

"It's not really open. But it's not closed either. I think it needs some kind of energy to activate it, but I'm not sure what would happen if we attacked it."

White Feather said, "The problem isn't opening it. It's closing it down. Can we drain the water?"

"Not without touching it. And we definitely don't want anything with energy touching it."

"I can blow it out of there," he replied.

"Would that move the portal? Or destroy it? It might change how it worked." I shrugged. "I don't know."

Lynx disappeared outside and returned with a large rock. "Nothing attached to us. Not magic. You witches waste too much time."

"But that rock is earth," Adriel said. "It holds some magic!"

Lynx didn't wait a millisecond longer before he tossed the boulder directly into the water.

The tub was half full. The rock was heavy. Water should have splashed out onto the already dirty carpet, but the rock hit and then sank slowly. It was still on this side, but it took on an odd grayish cast amidst the ripples.

I flicked my fingernails and slid sideways.

The rock had changed the portal. I could now see the mist, the fog that was always In Between. The shadows shifted.

Spook barked.

I ignored him in favor of trying to make out the shapes...Spook barked again. There was an odd sound of music, not the demon kind, but...was that Troy? No, not Troy. Why was I so confused?

Kyle was a ghost of his former ghost self. His back was hunched, much as Troy's had been when he was drained. He was trying to play, but there were notes missing. He may have banished the demon, but it had cost him. Unless he obtained new strings, he couldn't repair himself. His music was part of his soul.

Spook barked again, and this time he dashed right through me, startling me into floating backwards. How had I gotten so close?!?

Lynx was yelling. "Shadow! Shadow, breathe!"

No, this portal wasn't open, not exactly. But it had a vortex that slowly sucked energy into it.

I sank back into myself, staggering.

Lynx had hold of my shoulders. He didn't stop shaking me. "You stopped breathing! Don't do that!"

Adriel's bracelets were on fire. "I can't ground here," she said through her teeth. "This place is contaminated."

White Feather threw open a window. He used the fresh air to blast out two more windows at the back of the house. Old books and piles of paper scattered across the couch fluttered in the breeze.

"Keep breathing," Lynx ordered.

When I tried to speak, I realized I had half floated free again. I hadn't meant to do it.

He snapped his fingers in front of my face, but my eyes were wide open and staring at nothing.

The swirling gray was pulling things into it. Not just me, but the breeze that blew through and the line of blue where Adriel had tried to ground. She was connected to it. The scattered bits of her power slowly rotated closer to the center of the gray vortex.

I did the only thing I could think of. I reached for Adriel's bracelet and slashed my hand through the energy, sucking a hole through it.

The spark tossed me backwards, slamming me into myself so fast and hard, I knocked myself and Lynx to the floor.

White Feather had the door open now.

Spook ran back and forth between me and the tub, whining.

I stared at Lynx. "Kyle was there attempting to play his guitar, but the strings are broken." I frowned. "He knows it's broken. Maybe he was trying to tell me something. Do guitar strings have any energy? Do you think we could throw strings through there? Maybe he can close it if he has the strings?"

"You ain't going near that thing again." Lynx's ears were back. His voice was flat. He reached into his pocket.

I sat up.

Adriel pulled her pack around and extracted several guitar string envelopes. "I bought a whole set because I didn't know which ones he might need, and I wasn't sure when we might see him."

Lynx had the set he had bought already out. He had insisted he carry one set, and I carry the other.

"Don't ground again," I told Adriel. "It goes straight into the vortex. Spook—" I put my hand out to the dog. He hopped my way, but stayed out of reach. "No transfers of energy."

"Metal is never inert," Adriel said tersely. "Throwing these strings in there might make it worse, like the rock did."

I threw the packet, but I didn't dare slip sideways to do it. Lynx had tossed me the braid. He hadn't gone sideways.

The strings bounced off the water and landed on the other side of the tub.

"What happened?" Lynx asked.

I gripped his hand tightly and dared a peek sideways. The vortex was dark in the center. "Let me try yours."

He handed me one.

"Spook, ready?" I asked.

Lynx growled. "Shadow..."

I threw the packet, trusting Spook to jump between me and the portal if need be. I winked sideways as it hit the water, already diving back to myself. The strings were metal, not wood or life, but Martin said the portals were open walkways between worlds.

When the string hit, there was a flash of black. The rim of the tub dimmed with the same darkness. "Uh-oh." I was dizzy from the transfer. Luckily I was still sitting. "This portal is different. I don't know how Amy opened the portal that I used to return here, but I'm guessing she used Troy's life energy, not his death."

Adriel caught on first. "And this one used blood or death?"

"Maybe both. It's black, not gray. When I looked into the portal from In Between there was color. This one is gray, but it turned black as soon as the string hit."

"The rock sank. The strings bounced," Adriel said.

I shook my head. "I don't know why. Maybe because Kyle is on the other side. He looked terrible. He can't play. Without his music, he's fading."

"Maybe it appeared that way because of this portal," White Feather said.

But I knew how much energy was required just to remain sane In Between. "He won't attempt to reach us through that thing. We need to destroy it."

"These old tubs are iron inside. How the hell are we going to destroy it?" Adriel muttered. "Can't use water. It's already part of the problem. Can't use air. Can't use earth."

"Melting it would be damn near impossible," White Feather added.

"Shoot it full of holes," Lynx declared.

"There is a drain," Adriel said. She turned to me. "Would that work?"

White Feather muttered, "Whoever built this never intended it to be unplugged."

"Amy had to have a way to transfer herself back and forth from In Between after Martin destroyed the other portal."

Lynx waved his hand in front of my eyes. I followed his hand, if for no other reason than to reassure him. Satisfied, he got up and went outside again.

White Feather pulled out his cell and dialed his brother. "Gordon has something that will shoot through this thing."

When Lynx returned, he carried my longest staff, the one with the pointed end. "It's an old tub so it has to have a drain."

"What will happen when the water drains out?" Adriel asked me as though I had an answer.

"The drain unplugged would break the circle. And wood...it might suck the staff right through."

"Breaking the circle is definitely good," she decided.

White Feather hung up. "Gordon's on his way."

I stood behind Lynx ready to pull him back in case he broke through and something grabbed him. I didn't know if I could save him, but if he was sucked In Between, I was going with him.

Spook waited next to him too.

"Should we try to destroy anything that comes at you?" White Feather asked.

"I really don't know. It might be a good idea if you can keep the water back," I said.

Lynx was already poking under the tub with the staff. There wasn't much room for him to maneuver. "It's plugged with something tight," he muttered. "I need a curved staff."

White Feather said, "Hang on. I'll bring the crowbar from the car."

Lynx ignored him, but had no luck dislodging whatever was stuck in the drain.

White Feather knelt next to him and poked at the plug with the bar.

Adriel watched for a second and then suggested, "Power hitting it from the outside would travel around the circle or be absorbed. It's just a circle, like any other circle. Blood circles require blood or death to activate. So while power may be absorbed, it also stands a chance of bouncing or breaking through, right?"

No one had an answer.

White Feather grumbled when she put her hand on the crowbar. "Let me hit it. I can push earth power through the metal."

Her eyes locked with his. Lynx glared at me as though I had somehow suggested I hit it instead of Adriel. I wasn't about to offer. Well, I would have, except in this case, it wouldn't help. My sideways energy was too easily drawn into the vortex. If this thing fed on death, it could easily feed on souls, and it wasn't getting mine. It had sucked in Adriel's power, but it was probably only collecting stray pieces. Of course, if it collected enough of her, it might reach for her soul too.

"No," White Feather said. "Put one of your delayed explosions on the end. I'll jam the crowbar up against the seal, and we'll all hightail it out of here."

She nodded her head in agreement, reached behind to her pack, and without looking, removed a packet.

White Feather drew the crowbar in and she attached it. "Okay, everyone back."

I didn't need to be told twice. The only reason Lynx didn't beat me outside is because he was herding me and Spook from behind.

"Fifteen seconds," Adriel said.

I started counting. When I hit three, Adriel was in the doorway. When I hit four, she and White Feather were flying through the air. Lights exploded behind them.

Lynx grabbed me, but I was already rolling, knowing something had gone terribly wrong.

The entire house might have blown if White Feather hadn't already opened the windows and doors. As it was, part of the roof blew off.

For a few seconds, there was a calm, but before relief had a chance to set in, a large dark shadow blotted out the moon and the stars.

The roof crashed back down, disappearing behind the wall of the house. Oddly, instead of a crash, there was a loud splash.

The front part of the house, along with the roof, was sucked into the vortex as the water drained.

"Wow," I whispered.

"I thought you said we had fifteen seconds!" It was White Feather's voice, but he wheezed.

I sat up, wincing as my face brushed a rosebush. I scooted closer to the lilacs before trying to extract myself from the bushes. The lilac was missing all of its leaves.

"Should...have had more time," Adriel panted. "I think that thing tried to toss the magic away and that set it off early. Thanks for the landing."

"I'm used to forming bubbles around you. You're always flying through the air," he grumbled.

Lynx found my hand and pulled me up.

"Where's Spook?" I worried.

The dog woofed from somewhere behind the Mustang.

"We need to give Kyle new guitar strings," I said. There were probably other things I should have been worried about right now, but Kyle's gaunt face haunted me. Troy had looked like that.

"There were books in there," Adriel said. "We should have secured them first."

Lynx peered through the open hole that had been a house. "You think that portal is closed?"

The tub was cracked in half. Not only was there no water, the circle that had been the tub was fractured. "You want me to check sideways?" I offered.

"No. Let's go deliver those strings." He didn't release my hand. "You got this?" he asked the other two.

White Feather had one hand on his head, the other on his wife's shoulder. "Yeah."

"Where are you going?" Adriel demanded.

"Kyle's wife. She has his guitar. With it nearby, we should be able to pass the strings to him," I said.

"Now? It's after one in the morning!"

"It can't wait," I said.

"Now Lynx has her thinking all these jobs have to be done at night," Adriel muttered as we hurried past.

Chapter 38

I expected sneaking Roberto out of the School for the Deaf in the middle of the night would be difficult, but Lynx pulled into a cemetery next to the school, looked in the backseat and said, "You wanna get him or should I?"

Spook barked and disappeared.

"Roberto's in the cemetery? What's he doing in the cemetery?"

"He talks to ghosts. It's the only place he can hear people and have regular conversations. I've been telling him he needs to hang out with a better crowd, but he still comes here a lot. Even if he's not out there tonight, Spook will find him, and the cemetery is his route out of the school."

I thought about the tunnels we had just been in and hoped for Roberto's sake that none of the tunnels connected to the cemetery. That was just too creepy to consider.

Within ten minutes, Roberto joined us. He and Spook hopped in back.

Paula was less wary of us this time, despite it being the middle of the night. She had obviously given birth because her tummy was deflated.

I explained the reason for the late-night visit. "Kyle needs new guitar strings."

Her eyebrow, one with an earring in it, quirked up. "Really? Right now?"

I nodded.

"Okay, I guess. You were right about the money."

I nodded and introduced her to Roberto. "He's here to facilitate the communication. And this is Lynx. My name is Shadow," I reminded her.

She opened the door wider to let us in. The house was small, but neatly kept. "How did you know I had moved in with my mom?"

I hadn't asked Lynx how he knew. He didn't offer an explanation either.

Paula's mother stood in a robe at the head of the hallway. A crib was in the living room next to the couch where it was obvious Paula had been sleeping.

I was happy to see Kyle's guitar leaning against one edge of the sofa.

"The baby is sleeping. You won't wake her, will you?"

She placed herself between us and the crib as though she didn't want us too near her baby. I couldn't blame her. We were a strange crew. Neither Roberto nor Lynx had spoken other than to nod during the introductions.

"Let's do this," I said.

"Don't you want to know about the money?"

"The money?" I repeated.

"I did find it. Kyle must have been saving for a long time. It's really helped a lot." She took a shuddering breath. "God bless him. I miss him."

Roberto signed something, and Lynx translated. "Roberto doesn't need any money, but he would like to hold the guitar."

"Oh." She blushed with embarrassment. She started to walk around the crib, but caught sight of her mother and stopped. She looked back at us, her body still between us and the baby. "Go ahead." She motioned towards the guitar case.

I thought maybe Roberto would play the guitar, but he didn't even open the case. He just sat on the couch with it across his lap. I wondered if the call was like that of a séance, or if Kyle would just feel the pull.

When the weave shifted, it was more peaceful than it had ever been before. Roberto knew his stuff. Instead of fighting the weave, Roberto somehow invited the gray of In Between into the room with us.

Kyle was there, his guitar across his lap. It was the first time he hadn't been playing it since I'd visited him from this side. He was still crying, though.

"We...I...your strings." I tossed the packets, remembering to go sideways and snap the bundle away from me. The bundled packets, tied with twine, slipped through.

He missed them, probably because he couldn't see well through the tears. Or maybe it was because he was only a shadow of his former self.

"Careful, Kyle," I warned, still sideways. "Don't let anything there feel your sorrow."

He nodded, but he only had eyes for Paula. "I'm sorry. I didn't leave you on purpose."

"I know." Her voice was thick. "She looks like me."

"I know."

I searched the gray around him, worried.

"Can you come again? More often? Oh, I never thought I'd see your face again!" Paula was now bawling, too. She reached into the cloud of gray, snapping Kyle out of his misery.

"Don't! Paula! You don't belong here. Lisa needs you."

"She needs you too!"

"I—" he looked at me, the desperation leaking to our side. "I saw you at the other portal through the water. I wanted to cross. I remembered how you did it, but when I tried to play, thinking it would open it, something was wrong. There was no music."

"Kyle, you can't come back." Tears dripped off my own chin. "You'd be like Amy, not like me."

He picked up the strings I had thrown and unraveled one of them. The gray held bits of energy around the metal, glints of not-gray. He stared longingly at Paula and sighed. "I belong here now. And maybe it will be better now that I have the strings. I haven't been able to play."

"We'll listen for the music," I said softly. "The music is still here. We'll find it."

He smiled. "Yeah. That's good. Never forget the music."

Roberto's hands clenched once, and the guitar nearly slid off his lap. The weave drifted closed, slowly.

The ticking of a clock on the wall broke the silence, but none of us spoke.

Kyle must have restrung his guitar quickly because within seconds, the music floated through.

Paula put her fist against her mouth. "He's not coming back, is he? Not ever."

I shook my head. "And the weave is dangerous for him. Make your peace with him. That will make things easier for him for as long as he stays In Between. He needs to know you're okay."

"Will he always be there? Waiting for us?"

I hesitated. "No one knows. There might come a time after you let him go that he moves on to a better place." I stared over at the crib. Lisa's eyes were wide open and her little hand waved. "You'll know when that happens."

We didn't stay, but part of my heart was lodged somewhere In Between.

Damn. Sometimes living hurt almost as much as being dead.

Chapter 39

It took us nearly a week to clean up the mess in The Monastery and the tunnels, but the free food was fabulous, and Tino paid us for the work. I wasn't certain the exchange was fair, but being low on cash, I didn't turn down the offer.

Adriel reset the spells, including illusions, on the exits, but she muttered a lot about, "No real way to stop a demon."

The gargoyle seemed content with his new circumstances, and Tino certainly didn't complain about having a new resident. Horacio not only helped clean up, he worked a side deal to perform security by perching on the roof at The Owl. He was there more than once when we left there after eating. Anyone else who saw him probably assumed he was a new statue.

Who knows what people thought on the days he was missing, or when they saw me waving at him like an idiot?

Adriel had discovered that the most important books and notes were hidden under a floorboard in what was left of Julia's bedroom. She took them to someone she called Granny Ruth. The gist of the records revealed that Julia and Amy had studied the occult hoping for a cure for the cancer. Sometime after they started studying, Amy became attached to the idea of not just bargaining for a cure, but for capturing the power of a demon.

The notes became increasingly desperate and rambling after the demon call.

One morning before we started our clean-up chores, Adriel handed me a piece of paper. "Blood donors from the center where Amy worked. Your name might be on the list."

I stared down at it. Before I could read any of the names, a very small spider skittered across the page.

"Oh, sorry. One of Granny Ruth's. You get used to them." Adriel put her finger back on the page, allowing the tiny spider to crawl onto her fingernail. She carefully released it on a nearby statue.

She turned back to me. "Granny Ruth and I copied that page from a printout we found stuffed inside one of Amy's grimoires. Near as we can guess, Amy was keeping track of blood donors as possible victims to possess. She noted athletic, healthy people in particular, men or women."

"You think I was there to give blood?"

Adriel rubbed her bracelet. "You were attacked at the park nearby. Maybe you stopped in to donate, and Amy liked your stats. You were in good shape when you were first admitted, according to Patrick."

"I didn't have my staff or any other weapon. I must have felt safe. A hospital seems like a secure place."

White Feather, carrying pieces of hardwood flooring, paused on his way by. "And a blood bank probably wouldn't be too keen on your walking in there with a weapon for knocking heads."

"Or maybe I wasn't as paranoid as I am now." My staff was never far from me these days. I scanned down the list, but none of the names called to me. Some names had been crossed out. There were doodles and stars next to others.

"Gordon is running background checks on all the names. I'll let you know what he finds out," White Feather promised.

"Based on the notes, I'm almost positive Amy died when she tried to possess you. She lived in her own corpse until it started to turn zombie, which wouldn't have taken more than about three days. Then she hopped over to Ted." Adriel shuddered. "It appears they tried another demon calling to learn the secret to opening and closing the portals. She used that knowledge to travel back and forth. Her mother knew the danger of allowing Amy to possess her so they hunted for other victims instead."

"And Amy spent her time hiding behind Troy and helping Julia prepare Espy. I hope Espy was the only other victim."

Adriel clutched her bracelet harder and rocked on the balls of her feet. "Yeah. You were probably the first. Ted was the second. The notes didn't indicate anyone else helped them, but Amy or her mother stole the two grimoires from somewhere. The original owner might have been a victim too. By the time Amy possessed her mother, it was a last resort for both of them."

"Did the grimoires really promise that Amy could keep herself alive by calling a demon?" I asked.

Adriel shook her head. "Grimoires can't be trusted. Their text doesn't change exactly, but there's a magical element that allows some people to read certain things. Another person might not see the text at all or see only parts of it. From the notes I saw, Amy dreamed of more than just a healthy body. She had copied text that described demons with flames of gold. There were a lot of dollar signs next to that note and a line that said, 'Who needs college when you can have a free lunch?'"

"Crap." I could have told Amy that anything burning along that soul-sucking blackness might be golden in color, but that didn't mean it would buy you lunch. It might *invite* you to lunch as the main course, but it wouldn't be the one paying.

At three in the afternoon the next day, Lynx decided the monastery storage room was close enough to merely "dusty and decaying" as opposed to "requires more repair or it will fall down." He didn't bother to tell the others we were leaving. He just took my hand and squeezed my fingers. I followed without releasing his hand.

He drove to Martin's canyon, the one I'd seen In Between.

Spook came with us. According to the updates Espy had been texting Lynx, Spook had been over to visit her several times.

After we hiked less than a quarter of a mile, Lynx loped off to check the trail ahead.

Walking across the sand, I felt Kyle and Martin grin with approval. I didn't miss Martin's crooning, but every now and then, when the breeze swirled a certain way, picking up the heat of the rocks, maybe I could hear him mixing it up with the earth he so loved. Of course, it was completely possible that he was peeking through the edge, watching. I'd done it enough times, wishing I could cross, seeing people who could not see me.

I smiled and saluted the big blue sky. "Don't worry. I'm not wasting a single day."

Lynx reappeared behind me as suddenly as he had disappeared. He moved fast, especially in the desert. "You talkin' to yourself again?" he asked.

"How do you shift and stay in your clothes?" I asked, ignoring his teasing.

His eyes lit up with the supreme smugness only a cat possessed. "I learned the trick just last year. Tara," he hesitated, but then continued. "She's White Feather's sister. The healer."

"I remember." Lynx never seemed comfortable around her, but he'd tell me about it in his own time if it was important.

"She did this thing with tat ink, extracting it from White Feather when he was infected with a bad spell. She figured out how to do it after studying the way I shifted. But I figured if something foreign could be expelled, I could grow through it too."

"So you just grow your cat through your clothes?"

"Pretty much. Took some practice, and there's a few tricks to it. Only works on cotton and hemp; earth stuff. Silk blocks magic, plus the weave in it is too tight."

"No wonder your clothes look stretched out all the time."

He shrugged. "I buy a lot of t-shirts. Doesn't work with shoes either, so I have to go back and get them all the time."

That explained why he was often barefoot.

Lynx stared off into the canyon. "Were you talking to Martin? I don't see him."

"I haven't seen him either, but he might be here. The weave thins without opening. I said hello to him and Kyle and maybe Troy just in case they were around. You can't abandon people just because you're on a different side of the weave. They're part of my family."

Spook trotted over and put his head under my hand.

"And you had to adopt a three-legged dog, too? You couldn't adopt a cat instead?" Lynx's whine didn't hold any real heat.

I smiled. "I adopted one of those too."

His eyes locked with mine.

Cats can out stare anyone, but he did blink. Lynx made a grumbling noise that was more purr than bite. As he turned his body, he brushed against me. "You planning on staying around for a while?"

I didn't know if he was asking whether I planned on staying alive or staying with him or staying in the canyon. "As long as you let me?" I guessed.

He leaned close again. "Right around forever then."

I put my head on his shoulder. "I can live with that."

Other Works

Tracking Magic (Max Killian Investigations) contains the first story about Troy and Cinderspark.

The Sedona O'Hala series (**Executive Lunch, Executive Retention, Executive Sick Days, Executive Dirt**) is a series of humorous cozy mysteries: Sedona must solve a few crimes while fighting her way up the corporate ladder; mostly she dangles from her fingertips just trying to survive.

If you're looking for a good romantic comedy give **One Good Eclair** and **One Smart Cookie** a try. The Nutrition "Mafia" series involves shenanigans at the highest level of fun, mystery and romance.

Catch an Honest Thief is a stand alone mystery, combining a stealthy caper in the New Mexico desert with high-tech gadgets. Alexia must try to save her career—and her life.

Dragons of Wendal series: Romantasy adventures with magic, shifters and a mystery to be solved. In the first, Zoe intends to learn magic, but the mages at the university might not be willing to teach her what she needs to know.

Soul of the Desert is an historical adventure of a boy on the run from the mafia. Which is worse, the guns of New York or the dangerous desert of New Mexico?

The Moon Shadow series is contemporary urban fantasy: **Under Witch Moon, Under Witch Aura, Under Witch Curse.** Adriel is an earth witch working hard to make an honest living. When she finds herself on the wrong end of black magic—it's either solve the crime or die trying. The Moon Shadow series is followed by the sidekick adventures, **Witch Way, Null Witch** and **Ghost Shadow.** The sidekick adventures are urban fantasy mixed with romantasy.

You can find Maria at her blog: www.BearMountainBooks.com. Come on by and say hello!